Discovering Gold

Romancing the
Californian Cowboys

S M SPENCER

Cover design by BookPOD

Cover images by iStockphoto

eISBN: 978-1-922270-18-4

ISBN: 978-1-922270-68-9

Related books in the Copperhead Creek Australian Romance series:

A Chance to Come True

A Chance to Get it Right

A Chance to Let Go

A Chance to Belong

A Chance for Snow

Related books in the Copperhead Creek Mystery series:

Murder at the Creek

Related books in the Romancing the Californian Cowboys series:

Striking Gold

PROLOGUE

Melbourne, Australia — December

Alex Mason pulled into her driveway and turned off the car's engine, then sat gripping the steering wheel as tears of frustration burnt behind her eyes.

Six years.

Six years of long hours, without any extra pay, to build the after-school and summer tennis programs.

Oh, and six years of promoting the club in her own time by walking the entire neighbourhood doing letter-box drops.

And what do they do to show her how much her loyalty has meant to them? Why, they shut the doors—two weeks before Christmas—with no warning. No notice for her. No notice for the other employees. And worst of all, no notice for all the families whose children were enrolled for the summer tennis program.

Her fists clenched and unclenched as she let her anger simmer.

What were all those kids going to do over the summer now?

She took two deep, calming breaths, determined to find some sort of silver lining in this.

Money wouldn't be a problem. They'd given her six month's pay and Liam was earning good money these days, so she didn't have to find a new job immediately. Maybe she could find somewhere else to set up the program? She could check with all the other clubs in the area and if she was lucky maybe one of them could offer her a court or two for a few hours a day. Or maybe the City Council or a local school could help her out. Or if she couldn't find courts, maybe she could think of something else they could do, something besides tennis. Maybe even something at Liam's golf course.

She closed her eyes, determined to stay positive. Okay, so the club was closing and she'd lost her job, but the world hadn't come to an end. At least she'd thought to save a copy of the list of all the parents' names and phone numbers. She'd think of something and then contact every one of them.

Taking a deep breath, she grabbed her handbag and box of belongings and made her way inside.

As she stepped into the kitchen, uneasiness washed over her but she brushed it off and set her box and handbag on the table. She'd make a cup of tea and start making calls because, with Christmas just two weeks away, there was no time to lose.

As she pulled a mug from the cupboard she heard something.

Had a faint sound had come from the other end of the house?

Standing perfectly still, she focused on the silence, questioning whether she'd actually heard anything more than the sounds of the house settling. Then, just as she convinced herself it was nothing, the sound drifted toward her again.

She held her breath, waiting for fear to swallow her. Only it didn't. Whatever she'd heard didn't incite fear, but rather curiosity.

She crept down the long hall toward the source of the sound, searching for anything out of place, ears straining for more sounds. A muffled voice wafted toward her, dragging her closer to her bedroom door. Had Liam come home? She hadn't checked the garage—had he put his car away?

When she reached the door it stood slightly ajar. She pressed a finger to it, reluctantly, watching as it slowly swung open enough for her to see inside the room.

Her heart sank as she took in the scene before her; Liam's muscular back, tangled sheets, feminine hands clinging to his bare shoulders, a shock of long blonde hair trailing across the pillow.

She shrank back, unable to tear her eyes away. Short sharp gasps of air filled her lungs, but she couldn't exhale. She clasped her stomach, hard, doubling over, and somehow the movement pushed her breath out. She gulped in air and immediately regretted it—it tasted of massage oil and sweat. She stared at them, expecting them to turn and look at her. Had their groans and heavy breathing drowned out her desperate gasps? A herd of raw emotions thundered through her, yet she still stood paralysed—drawn to watch even though repulsed.

This couldn't be happening.

She blinked, slowly, and then rubbed her eyes but the sight before her remained unchanged. When she cleared her throat, she expected Liam to look up, but he didn't react.

She coughed, louder.

Still nothing.

She grabbed the handle of the bedroom door and pulled it shut with a bang. Stepping back, she leaned against the wall for support, listening to her thunderous heartbeat as she waited for the inevitable tears to flow. Only no tears came.

She gritted her teeth and took a few short breaths, gaining strength as anger once again welled up inside her.

Strained voices finally filtered through the closed door. They were followed by shuffling and the slamming of the ensuite door. A moment later the bedroom door squeaked open. Liam stood there wearing nothing but his boxers and a vague excuse for a smile. He blinked too quickly; uncomfortably.

'You're home early, honey. I ... uh ... wasn't expecting you.'

Huffing out a breath, she stepped into the centre of the hallway shaking her head back and forth slowly. She couldn't look at him so she focused on a photo of the two of them; one taken on a sunny Queensland beach. It was their honeymoon, almost ten years earlier. Her brow tightened as she remembered the photo being taken—remembered her thoughts at the time, that she'd married the most wonderful man on the planet.

She'd been planning to suggest they go back to the same beach for their anniversary.

Biting her lower lip so hard she tasted blood, she focussed her mind on him. Suddenly a series of images flooded in; the beeping of text messages at odd hours; the hesitation on his face each time he told her about workshops that would take him out of town; and the unexpected surprise of finding freshly washed sheets on the bed last week. How long had this been going on? How long had she failed to recognise the signs that seemed so clear now?

Her forehead tightened further as she tried to think faster, to put things into perspective. When did they last have sex?

For the third time today, a wave of anger washed over her. She closed her eyes, shaking her head, wanting everything about this day to be a dream, but knowing it wasn't.

When she opened her eyes he'd moved closer. He reached a hand out toward her but she raised her hands, palms facing him, as she took two quick steps back. 'Don't.'

His hand dropped to his side. His eyes pleaded. 'Babe, it's ... not what you think.'

'It's not what you think.' She repeated his words, unsure whether out loud, or in her mind. She swallowed hard, and then, lifting an eyebrow, she turned to gaze down the hall looking for some sort of inspiration. She twisted her wedding band round and round as she tried to find the right words—any words—that would adequately express her disgust and mortification. There were none that could do her feelings justice. 'Right, so it's not what I think. Then what is it, Liam?'

He stared at her, an awkward half-smile twisting his face. It was the first time in all the years she'd known him that he struggled to speak. He was the smoothest talker she'd ever met, and she'd adored his non-stop chatter, his flirtatious grin, his winks and caresses. All those little things that had made her believe she was the centre of his universe.

When he finally broke the silence his words were anything but smooth. 'She ... I ... I mean we ...'

She huffed out another breath and swallowed hard. Then it dawned on her that, surprisingly, she was amused by his discomfort.

A sense of calm washed over her. Maybe, on some level, she had known.

About Liam's cheating.

About the club owners' plans to sell out.

About the rug being pulled out from under her very existence for the second time in her life.

'You know what? I don't even want to hear your explanation. It doesn't matter.'

The man in front of her ran a shaky hand through his hair, blinking rapidly as his mouth opened and shut like a beached fish.

He was a stranger. A man she didn't know.

And importantly, a man she no longer wanted to know.

CHAPTER 1

Sixteen months later

Alex wiped the sweat from her brow as she leaned up against her car, catching her breath. She'd just finished jogging the five kilometre track that circled Albert Park Lake and as she inhaled the fresh morning air she took in the colours of autumn. The trees had already started dropping their leaves, and those still clinging to the branches were turning various shades of red.

A wry smile touched her lips as she stared at the leaves on the ground. Their lives were over, their rich colours faded to dull brown. They'd soon be nothing more than dust on the wind. She swallowed hard as her shoulders drooped. She'd turned thirty-one on her last birthday, edging closer to the day when her own colours would begin to fade, and what did she have to show for herself besides a failed marriage and a ruined career?

She wiped her forearm across her face again, and grunted with frustration. Where were her endorphins today? Running usually gave her a lift, yet today she'd needed to remind herself once again that she was neither the only person in the world to lose a job without warning nor the only woman to have been cheated on by a husband. She wasn't even the only athlete to have a career come to a grinding halt due to an injury.

Trying to lift her spirits, she made a mental checklist of the positives. The divorce was finalised. She had a good job now—okay, it was long hours, and somewhat mind-numbing at times, but the pay was good. She was ahead on her mortgage payments and if she continued to work hard for another few years she could consider a less demanding job; one that would allow time for other parts of her life.

Pulling the band from her hair, she bent over and combed her fingers through her long damp tresses, wondering what had brought on today's trip down self-pity lane. When she straightened up, she looked toward the lake and a slight smile pulled at her cheeks. A group of small dinghies bobbled across its surface, the tiny little boats carrying small children learning to sail. A fresh gust of wind brought with it the sound of their laughter. That must have been it. The sound of young children enjoying themselves always triggered a twisted jumble of pleasure and pain.

She sighed, forgiving herself for her less than cheerful thoughts. Then, remembering the card from the post office saying she needed to collect a registered letter, she checked her watch, noting she had plenty of time to get to the post office before mid-day.

But for the life of her she couldn't think who'd have sent her a registered letter. Unless she'd won the lottery?

~~*~~

'You aren't going to believe this.'

Alex sat at her kitchen table, facing her sisters, Casey and Taylor. The twins were younger versions of her; each had flame red hair, green eyes and a smattering of freckles across their cheeks. What set them apart these days was Casey's short cropped style, whereas Taylor and Alex both still wore theirs long.

The twins both smiled and rolled their eyes.

'So tell us, already. I can't stand the suspense.' Casey picked up one of Taylor's mini sausage rolls, dunked it into the bowl of tomato sauce, and popped the whole thing into her mouth.

Alex placed an envelope on the table in front of them. 'Did either of you get one of these?'

The twins looked at each other and shook their heads in unison. Casey spoke. 'I didn't have any mail yesterday, but I'm not sure my postman comes every day.'

'Me neither,' said Taylor. 'What is it? It looks official.'

Alex removed the letter and began reading aloud. The beginning identified the sender and explained the firm had been engaged to handle the estate of one Steven Mason of Masons Flat, California. Alex read quickly at first, and then slowed when she got to the important bits.

Steven Mason, a man whom neither Casey nor Taylor could possibly remember, had named the three of them as the joint beneficiaries of his entire estate.

Taylor quirked an eyebrow. 'I don't get it. Who was Steven Mason?'

Casey looked over to Alex with a question on her face. 'I don't get it either. I have this vague recollection of his name ... maybe ... but who was he ... and what, exactly, have we inherited?'

Alex shrugged her shoulders, and then an eyebrow quirked involuntarily as a smile crept onto her face. 'Steven Mason was our great uncle, and it looks like we've inherited a gold-mining town called Masons Flat.'

CHAPTER 2

'Welcome to Sacramento. On behalf of the Captain, and all the crew, we thank you for flying with us and hope you have a lovely stay in our beautiful city.'

The moment the seat belt sign went off, Alex stood and threw her arms back to open up her shoulders. Then her left hand reached up under the collar of her jacket in what was practically a reflex action. She pressed her fingers into the tight deltoid muscle and even through the fabric of her tee-shirt she could feel the scars with her thumb and forefinger. The old injury always bothered her more when she was tired.

A half hour later she was waiting at the taxi stand and soaking up the warmth of the California sun. She looked up, watching as the clouds changed shape, floating along on air currents that never made their way to earth. It had been a long flight, but well worth it, leaving Melbourne's increasingly colder weather behind to arrive in California's spring.

It never failed to amaze her how the time difference worked—how she could arrive in California on the same day she'd left Australia—and nearly the same time. It was as if the trip had taken only a blink of an eye except that her body knew it had been nearly twenty-four hours since she'd left her house, even if the clocks begged to differ.

She smiled, imagining her sisters still tucked into their warm beds with their partners, doonas up around their chins. She'd get her head around the time difference eventually, but for now she was simply looking forward to a long walk to stretch her legs, followed by a shower, a proper meal, perhaps an hour or two in front of the telly, followed by a soft bed.

~~*~~

Alex woke to a beautiful blue sky, feeling excited and re-invigorated. The bed had been as good as she'd hoped, and she'd slept better than

11

she had in a long time. Maybe it had something to do with feeling at home in California; after all, she was born right here in Sacramento.

After a quick jog along the streets of Old Town, she showered and had a leisurely breakfast. A half hour before she was due at her appointment, she headed across to the Capitol Mall which had been blocked off for a street market. Stands displayed an impressive array of fruit and vegetables, such as cherries, tomatoes, zucchinis, squash, melons and apricots, as well as fresh flowers and wine. The whole street buzzed with activity, providing a pleasant contrast to the high-rise buildings on each side of the mall. She peered into one of the stands, amazed by the size of the strawberries on offer. She smiled at the vendor, wondering if everything in California was bigger and better than anywhere else.

She tore herself away, and it wasn't long before she found the building and made her way up to the sixth floor.

A tall man with a full head of grey hair, sporting horn-rimmed glasses and an expensive looking suit, said good morning to her as she stepped through the doors. He flashed a warm smile when she replied, then switched his cup of coffee to his left hand, and extended his right. 'Ah you must be Alex Mason? We don't hear a lot of Australian accents in here. I'm Damien West. How was the flight?'

'Long.' She replied, shaking her head. 'But it was fine, thanks for asking.'

'I haven't ventured as far as Australia, but it's on my bucket list for when I retire. Now, before we get started, can I offer you a cup of coffee?'

A few minutes later they were seated in a quiet room in front of a rather thick file. Mr West put his hand on the file, but stopped short of opening it. 'I take it your sisters were unable to make the trip?'

Alex shook her head. 'Neither of them could take the time off work.'

'I understand; it was rather short notice. But you had no trouble?'

She tilted her head, wondering how honest she could be with him, but decided there was no point being anything but honest. 'My employer wasn't going to let me take the time off, so I quit. I was getting tired of the job anyway—this gave me a good excuse.'

Mr West's smile made her wonder if maybe she and her sisters were going to be so rich that it wouldn't matter if they all quit their jobs. But when his smile faded as he opened the file her heart dropped.

'I see. Well, perhaps we should get started. I think it'll be best if we keep it simple for today. We'll focus on bringing you up to speed with what you've inherited, and I'll give you an overview of the steps we'll need to take over the next few days. Then you can go away and think about it, and come back to me with further instructions.'

'Instructions?'

'Alex, the three of you have inherited a significant amount of assets and you'll need to determine the best type of ownership structure. We can assist you with everything if you wish, or you may prefer to use your own representatives.'

'Representatives?'

'Yes—accountants and lawyers. Then again, it might be best if you engage someone who understands both US and California taxes and laws. You may wish to consider using your uncle's accountant, given his knowledge of your uncle's assets.'

Alex put her elbows on the table and leant her head down. Lawyers, properties, taxes—this was sounding an awful lot like her divorce. She took a deep breath and looked up at him as she attempted to stifle a yawn.

He chuckled softly. 'I'm sure it seems complex at the moment, but it will all become clearer as we go through it. For now, how about I just give you an overview, and a summary to take away with you to read at your leisure and discuss with your sisters?'

Alex sat up straight, summoning all her wits. 'My sisters have given me full authority to do as I think best, so apart from any signatures you might need, I'm pretty sure I'll be able to handle everything myself.'

As he raised an eyebrow, he began organising the papers in front of them.

Frowning, she willed herself to pay attention as he began to talk her through the numbers, but her mind kept wandering, going round and round as she tried to recall when and how she'd met this uncle. They'd moved to Australia when she was in the first grade, and she was fourteen the next time they visited—when she and the twins came over to see their father. She didn't think she'd met this uncle on that visit. Of course, her father lived and worked in Sacramento, so it was possible he knew little about Masons Flat. Was it conceivable that he hadn't been aware of what he might one day inherit? Or was he just not terribly interested because it wasn't worth much in any case? She frowned, suspecting the latter was more likely. Her heart sank further as it occurred to her that she, Casey and Taylor may have inherited nothing more than tax liabilities. Maybe that was why Mr West said they needed an accountant.

She looked up when Mr West stopped talking, and she wondered just how much she'd missed.

'Now, as I mentioned in the letter, you and your sisters are the only beneficiaries.'

'Yeah, about that ... do you mean to say he didn't leave anything to any friends or other family members?'

Mr West nodded. 'Not one. I questioned them at the time when they changed their wills, but they were determined everything should stay in the Mason Family.'

'They?'

'Your grandfather and his brother, your great-uncle. The two of them came to see me, shortly after your father died. They were each other's beneficiary, with your father next in line. However when your father died ahead of them, they came in together and changed their wills, replacing the reference to your father with you and your sisters as joint beneficiaries.'

It seemed odd that her grandfather hadn't advised them. Would he have thought them too young to understand? Even so, surely he could have written to their mother after their father died? When they'd confronted their mother with the legal letter she'd claimed complete ignorance about Masons Flat. Then again, their mother had about as much business acumen as a gnat, and her new partner, Frank, the never-wanna-grow-up-surfer-slash-hippie had even less, but still, wouldn't her mother have at least twigged to the possibility that her daughters might inherit something one day?

Mr West smiled, reminding her of a school teacher. 'You look like you're fading. Had enough for today?'

'Yes, sorry, I am struggling a bit. But just to clarify, are you certain there are no other relatives?'

He cocked his head before answering. 'You're the only surviving Masons from the original founder. There may be distant relatives somewhere, but none your grandfather and great-uncle wanted to include.'

Alex took a deep breath, still shaking her head in disbelief. 'And my uncle never married? Had no children?'

'No, he never married, and he had no children.'

'I'm sorry I seem so surprised ... more like flabbergasted, actually. It simply wasn't ever on my radar.'

Mr West frowned slightly. 'At least it's a good surprise, yes?'

She grimaced. 'I don't know. Is it?'

A proper smile now touched his lips, and his eyes twinkled. 'Of course it's a good surprise.'

Twenty minutes later Alex sat at her hotel table, holding a fistful of keys in one hand and some documents in the other. She looked back and forth between the two, overwhelmed by her change in circumstances.

She and her sisters were now the proud owners of seven buildings in the main street of Masons Flat, which included a saloon, a boutique hotel and five other shops. There was also the home her uncle had been living in right up until his death, and some other assets that she would no doubt get her head around at some stage.

~~*~~

Alex pulled out of the rental car agency in a bright red convertible Mustang at eight-thirty the following morning, over the moon that they'd had the car she'd requested, and excited that she'd be in Masons Flat well before noon and could have lunch at the hotel.

She looked over her left shoulder, then her right, then her left again before pulling out onto the road and settling in behind a small sedan. Driving on the right side of the road was a little tricky at first, but the mantra a friend had given her seemed to help. Every time she made a turn onto a new street she repeated the phrase—*body in the middle ... body in the middle*—and it wasn't long before it started to feel less foreign.

She'd studied Google Maps the night before, and even though it was a slightly longer drive via Placerville, she'd decided to take that route. She had fond memories of stopping in Placerville for a hot chocolate when her father had taken her and the twins skiing to Lake Tahoe. She'd been nearly fourteen and her sisters eleven when they'd come to stay with him that Christmas. It was the last time any of them had seen him.

As she pulled into the small town, she breathed in the familiar scent of clean mountain air. She parked, got out and walked along the main street, poking her head into cafés, some gift shops, and a marvellous old hardware store. She liked to think she remembered some of the shops, but in truth she wasn't certain. In seventeen years things had no doubt changed.

After stopping for a cup of coffee, she did a quick walk along both sides of the street then returned to her car, dropped the roof down, and followed the signs to Highway Forty-Nine.

The two-lane road wound its way past farms and paddocks dotted with cattle, reminding her of the country roads at home. She slowed as she made her way through small towns that had an air of familiarity, surprised to see the odd stand of gum trees here and there. Had she been along this road when she was young? Or were California and Victoria just not all that different from each other?

A few minutes after eleven Alex spotted the sign for Masons Flat. The tree-lined road made its way past a few homes before arriving at a narrow bridge where a sign read *Welcome to Masons Flat*. She crossed the bridge, drove up a bit further, and found Main Street.

She'd arrived. She was in her town—the town that carried her family's name.

After parking in the front of the Masons Hotel, she got out of the car, and stood looking at the lovely old building. The two-story wooden structure, painted cream and dark green, had a verandah that ran all across the front of the upstairs. There appeared to be four sets of double-doors opening onto the verandah, where she imagined hotel guests could enjoy breakfast at small tables. The downstairs appeared to be the restaurant and bar. A row of flower boxes at the front, full of mixed blossoms, suggested the people who ran the business cared about it. The only thing it might need was a coat of paint, and she suspected that as the building owner it might be her responsibility.

She smiled as she read the sign saying food, lodging and spirits. She'd go for a wander and come back a bit later to have lunch and introduce herself to the manager. She snapped a few photos with her phone, and then made her way slowly along the wooden sidewalk which looked as though it had been there a hundred years. She and her sisters owned the hotel, and the five buildings alongside it. Did the shop owners have to maintain this sidewalk? There was so much she would need to understand.

Next door to the hotel was a small candy and ice-cream shop. When she opened the door to have a quick peek inside she was met with the mouth-watering scent of chocolate and roasted nuts. A young girl at the counter caught her eye, so she smiled, said hello and then stepped back outside. The next shop sold antiques and collectibles. A quick peek inside that door revealed the less appealing scent of musty fabrics and old furniture. There was a woman at the back who appeared busy with some stock and didn't even acknowledge her, so Alex ducked back out quickly. The next shop was vacant, followed by a clothing store with western boots and jeans in the window, and then the last of their shops was another vacant one. One of the first things on her agenda would be to find tenants for those empty shops. They'd be far easier to sell, and fetch a much higher price no doubt, once tenanted.

Beyond their shops on the same side of the road there was a steak house restaurant, a car park and then what looked to be two more empty shops. After that the street became residential, with small cottages set back behind established gardens. She snapped several more photos, and then made her way to the other side of the street.

On this side stood the town hall and an ornate church, followed by various businesses including some cafés, a largish shop with a sign that read hardware and homewares, a gift shop, barber, and what looked to be an upmarket jewellery store. There was also a mini-mall with a directory board showing some professional suites as well as retail.

At the corner, directly across from Masons Hotel, stood the Gold Nugget Saloon—temporarily closed, according to the lawyer, due to a fire which had completely gutted the kitchen. This was the only business her great-uncle had personally managed. Past the saloon were a couple more shops that were not only empty but heading toward dereliction.

It seemed surreal that three weeks ago she'd wondered how many more years it would take to build up enough equity in her apartment so she could take a part-time job and have time to get back into coaching. And now here she was, a significant property owner, albeit in a relatively unheard of Californian town. Then again, until she spoke to the accountant she probably wouldn't know exactly what everything was worth, but even so, she and her sisters owned nearly half of the Main Street shops, and if property values here were anything like Melbourne's, they should be laughing. She might even be able to afford to get rid of the apartment and buy a house again. That meant she could have a yard, and having a yard meant she could have a dog. Images of a home in one of Melbourne's leafy green suburbs filled her mind and her heart.

Shaking her head, knowing full well she was getting way ahead of herself, she began to make her way up the street toward the saloon. Just then an old pickup pulled up at the front of it, and the driver went inside through what she would have thought should be a locked front door. Her brow tightened as she recalled what Mr West had said, that works had come to a standstill when her uncle died. That being the case, no one should be going inside, tradesman or not.

CHAPTER 3

Travis Gold's jaws were still clenched as he drove into town. He'd spent the morning watching the veterinarian stitch up the leg of one of his most promising fillies when he should have been working her in the arena, getting her ready for the big rodeo. That she'd injured herself was bad enough, but that he knew exactly what part of the fence she'd have done it on made it worse. He'd spotted the damaged fence the day before and neither he nor his brother had gotten out there to fix it.

As he turned into Main Street he was surprised to see his brother's old F100 pickup at the front of the saloon. He didn't share Denver's love for the old rust bucket, but who was he to criticise someone's choice of transport when he was driving a Range Rover in what was almost exclusively Ford country.

Pulling to a stop behind Denver's pickup, he jumped out shaking his head, once again questioning his brother's decision to get involved with the saloon. Firstly, it belonged to the Masons. Secondly, why spend time at the saloon when there were things that needed doing around their own property—like getting ready for the rodeo, and like fixing that fence before one of the horses got hurt. But besides all that, with Old Man Mason gone there wasn't even any guarantee he'd get paid. What was he doing there now?

He stomped toward the saloon's entrance, determined to pull Denver out of there and set him onto more lucrative tasks, but as he approached the door he heard muffled voices and his footsteps slowed unconsciously.

'... rockabilly? It's heaps of fun to dance to.' That was Denver.

He couldn't hear the response, but he did hear soft laughter. It floated out the door bringing back memories of the laugh he'd grown up listening to. It couldn't be his mother's though—her funeral had been almost five years ago now.

When Travis stepped inside the saloon he came to a dead halt, allowing his eyes to adjust to the dark interior. The pair immediately stopped talking, and turned to face him.

Denver stood taller as he spotted him, and even in the limited light Travis could see the change come over Denver's face. Guilt never was his colour. The woman simply stared at him, an eyebrow quirked with curiosity.

Travis tried not to scowl, but he wasn't sure he'd succeeded. The woman's red hair could mean just one thing; a Mason had come to town—probably to claim her inheritance.

'Oh, er ... hey Travis. How's the filly?' Denver smiled, but his voice betrayed his guilt.

Travis wondered if Denver felt guilty about the filly, or about what he'd been telling this woman. Either way, it didn't matter. 'Tom says there's a good chance there won't be any permanent damage, but she'll be out of work for a while ... couple months at least. Worst case, could be up to six months.'

'Blasted mares and their kicking out.'

Travis scowled again, intentionally this time. 'You meant to say blasted fence, and blasted people for not fixing it, right?'

Colour flooded back to Denver's face. 'I've got those standoffs in my pickup. I meant to drag them out yesterday.'

'Yeah, well, no rush now is there? The damage has been done. I've moved the rest of the horses out to the back pasture, and she'll be in a stable for at least a couple of weeks.'

Denver looked down, scuffing his feet, then seemed to remember his manners. He looked at the woman beside him, then at his older brother. 'Oh, you two won't have met. Travis, this is Alex Mason. She's come all the way from Australia to have a look at the properties her uncle left her. Alex, this is my brother, Travis.'

Travis now turned to study the woman. She was tall and slender, with an athletic build. Her chestnut coloured hair, hanging just past the top of her shoulders, looked soft and silky but it was her eyes that really caught him off guard. Flecks in her green eyes sparkled like fool's gold.

He tore his eyes away from hers and cleared his throat, and then he took a step forward and held out his hand tentatively. He wasn't certain he wanted to touch her, in fact it seemed almost foolhardy, but if he was anything he was a man with manners. And right now he wished his father hadn't been so hung-up on manners—hadn't drummed them into his two boys from the time they were old enough to talk.

'Pleased to meet you, Alex.'

He'd shake her hand, but that didn't mean he had to make eye contact again. Instead, he stared at her hand as she reached forward and placed it in his.

'Likewise, I'm sure,' she said, her Australian accent sounding as smooth as her hair looked.

Her soft hand was at odds with her surprisingly strong grip. After a few seconds she pulled her hand back. Had she found his calloused hand disgusting? Good. Because if she did find him disgusting, maybe she'd find all the hardworking people here in Masons Flat disgusting, and sell everything. Quickly. And that could only be good for him and Denver.

Looking up, he briefly met the woman's gaze again, and then turned back to Denver. 'Look, I've gotta get going. I just spotted your pickup, and wondered what the ... uh ... what you were doing in here.'

Alex spoke before Denver had a chance to reply. Travis turned back to face her again.

'I won't stay either. I want to have a look around town before heading back to Sacramento, so I should keep moving too.'

'You're not staying at the old man's house?' Travis regretted his question as soon as the words left his mouth. Why should he care where this woman stayed? Why give her the impression he cared?

Her eyebrows rose inquisitively. 'No, I'm staying in Sacramento—at the Tower Bridge Inn. In fact I haven't even been over to look at the house yet. I've only just arrived a little while ago.'

'Right. Well then, welcome to Masons Flat. And safe trip back to Sacramento,' he said as he quirked a brow impatiently.

She tilted her head, as if taking his measure, then, out of nowhere, came this beautiful smile. 'Thank you.'

Her smile was contagious, but he did his best to suppress a response, instead simply nodding. He turned to Denver and shrugged. 'I'll see you back at home. We've got a lot to do today, you know that, right?'

Denver cocked his head. 'Yep, I'm heading out soon.'

Travis turned on his heel to leave, but before going he took one last look at the redhead. She was exactly the kind of woman he didn't need in his life, and yet every fibre of his body yearned to be near her. All he could hope was that she'd sell everything quickly and go home.

~~*~~

Alex breathed a sigh of relief the moment Travis Gold walked out the door. She wasn't sure she could have put up with him much longer. His eyes were most likely brown, but in the dimly lit saloon they'd looked black.

And intense.

Way too intense.

Now, with him gone, weariness squeezed in on her. Had putting up a strong facade drained all her energy, or was it the jetlag still?

She turned when Denver let out a loud sigh. The resemblance was strong between them—both having dark hair and eyes—but Denver lacked his brother's intensity. Denver seemed nice. And the apologetic look on his face made her wonder if he'd found his brother as difficult just then as she had.

'Well, that was ... intense.' She huffed out a breath, trying to make light of the awkwardness.

'Yeah, sorry about that. He's not always so abrupt. I think he's pretty upset about that filly.'

'Yes, I'm sure he must be.' She hesitated before allowing herself to ask the next question. 'Although I did get the feeling he wasn't too impressed about you being here in the saloon. It wouldn't have had anything to do with me, would it?'

Denver shook his head as a deep frown appeared. 'No, it's just ... he never liked me working on the saloon.'

'Really? And why's that?'

'It goes back a long way ... you see, the saloon used to belong to our family, and our Dad carried a real grudge about how we lost it. Travis, now he's head of the household, well he's kinda sensitive about it, too.'

'Oh?'

Denver's eyes darted back and forth for a moment before he continued. 'Besides, he's never been the same around women since his divorce.' He shrugged his shoulders, and quirked a smile. 'I probably shouldn't have said that.'

She smiled warmly, hoping he'd continue. 'I won't let on that I know.'

His quirky smile softened, and he let out a sigh. 'I don't think he trusts many women anymore.'

'Messy, I take it?'

'Yeah, she ran off with a bull-rider.'

So, they had something in common—cheating spouses. Not exactly a great basis for a meaningful friendship, but it least she didn't take his rudeness quite so personally now. 'Someone he knew?'

'Yeah, kinda.'

And that had to be worse. At least she hadn't known her replacement.

'Well, I'm glad you don't think it was about me.'

Denver started to say something else, but gave her an uncomfortable smile instead. She wanted to ask him more about how the saloon's ownership changed, but decided not to pressure him for further information. She'd ask the lawyer if he knew the saloon's history. Or maybe the accountant would know. There was no point putting Denver off-side with too many questions, although there was one more she needed to ask.

'Given the works have stopped, what were you doing in here today?'

Denver's face lit up. 'Ah,' he said, holding up a finger in a *wait just one moment* gesture as he dashed back into the burned-out kitchen.

Alone now, Alex took the opportunity to look around the saloon. A fine layer of dust covered just about everything, but even with the dust, the room seemed to hold memories of better days. She reached out, and traced the well-worn edge of the bar with her fingertips, imagining people leaning up against this bar, in the days well before she was even born. She looked up, taking in the huge mirror across from her. The beautiful piece was set in an ornately-carved dark wooden frame. She leaned toward it, frowning, noticing damage in one corner, and wondering how it might be repaired.

Reaching down beside her, she pressed her hand onto a stool. She swept her hand over it, removing the dust to reveal rich burgundy leather, slick and shiny with years of wear. She sat for a moment, turning to take in the rest of the room. A large tarp in one corner covered what appeared to be a pool table; in the other was a small dance floor complete with another covered object that by its shape and location must surely be a juke box. Tables were scattered throughout the rest of the saloon, with chairs covered in the same leather as the bar stools.

She closed her eyes, letting her imagination take over, and could almost smell freshly cooked burgers and fries. She listened with her heart, allowing the tinkling of ice dropping into glasses, the laughter of patrons, and music from the jukebox surround her. She'd never been much of a bar-goer, yet this saloon didn't feel like a stranger to her.

Then there were footsteps—was it customers going to and fro, buying drinks, heading to the pool table maybe, or to the dance floor?

Her eyes flew open at Denver's voice. He'd stopped beside her with a tool belt in one hand and a sander in the other. 'I'd left my tools behind. Hadn't needed them until this morning, and then I remembered this was the last place I'd used them.'

It took her a moment to reorient herself, and then she smiled. 'Oh, so you aren't a full-time carpenter I take it?'

'Not any more. I used to be, but when Dad got sick, Travis and I moved back home and I had to help running the place, so I only do a bit of carpentry work now—the odd bit on our properties, and for friends and that. This morning I was working on ... I was doing some work at our place, and remembered this was where I'd left my sander.'

'Oh, so if you're not really doing carpentry work any longer, why did my uncle engage you to look after the saloon repairs?' It seemed odd that her uncle would employ him if he wasn't really doing that sort of work any longer; especially given the saloon was the basis of contention between them.

When Denver was slow to respond, she tilted her head, staring at him until he answered.

'He didn't really ... his insurance company engaged a contractor, but Old Man Mason wasn't happy with the quality of some of the work they'd done, so he asked me to oversee it—just check on the work from time to time and keep an eye on things.'

'But if you were just overseeing it, why the sander?'

He shuffled his feet for a moment before answering. 'I can't help myself, you know? There was some work the boys weren't doing right, so I just thought I'd touch it up.'

She smiled, appreciating his dedication. But it still didn't answer why he'd even been asked to be involved. 'But why you? Surely, there are other good carpenters in the area?'

'Yeah, of course there are ... but ... well ... Travis and I had made an offer to buy the saloon, so he knew we'd have a special interest in making sure the repairs were done properly.'

Alex stepped back, his unexpected admission surprising her. So, these brothers had put in an offer to buy the saloon—one that hadn't been accepted. Perhaps that explained why Travis was still sensitive about it.

Regardless of the saloon's history, she wasn't going to let that be a factor in her decision making process. She liked the saloon—liked the feel of it—and was beginning to wonder if it mightn't be worth hanging onto. And if that were the case, it might be an option to hang onto all the other properties as well. Maybe this wouldn't be a sell-up-and-go-home exercise after all.

'Right. Well, before we go can I have a quick look at the damage in the kitchen?'

CHAPTER 4

Alex was immediately invited into the dining room of Masons Hotel by an older man with a waistline that suggested the food they served must be excellent.

She ordered a Caesar salad and one of those brilliant iced-teas that the Americans were so good at, and sat watching the other patrons in the cheerful dining room.

When her lunch arrived she pulled out her phone, took a couple of photos, and emailed them to her sisters. It was still too early to ring—they'd probably still be sound asleep—but she put a caption on the email saying she was dining at their hotel, and followed it with a row of smiley faces.

When she finished her meal she walked over to the register to pay, and the man who'd served her appeared straight away.

'The salad was lovely, thank you,' she said with a genuine smile.

'I'm so glad you enjoyed it. We certainly aim to please our guests.'

'Yes, well, about that ... now might be a good time to introduce myself. I'm Alex Mason, Steven Mason's great-niece—which actually makes me the owner now.' She held out her hand, which he grasped in his larger one.

'Alex, it's a pleasure to meet you. I'm Sam Johnson, and lunch is on the house, of course.'

'Oh, no, I'm more than happy to pay. The meal was lovely. I just wanted to introduce myself, given we'll no doubt have plenty of dealings in the future.'

'No, I insist. My treat. I'm just surprised I didn't realise who you were. The family resemblance is rather strong.'

'Thank you, Mr Johnson, but it really isn't necessary.'

'Just Sam, please, and I won't be taking your money. Not this time, anyway.'

She smiled again. 'Thank you, Sam. The hotel is lovely, and the flower boxes out the front are such a nice touch.'

He beamed at her words. 'My wife does them. I'll tell her you admired them—she'll be tickled pink that you both noticed and mentioned them.'

'She isn't here today?'

'No, she's here on the weekends, but this time of year I can pretty much handle things without her during the week.'

'Oh, so you don't live on the premises?'

'No, we have a night manager who lives here in exchange for being on call at odd hours.'

She quirked a brow. 'I don't suppose I could have a look around?'

He rolled his eyes. 'How stupid of me. Of course you'd want to have a look. Follow me. We'll have a quick look upstairs, and then I'll show you the kitchen and back rooms.'

Sam led the way as they climbed the well-worn carpeted stairs up to the floor above. With each step the floorboards squeaked in protest, and Alex wondered just how many times they'd borne the weight of guests and workers over the years. She allowed her hand to trail along the carved wooden handrail, noting the grooves in sections where the wood must have been softer and more prone to wear. How many hands would have done exactly what she was doing now? The wood was as smooth as glass, much more so than any sandpaper could have made it.

When he reached the top of the landing Sam stopped for a moment to catch his breath.

Alex stopped on the step below him, and pointed to some old photos hanging on the wall beside her. 'Do you know who the people are in the photos?'

'I know most of them. This one here, this is David Mason, and his wife Sarah. And the two little chaps with them are your Uncle Steven and his brother, Joe. Now I'd say Joe must've been your grandfather, right?'

When he paused, and looked at her for acknowledgement, she nodded.

Then he continued. 'The boys mustn't have been more than six or seven in that photo.'

Alex leaned forward, studying the photo carefully. Being black and white meant she couldn't tell if they all had the red hair that ran in her family, but she suspected they probably did.

28

Now she pointed to the photo just down from where she was standing. 'And this photo, with the three men?'

'Ah, that's the three town founders—Thomas Mason, Mr James and Mr Gold. The tallest of the three men is Thomas Mason—I know that because there are a few more photos of him in some of the bedrooms.'

Alex stepped down to study the photo closely. It was like she was looking at a photo of her own father, the way he looked when she last saw him. The man was taller and more rugged than her father, but the family resemblance was strong—his sharp nose and deep-set eyes. She drew in a breath, suddenly missing her father. She hadn't known him well, and regretted that now more than ever.

'Would you like me to show you a couple of the bedrooms? I shouldn't be away from the front desk for too long, in case anyone comes in.'

They had a quick look in the guest rooms—which were each different, yet lovely in their own way—with their individual balconies that overlooked the street. She'd probably enjoy staying in one herself, and that was a good sign. When she told Sam as much he beamed.

After they'd made their way back downstairs and had a quick look at the kitchen and said hello to the cook, Alex turned to say goodbye. 'Thanks so much for the tour, Sam. It's a beautiful old hotel and your presentation of it is top-notch, that's for sure. Speaking of presentation, are there any repairs you need done? Anything you should let me know about?'

'Not really. Things do come up from time to time, but there's nothing at the moment. Besides, I fix what I can myself. I'm not bad with a screwdriver and a hammer when I need to be.'

'Well, don't hesitate to let me know if there's anything I should be aware of.'

He walked her to the front door and Alex was about to leave when she thought to ask. 'It seems awfully quiet for such a nice day. There have hardly been any cars in town.'

'It is a bit quiet today, but it's early in the year. Things pick up once the kids get out of school and families start going on vacation—that's when we start to see more tourists. Plus the County Fair and the big Jumping Frog Jubilee over in Angels Camp is coming up in two weeks. We always get a bit of overflow then. It'll make the town busy.'

She looked at him blankly. 'Jumping Frog what?'

Amazement crossed his face. 'Don't tell me you haven't heard of it?'

'Uh, sorry, no, I have no idea what you're talking about.' Was this some sort of gag they pulled on newcomers? Jumping frogs? Right up there with Australia's legendary Drop Bears, no doubt.

'It's only the biggest weekend around here. People come from all over the country, and even Canada, to enter the Calaveras County Jumping Frog Jubilee. Not to mention the Frogtown Rodeo.'

Her forehead tightened involuntarily. 'You're serious, aren't you?'

'Of course I am,' he said, shaking his head and shrugging his shoulders. 'Look it up on the internet if you don't believe me. It started ages ago. Mark Twain wrote a story about it back in the eighteen-sixties, and it became an annual event sometime in the nineteen-twenties. We're fully booked for the whole time, plus a couple days either side of it. And I expect it'll stay a bit busier from then on.'

'Well ... I truly did not know.'

His face broke into a wide smile. 'Well, now you do. And you can't miss it. Even if frog jumping isn't your thing, the rodeo is worth going to. Lucky you've got a place to stay as I doubt you'd find a room anywhere around here at the last minute.'

For a moment she didn't know what he meant, and then it dawned on her. Her Uncle Steven's home was hers now. She'd go have a look at it before she left town. She smiled at him and started to move to the door but could tell he wasn't finished. 'And?' she prompted him.

'And then there's Denver Gold's big thirtieth birthday bash next weekend. He's throwing a huge party—live music, barbeque, and dancing. Lots of dancing. Everyone's going. It'll be a great way to meet everyone from town, and then some.'

Now it all made sense. Denver's flirting, and asking her about rockabilly music. Perhaps he'd have invited her if Travis hadn't interrupted them.

~~*~~

Staying in her uncle's house—her house—hadn't been something she'd contemplated. He hadn't died in it, but from what the lawyer said he'd been rather unwell for several months in the lead up to his death which meant the house could be a horrible mess. And it had been locked up for several weeks now, which meant it probably smelled. She wrinkled her nose at the thought, and then made the short drive down Mason Street until she found the address.

She parked out the front and stood gazing at the house with wide eyes.

When she'd been told she'd inherited his house, she'd imagined some sort of rustic cabin, or miner's cottage. Old, like him, and probably in need of significant repairs. She'd expected an unkempt garden full of weeds, and perhaps a broken down car out the front.

However, what she found was the complete opposite.

The house was modern, constructed from a combination of corrugated metal and masonry walls, with huge windows all around. It seemed like it might have been specifically designed for the land it sat on, capturing the views across a wooded area to the hills in the distance. At the front it had a well-designed low maintenance garden, and there were no cars at all, let alone a broken down one.

Then it occurred to her that she could have gotten the address wrong. She double checked her notes and looked at the letterbox at the front. This was definitely the right address.

She walked past the house along the side street—Blue Gum Road— where she now saw the driveway leading to a garage at the back of the house. Just past the driveway was a huge hedge that separated the home from its neighbour. When she stopped to have a look at the neighbouring home, similar in style but larger, she wondered if both houses might have been built at the same time, by the same builder. Perhaps her uncle and the neighbour had gotten a better deal that way.

She made her way to the end of the street, noticing the rest of the homes were more in keeping with what she'd expected to find—modest homes, but older, some with nice gardens, some less loved, and yes, some with broken down cars in the front gardens.

Arriving back at her uncle's house, she walked up to the door and dug out the keys the lawyer had given her. He'd said it would be fine if she went into any of the untenanted properties. They were, after all, hers now.

As she entered the house she found herself in a light filled entry hall that had a huge living room off to the right and what must be the master bedroom to the left. Further along, the entry hall led to an open plan kitchen and family area. She suspected there would be further bedrooms and utility rooms beyond that.

She stood there in awe. The house smelled of lavender. Then she remembered something Mr West had said about her uncle having employed both a gardener and a housekeeper. Whoever had been doing the housekeeping had done a brilliant job, and she couldn't fault the gardener either.

Making her way toward the back of the house, she located her uncle's study. She entered, surprised at how organised it was. A large mahogany desk sat facing a window that overlooked the large park across the road. Cabinets, also made of mahogany, held files and binders that were all labelled. A filing cabinet sat in the corner, with pull out drawers filled with loose files. She'd have to go through the files at some stage over the next week, but not this minute.

As she continued to explore each room the house grew on her, and she got a sense that not only could she see herself staying for the rest of her visit, she could actually see herself living in this house.

And just as that thought started to develop there was a rap on the front door. Had someone seen her come in? Perhaps the local welcoming committee?

CHAPTER 5

Travis couldn't get the image of Alex out of his mind. He'd been trying to focus on his horses, but every time his concentration lapsed for even a moment her green eyes were there—flashing—igniting something he wanted to leave buried deep.

Not having a woman in his life was a decision he'd made after his divorce—he didn't need that kind of heartache ever again—but even if he did, the last woman he should be getting fixated on was Alex Mason. For one thing, she didn't even live in the country. And for another thing, she was a Mason.

He dismounted and rubbed the young gelding's neck before tying him to the hitching post. The gelding was ready, so the last-minute substitution wasn't a huge issue for the rodeo, but the filly would have brought a better price. This gelding worked well, but he didn't have anywhere near the visual appeal of the filly.

When he spotted Denver driving up, he called out and waved him over.

Denver parked, then approached with the stand-offs in his hands. 'Thought I'd go fix that fence while I'm thinking about it,' he said, stopping next to him and rubbing the gelding's nose.

'Good idea. It won't take more than a few minutes. What else have you got planned for the day?'

Denver looked at him sheepishly. 'I wanted to work on the dance floor and bandstand. Party's in just over a week, you know. You haven't forgotten about it, have you?'

Travis huffed as he shook his head. Forget? How could he forget the party that Denver talked about daily? He knew it was important to Denver, so he was trying to be enthusiastic, but one side of him knew he'd cancel it if he had his druthers. 'How could I? Look, you work on the dance floor, and I'll put this guy out and then go check the cattle.'

'You sure? I can go check them as soon as I'm done; it won't take me long.'

Travis had to laugh at that. Nothing would take long, where Denver was concerned. He was a glass-half-full sort of person if ever there was one. He patted his younger brother on the shoulder. 'Go, before I change my mind.'

Travis waited for Denver to walk off, and when he didn't, Travis asked the question that was burning inside him. 'And did you invite her?'

Denver looked at him with the innocence of a two-day old foal. 'Invite her? Who are we talking about?'

Travis scowled. As if he didn't know.

Denver barely concealed a sly grin. 'Oh, her, yeah, I thought about it, but then you walked in and we never got back to talking about music and dancing. Do you think I should've mentioned it?'

Travis did his best to keep all emotion from both his voice and his face. He wasn't sure he managed, however. 'It's your party, little bro. You can invite whoever you want.'

Denver looked over his shoulder toward the back pastures, a slow smile creeping onto his face. When he turned back to him, he lifted an eyebrow. 'You seem rather interested in her. Has she gotten under that tough skin of yours?'

'Watch it, Den, or I might change my mind about things.'

Denver let out a huge laugh and started back toward his pickup. 'Yeah, reckon I'll invite her. Wish I knew how to get a hold of her.'

'You do, you big oaf. She told you. She's staying at the Tower Bridge Inn.'

'Oh yeah, she did too. How'd I miss that?'

Travis didn't reply as he went back to grab the gelding to untack him and put him out, but he did think about the conversation. The thing was, he was uncertain whether he was excited or terrified.

~~*~~

Alex peaked out the living room window where she could just make out the profile of a tall man wearing a dark blue suit. He looked out of place on this warm day in this casual small town, but nothing about him seemed menacing.

She opened the door, finding him talking on his phone. He quickly apologised to the caller and shoved the phone in his pocket before reaching out his hand and pasting a huge smile on his face.

'Ms Mason, I assume?'

She stared at his outstretched hand for some time and then looked up at his face. 'Yes, and you are?'

'Phil Marshall, of Marks and Marshall Realty, at your service.'

Estate agent. She placed her hand in his, gave it a quick shake, and then pulled it away. She'd take Travis Gold's calloused working-man's hand any day over this man's damp one. The thought startled her—it had come out of nowhere.

'What can I do for you Mr Marshall?'

'Call me Phil, please. And it's not what you can do for me; it's what I can do for you. Have you got a few minutes to talk?'

Alex wanted to say no, but that seemed far too rude. Instead, she cocked her head and bit her lip. 'A few minutes. Sure.'

He hesitated for just a moment, as if expecting her to invite him in. When she didn't, he continued. 'Great. I've had a bit of interest in this property—several people have asked if I know what the owner is going to do, and I don't think you'll have any trouble getting quite a good price. Shall I put together a proposal for you?'

'I beg your pardon?'

'Oh, well, naturally I assumed you'll be selling this property, along with the others in town? I understand you're Australian, and ... well, correct me if I'm wrong, but I assumed you'll be selling everything.'

'That is a rather bold assumption, Mr ... I'm sorry, I've forgotten your name.'

She hadn't forgotten it. She just wanted to shrink his ego a bit. His shoulders dropped as he took a breath, telling her the ploy had worked. He seemed much closer to her height now.

'It's Marshall. Phil Marshall, of Marks and Marshall Realty.'

'Yes, of course, Mr Marshall. I haven't decided what I'll be doing with any of the properties. I only arrived in the country a few days ago, so you'll appreciate I will need a bit of time to digest everything and make some decisions.'

He fished in his pocket and pulled out a business card. 'By all means. My apologies if I've overstepped the mark. I was passing by and saw your car. I knew who it must be, you know? Anyway, I wanted to make sure you know I'm here to help, in whatever way I can.'

She took his card, glanced at it, and shoved it into her jeans pocket. 'Thanks, again. I appreciate your willingness to help, *in any way you can*. I may just take you up on your offer, once I've had a chance to make some decisions.'

'I hope you do, Ms Mason. I sincerely hope you do.'

~~*~~

Travis hosed off the young gelding and put him in a pen with a flake of alfalfa. He'd worked hard and deserved an extra feed before going out into the pasture with the rest of the youngsters. He watched as the horse began eating, enjoying the sound of his munching. There was something about the sound that always relaxed him.

Well, usually.

Today it wasn't working. All he could see while looking at the deep green alfalfa leaves was a pair of flashing green eyes in a face bordered by flame red hair.

He wondered if Denver would invite her to his party. Even if he didn't, Masons Flat was a small town. If she planned on hanging around for any length of time, he'd see her again.

Not that seeing her was a good idea.

In fact, it was without a doubt a bad idea.

So why did his heart race at the thought of her? What spell had she cast on him that kept her floating across his mind?

He walked into the barn, glanced at the filly's bandage to ensure it hadn't slipped, and then went inside to grab the keys to the Kabota rural terrain vehicle, or The Beast, as he and Denver usually called it. He'd check the cattle and focus on his chores. Then he'd work another of the youngsters, and with a bit of luck, he'd be able to push all thoughts of Alex Mason aside.

~~*~~

Thinking about Travis Gold's handshake had been a mistake as now she couldn't get those dark eyes of his out of her mind. She'd met men who were more handsome than him, indeed she'd married one. But she'd never met a man who had brought out such an immediate and strong physical reaction in her, and it had her on edge.

As the estate agent drove off, Alex let out a sigh of relief. She'd never been attracted to men like him—forward, and full of false compliments. Or had she? Wasn't Liam a bit that way? Hadn't he won her over with his charm and compliments?

A wave of nausea surprised her as memories of the way her marriage had ended came flooding back. She'd been such a fool. Why couldn't she have seen then what she could see so clearly now? Was it just the contrast to a serious man like Travis Gold that made her realise those overly charming types weren't for her?

She did a mental face palm. Why was she using Travis Gold, a man she barely knew, as a comparison to anyone? She frowned, once again blaming the jetlag for her inability to stay on topic. She was here to investigate her assets and make some decisions. And now that she could see how nice this house was, her next task would be to get shifted in. Why pay for a hotel in Sacramento when she could stay here?

As she continued her walk-through of the house, she liked what she saw until she reached the laundry and dread washed over her. The back door was ajar. She reached for the doorknob and when it didn't turn in her hand, she knew that meant it was locked, but when she pushed it shut it popped right back open. It wasn't catching properly. She looked at it carefully, and her heart sank further. It didn't have a deadlock, just the flimsy lock in the door handle.

At least there was a screen door. She tested it, disappointed to find that not only was it not locked, it didn't even have a lock.

Country people were often less concerned with security than city people—she knew that, as it was the same in Australia—but this was a relatively new house. Her uncle must have been completely blasé about security not to have a deadbolt, or at least a locking screen door.

She couldn't stay in the house this way. She'd have to get it fixed before she could move in, and that meant she'd need either a locksmith or a carpenter; quickly.

CHAPTER 6

Alex knew a carpenter who claimed to be pretty good at his job. And no doubt Sam could tell her how to contact him.

When she dropped in, Sam greeted her with a warm smile. 'I didn't expect to see you again quite so soon. Couldn't get enough of our fine offerings?'

She chuckled. 'Lunch was superb, but I'm actually here for some information.'

He ducked his head conspiratorially and whispered. 'You've come to the right spot if information is what you're after.'

As the expression *small town gossips* came to mind, she decided she'd spare the details.

'I stopped in at my uncle's house ... well, I guess it's mine now, but anyway ... I wondered if you knew who did his gardening and housekeeping?'

'Oh, the housekeeper would be Hilda Weston. She does some of the cleaning here for us as well. Why, is something wrong?'

'No, not at all. I'd like to speak to her about continuing, that's all.'

He let out a sigh. 'She'll be pleased to hear that. Here, I'll jot down her name and number for you. I'm not sure about the gardens, but it might have been the neighbour.'

'Thanks, Sam. Oh ... and while I was there I spotted a few things that need fixing and I recalled Denver Gold being a carpenter, but I don't know how to get in touch with him.'

'Denver? Well, his place isn't far from your uncle's. Probably about ten minutes down the road. I don't have his number handy, but I can tell you how to get there.'

~~*~~

Alex followed Sam's instructions and stopped at the entrance gates. A large sign on the side stated *Welcome to Gold's Ranch, home of Gold's*

Hereford Cattle and T & D Golden Bar Quarter Horses. She was in the right place.

She drove through the gate and headed along the tree lined driveway. There were paddocks on both sides of the drive, and the one on the right held some of the cattle. At first, she wasn't even able to see the house but finally she spotted a structure ahead. The home was single storey, made of timber and stone, and looked massive. When she reached the circular drive at the front, she realised that although the house was quite large, what had appeared to be another wing of the house was actually a huge barn.

Parking, she got out to have a look around, and that's when she spotted a rider in an outdoor arena off to the right. Her instincts told her it was Travis, not Denver, but her feet seemed to have a mind of their own as she found herself walking toward the fence.

She knew nothing about horses other than what she'd seen at the races and the occasional agricultural show, but something told her that both this horse and its rider were special. Travis seemed as one with the horse as it ducked and weaved in the enclosed arena, chasing the cow in what was almost like a game of cat and mouse as the cow looked to be enjoying the game as well. She didn't once see Travis lift his hands or give the horse any instructions, so as far as she knew it might be done with mental telepathy.

She stood there for several minutes watching him before he noticed her. When he finally looked over, the cow had been coerced into a small pen, and the horse stood guard at its entrance. Both the horse and the cow looked worn-out, and she wondered how long he'd been at this before she'd arrived.

He dismounted, gave the horse a pat on the neck and then walked over and shut the gate of the pen. Then he turned and walked toward her, leading the horse behind him.

'We meet again. Twice in one day,' he said in a monotone that didn't give away his feelings about seeing her.

Somehow, he seemed less intimidating than he had earlier, taking up less of her personal space than he had in the confines of the saloon. Or maybe he was simply in his element here, making him seem more relaxed. But when he removed his hat and sunglasses, she could see his eyes; they were smouldering. Or was she imagining that?

'I ... uh ... was looking for Denver. I need a carpenter, and I've heard he's the best in town.'

Travis rubbed the back of his hand across his forehead and then put his sunglasses back on. 'Ah, right, and so he is. He's out at the back of the house, working on the dance floor.'

Her eyebrow quirked involuntarily, and she wished it hadn't. She reached up and pretended to remove some hair from her face.

'Is it okay if I go back there to find him?'

When Travis hesitated a moment, she thought he might say no. Then he put his hat back on, and reached behind him and patted the horse on the neck. 'Sure. I'd take you myself but I need to hose this guy off—he's had a good workout this afternoon.'

'Well, I'm far from an expert on horses, but he sure looked great. Did he do everything himself, or were you giving him signals I couldn't see?'

Now Travis smiled, and it changed his whole demeanour. 'He did most of it himself. I've been working with him for almost a year now. He has some of the best instincts I've come across.'

'Is he a horse you bred? I mean, I saw the sign when I came in, so I assume you breed horses here?'

He nodded slowly, and then turned to look over his shoulder toward the back of the house. The gesture felt dismissive; like he wanted her to go already, but when he turned back to her his words belied his body language. 'Yeah, he's out of a well-bred mare I purchased a couple of years back. He's her first and she's had two more who I hope will turn out just as good.'

'If you trained him, and you'll be training the others, they'll no doubt be as good.' She bit her bottom lip as she finished speaking. She knew nothing about breeding horses or training animals, so why had she even said that? Was it just the need to say something positive? An excuse to stand there and talk to him?

When he didn't respond other than to again reach back and pat the horse, she continued. 'Right, well I guess I better go find Denver and see if he's got some time to help me.'

Travis huffed. 'Oh, he'll find time, trust me.'

She frowned, not sure what he meant, but hoping he simply meant that Denver was a helpful sort of person. She liked Denver, but she wasn't interested in him. Or at least not in the way she could be in Travis, if she allowed herself to be. Which she had no intention of doing.

~~*~~

Travis watched her walk away, disappointed he hadn't thought of something clever to say to her. Then he kicked himself for that thought. After all, why should he want to impress her? He didn't need someone like her in his life—she was a Mason, and a city girl. But even if she wasn't either of those, he didn't need any woman to complicate his life at the moment. His life was fine just as it was—no woman, no trouble.

He ordered himself to stop thinking about her as he patted the gelding on the neck and led him out of the arena to the hitching post. Unfortunately, that spot provided an excellent view to the lawn area behind the house, exactly where Denver was building his dance floor.

Struggling to tear his eyes off her, he watched as Alex made her way toward Denver. When Denver stood to greet her Travis turned his back to them, removed the gelding's bridle, unsaddled him and carried everything into the tack room.

Inside, he took a couple of deep breaths and tried to think this through rationally.

The woman was a Mason, a member of the family who'd stolen the saloon and started a feud. All through their childhood, he and Denver had witnessed their father's frustration as he'd exhausted every legal avenue in an attempt to un-do the transaction. Then, when he was dying, one of his last wishes was that Travis promise to continue to fight for it.

And he had, just with a different approach. He and Denver had put in a written offer. Old Man Mason had agreed it was fair, yet he'd chosen to ignore the offer therein keeping the feud alive.

Travis sighed, wishing he could be more like Denver. Denver had pretended to go along with their father's wishes, but he hadn't really bought into the whole idea of there being a feud. Denver liked everyone.

When Old Man Mason died, Travis was certain the feud had gone to his grave with him. No Mason had ever turned up in town since Travis was old enough to pay attention, so the most likely scenario was that the beneficiaries would simply sell off the assets through their lawyers.

It made sense, and Travis had been happy—relieved even—to let go of the feud.

Until now.

By turning up here, Alex Mason had brought the feud back to life.

He took his hat off and rubbed his forehead in frustration. Perhaps Alex knew nothing of the feud. Maybe her coming to Masons Flat was simply because she wanted to do things in person rather than from a distance. Or maybe she didn't trust lawyers. She could still settle the estate quickly and go back to Australia. After all, what reason could she possibly have in keeping any of the properties?

Realising he needed to focus on business, he took a deep breath. He needed to stay on her good side, and hope this Mason was going to seriously consider their offer for the saloon.

He went back outside, grabbed the hose and ran cool water over the gelding, then put him into a small field with a couple of flakes of hay. He stood for a moment longer, gathering his thoughts, and then ambled over to where Denver and Alex were talking.

He had this. He would be nice to her, keep it business-like, and focus on getting the saloon back. He could do this to honour his father and put the feud to bed once and for all.

As he walked up Alex had her back to him, and Denver was laughing. When she placed her hand on Denver's arm just before speaking, Travis' jaws tightened.

'I'm looking forward to it, but the reason for the visit wasn't to wangle an invite to your birthday party, I wanted to ask if you could do some small repairs for me ... over at the house.'

'Repairs? Sure. Is tomorrow okay?' Denver might as well have licked her hand; he looked like a love-struck puppy.

'Tomorrow will be fine—say around one-thirty? I have an appointment first thing in the morning with the accountant.'

'That works.' Denver finally turned to look at him. 'Ah, Travis, I was just telling Alex about the party next weekend. She's going to come, isn't that great? And get this; she's never danced to rockabilly music, so this will be quite an experience for her.'

When she turned to him and smiled, his business-like demeanour faltered. He could kill his brother right about now. Instead, he smiled back, and tried to appear amused, which was difficult with clenched teeth.

He turned to Alex, pulling his business façade down again. 'I overheard you saying you were meeting your accountant tomorrow. If it's the same one your uncle used, maybe you can ask him about our offer to buy the saloon. Your uncle had been toying with the offer for ages, but he never committed to anything—mentioned something about the accountant advising against selling it.'

'Oh, the lawyer never said anything about any offers, but yes, the accountant is the one my uncle used, so I'll ask if he knows anything about it. Are you sure he gave the offer to his accountant?'

He looked away for a moment, taking his time, gathering his thoughts so he could reply calmly. 'No, I'm not sure of anything, that's just what he said to us. Our offer still stands, even though the place may require more work than what the insurance will cover. Think about it. It was a good offer. Talk to the accountant, then let us know.'

Her mouth smiled, but her eyes were like cold hard gems. Then the fire he'd seen in them the day before returned as she cocked her head. 'Certainly. I'll speak to the accountant about it.' Turning back to Denver, she changed the subject. 'Oh, is there a dress code for your party? I didn't bring a lot of clothes with me. I planned to do a bit of outlet shopping before I go home, and fill up my bags that way, but if I need something in particular, I'll need to have a look soon.'

'Dress code? I suspect there'll be everything from party dresses to jeans and boots, so it's entirely up to you. You ever hear of anyone setting a dress code for anything around here, Travis?'

When she turned toward him, Travis just shrugged. What did he know about dress codes? And why would he care?

She turned back to Denver. 'Great. Well then, I'll see you tomorrow around one-thirty. Corner of Mason and Blue Gum.'

Travis gritted his teeth as he watched the exchange—as if either of them needed to be told where that house was.

'See ya tomorrow, Alex.' Denver said, doing a mock bow and winking as he lowered his head.

'Yeah, see ya.' Travis raised an eyebrow, then turned to Denver, determined not to watch her walk away. 'We've got work to do, Den, how much longer do you need to work on this dance floor anyway?'

~~*~~

As she walked back to her car, Alex once again had the distinct impression she'd been dismissed. Travis might as well have told her to *piss off already*, the way he gave her the cold shoulder and turned to Denver. Then again, she hadn't exactly been warm toward him either. What was it about him that made her feel like she had to be so serious and business like?

The brothers were like chalk and cheese; Denver all smiles and jokes, and Travis serious and stern.

But it was more than that. Travis Gold was borderline rude.

And yet she still found herself drawn to him. One minute she felt as silly as a shy school-girl talking to the cute boy in class, and the next like a shrewd business-woman doing a deal. What was happening to her?

Was she simply over-tired? She still hadn't gotten into normal sleep patterns. That was the only explanation.

She keyed the hotel's address into the car's navigator, wanting to take the quickest route back to the hotel. Perhaps a good night's sleep would cure her odd behaviour around that man. Something needed to.

CHAPTER 7

Alex sat beside the rather rotund accountant, Gary Matthews, as he went through the profit and loss statements for the various buildings. The documents were similar to those she was used to looking at when she managed the tennis club, although these were a whole lot more personal.

The good news was that the properties as a whole showed a positive return. There were no mortgages on any of them, so the rents only had to cover rates, maintenance and insurance. And once they put tenants in the vacant ones, the situation would only get better. She and her sisters couldn't retire on the income but, if they decided to keep them, they weren't going to be out of pocket.

But that decision hadn't been made yet. There was still the option to sell everything. And that carried a lot of appeal as it would most likely give her enough money to pay down her mortgage and set up her coaching business.

With that thought in mind she asked the obvious question. 'Do you have valuations for the various buildings?'

'No, but I will need to get them done if we're to do your taxes for you.'

When Alex sighed, Gary raised his hand, frowning. 'But I seem to recall your uncle saying something about having obtained valuations a few years back. I always tended to go by the County's Annual Assessments and then bump them up a bit—for insurance purposes. Is that what you're after?'

'Sort of, but we're trying to decide whether we should sell everything and be done with it, or whether we should hang on to some or all of the properties.'

Gary quirked a smile. 'Really? You think you might want to sell?'

'Maybe. We have some decisions to make, obviously, but I need to understand the current market value of each of the properties—in the condition they're in right now.' She and her sisters definitely didn't have spare cash to throw at doing up the buildings.

'Well, funny you should say that because I have a realtor friend who would be more than happy to help.'

She frowned, biting her lower lip before speaking. 'That wouldn't happen to be a Mr Marshall would it?'

'Why yes, have you heard of him?' He broke into a broad smile.

She grimaced. 'He dropped in when I was visiting the house. I wondered how he'd known I was there.'

'Ah, well ... news travels quickly in small towns, you know that. But he and I go way back—we were in college together, you see.'

As interesting as that was, the fact that he and this agent were good friends wasn't exactly a tick in his favour. Exactly how much might he have told the agent?

'And does he manage the tenanted properties?'

'No, no, that's a chap out of Sonora. Thompson Realty, Ben Thompson.'

'I suppose I'll need to speak to him; I'm curious why those two shops have been vacant for so long.'

'I don't know him personally, as your uncle dealt with him directly. I think he was a friend, or perhaps the son of a friend. I did ask your uncle why they were still vacant, but all he said was that there wasn't much interest in them, and he didn't mind them being vacant until the right tenant came along.'

'And this Thompson fellow, does he manage other properties in town, or just ours?'

'I couldn't say,' he replied, shaking his head slowly.

She wondered if Ben Thompson managed the Gold properties, and if they owned any of the others that were vacant in town. Then, thinking about the Golds, she remembered their offer.

'Speaking of selling, have there ever been any offers received? For any of the properties? I mean, surely people in town knew about Uncle Steven's illness. Has anyone come forward with any offers to buy any of the shops or his home?'

'Nothing recently. There was an offer a while back, but your uncle never took it seriously.'

'And that was?'

'The Gold brothers. They wanted to buy the saloon.'

'I see ... and do you recall if their offer reasonable?' Alex asked, tilting her head with curiosity.

'Quite reasonable, based on what your uncle had said, but he didn't want to let it go. He liked working there as he said it gave him a way to keep in contact with everyone in town.' He winked, continuing, 'Personally, I think he enjoyed being a bit of a self-appointed gate-keeper on how much people drank.'

She wished she'd known Uncle Steven better. She only remembered meeting him once, when she was quite young—before they were whisked off to Australia. She remembered him being tall, with a deep voice, but not much else. Although it occurred to her that she might have heard her father refer to him as a bit of a loner—living out there in Masons Flat on his own, and never marrying. Yet, from what the accountant said, he didn't seem like a loner.

'Did he ever say *why* they wanted it? Why the Golds wanted to buy the saloon?'

Gary rubbed his jaw for a moment. 'Your uncle rarely talked about it, but I think it goes back to the way your family came to own the saloon. You see, your great-grandfather and the Mr Gold who was his contemporary were in a heated poker game one night—both drinking far too much. Gold threw what was then Gold's Saloon into the pot, and your great-grandfather threw in his hotel. Mason won, and Gold lost. Your great-grandfather then changed the name to Gold Nugget Saloon and refused to give it back. He'd won it fair and square. If Gold had won, you think he wouldn't have kept the hotel? Anyway, Duncan Gold, who was Travis and Denver's father, tried unsuccessfully to get the original transfer reversed. It was after he died that the boys put in the offer.'

'And Uncle Steven wouldn't sell it back to them?'

'Nope—like I said, he enjoyed owning it.'

She let that sink in. He'd enjoyed owning it, which meant she might too. 'Is that why it's on the opposite side of the street to all the other Mason properties?'

'Yes, exactly. Actually, are you interested in hearing a bit of the town's history?'

She looked at her phone. She had plenty of time. 'I would love to hear it.'

'In a nutshell, there were three miners, Mason, Gould and James, who made their fortunes in this area, and decided to set up the town together.'

'Yes, I saw a photo of the three of them at the hotel. The Mason was Thomas, but I don't recall the other two first names.'

'Nor do I. Anyway, Gould, who later changed his name to Gold, had most of the land on the north side of the street, Mason had most of the south side, and James had some on each side. Over the years James and his descendants sold their holdings, but the Masons and Golds kept theirs.'

'Did Mason and Gold buy up the James' properties, or are there other owners now?'

'Bit of both. Mason and Gold each bought a couple, and some were sold to others.'

Alex frowned, trying to visualise the street layout as Gary continued. 'And did you notice that the house is on the corner of *Blue Gum Road*?'

'*Blue Gum*?'

Gary smiled, raising an eyebrow.

Then the penny dropped. 'Oh, of course, I should have twigged that it was an odd street name for around here.'

Gary's smile widened further. 'Mason headed to Australia for the gold rush that followed the one here in California, and when he returned he planted a grove of Blue Gums, hoping to make a further fortune with the wood. He planted it to the south of what was then a very small town; the northernmost section of the grove is on the south side of Blue Gum Road.'

Alex smiled. 'Which is the park across from the house. So, my family had a connection to Australia, and I hadn't even been aware of it. My grandfather's great-grandfather, or would he be his great-great-grandfather?'

Gary shrugged, lifting his hands in an *I'm not entirely sure* type of gesture.

'Well, whatever he was, he'd been to Australia.'

'Indeed he had, along with both James and Gould. They all made more money over there, so when they returned, they decided to turn the small mining camp into a full-fledged town, and that's when Masons Flat was founded.'

She pondered that for a moment. 'And why was it called Masons Flat, rather than James or Gould?'

'Humph ... not sure. Perhaps they flipped a coin? If so, it would have been a gold one.'

He chuckled at his own joke, but Alex could feel a frown deepening on her face. Perhaps there were many reasons for this ongoing rift between the Golds and Masons. And perhaps the rift was deep enough for Travis Gold to try to drag down the value of the Mason properties for his own benefit.

Something that had been bothering her since she'd arrived finally found words.

'Do you know how the fire started, in the saloon? Could it have been arson?'

Gary shook his head. 'No, it definitely wasn't arson. Everything was thoroughly investigated. A grease filter caught fire and the whole kitchen went up in no time. They were lucky to get it stopped before it damaged more of the building.'

'I saw the kitchen ... all the damage. I just wondered if it could have been intentional.'

'Others thought the same, hence the thorough investigation, but there was nothing suspicious about the fire.'

'Okay then, it was just a thought.'

Alex took a deep breath and concentrated on the figures again. The buildings were generating enough cash to pay for themselves. And the situation would be even better if she could manage to find tenants for the two empty shops. She and the twins could keep them, if that's what they decided to do. It was going to be a big decision to make. And there would no doubt be a tax bill of some sort. The lawyer had alluded to it when he mentioned she might like to see an accountant.

She turned to Gary. 'I don't suppose you have any idea how much we're going to have to pay in taxes? I mean, if we decide to keep all the properties, for example, are we going to struggle?'

Gary frowned. 'Struggle? How do you mean?'

'Will we need to sell a few of the properties to pay the taxes? Do you have any idea what we'll be up for?'

Now he smiled. And it reminded her of the smile she'd seen on Mr West's face.

'Alex ... I thought the lawyer explained what you inherited?'

'He did ... sort of. Mind you, I don't know how much of it I took in—I think I was struggling to keep my eyes open.'

'Did he give you any sort of summary of what you've inherited?'

She dug into her shoulder-bag and pulled out the folded stack of papers. On the top was the summary sheet Mr West had prepared for her. She handed it to the accountant and watched intently while he studied it.

'Right. Now, this here ... see it?' He pointed to a line near the bottom of the page.

Alex leaned over to stare at the summary, focussing on the line he pointed to.

'What's it say, Alex?'

'Cash and cash equivalents: three million, seven hundred forty-two thousand, three hundred dollars and twelve cents.'

'Right. That's exactly what it says. Now, do you want to ask me the same question you asked a moment ago?'

Alex looked at him, dumbfounded.

'Alex?'

'Is that how much we've inherited? In cash?'

A slight smile touched his lips. 'Yes, cash in a variety of deposit forms. I wouldn't think you'll have a problem paying the taxes, Alex. Or at least, I can't imagine you will.'

'How could I have missed that?'

'I don't know. Have you studied the summary?'

'I thought I had. I mean, I guess I thought it was only the buildings, you know?'

'Yes, well, it's the buildings, and the cash. Not to mention if you turn the page over, quite a healthy stock portfolio. Your uncle was a very wealthy man, Alex Mason. And now you and your sisters are very wealthy women. Have you already engaged an accountant to help you through all this? Because you know we'd love to take you and your sisters on as clients?'

'We have an accountant, back home. But since I retired from professional tennis I haven't made enough to have to worry about US taxes. And my sisters have never had a problem. I suppose this inheritance might change things a bit—for all of us.'

He handed her his business card. 'Think about it. I'd be more than happy to work with your existing accountant if that helps. And by all means, if you have any questions, about anything, you can ring me ... anytime.'

Any wonder he'd been so happy to meet with her on a Saturday.

~~*~~

When Denver had pleaded with Travis to meet Alex over at Old Man Mason's place, Travis knew it was no accident. Even if there hadn't been the dead give-away of a twinkle in Denver's eyes, double-booking himself was not something Denver did. Ever.

But what he didn't know was why he'd been so quick to agree to do it.

He knew meeting her was a really dumb idea, and yet he'd jumped at the chance. He'd even raced to the shower to remove the layer of dirt from his skin after having spent the morning working with several of his young horses.

When he pulled up in front of the Mason house her red Mustang wasn't anywhere to be seen, but within a few moments she drove up.

At the sight of her, his heart started racing, and he cursed himself for being pathetic. Had Denver picked up on his physical reaction to this woman? Is that why he'd set up this meeting? And if it had been obvious to Denver, might it also have been obvious to her? He cringed at the thought.

As she walked up, he touched the brim of his hat in greeting and grunted a hello, hoping to disguise any hint of his feelings.

She cocked her pretty head, a slight frown creasing her forehead. 'Oh, isn't Denver coming?' Her disappointment was obvious.

'No, he'd forgotten he'd organised an electrician to do some work for the party. He sends his apologies.'

'Oh, I see. I, uh ... he could have come a bit later.'

Was she simply disappointed, or was she annoyed? 'He didn't know how to contact you to change the time.'

Her frown deepened momentarily in disbelief, but when she spoke her tone was completely business-like. 'Oh yes, of course. I'm just so used to confirming everything by text that I'd forgotten we arranged this in person. I'm sorry you had to come out of your way to meet me.'

'It's no trouble.' He pulled a screwdriver from his back pocket and waved it in front of her. 'I'm not entirely useless when it comes to tools.'

She looked at him blankly for a moment, and then indicated for him to follow her. 'Oh, okay then. It's the back door.'

When she raised an eyebrow and smiled, he had to remind himself to breathe.

CHAPTER 8

Alex wasn't sure how she felt about seeing Travis Gold right now.

She'd spent the previous evening alone in her hotel room, thinking about Denver's party. About getting a new outfit, and how she'd do her hair. She'd listened to some rockabilly music and gone through the dance steps she'd found on the internet. She'd expected to have plenty of time to get her emotions in check and be in complete control when she next encountered Travis Gold. She'd thought it would be fun to see him at Denver's party; from a distance. She'd even allowed herself to think about what it might be like to have a dance with him.

All that would have been on her terms, when she was prepared. Not out of the blue like this.

She tried her best to keep things business-like. That's all this was, after all. She'd engaged a tradesman to do some work. It wasn't her fault a different man had turned up.

He was right behind her as she showed him through to the laundry, his body heat practically scorching her as they walked along. Her arm lifted reflexively as she started to run her hand through her hair, but she forced herself to stop. There was something about body language and hair—and it wasn't the message she wanted to send him.

She stopped when she reached the laundry and turned to him. 'It's the back door. It isn't closing properly, and the screen has no lock. I'm too much of a city girl to live in a house that can't be locked up.'

He took off his hat and placed it on top of the washing machine. When their eyes met, she could see confusion in his.

'Did you say live in? As in, you're planning to live here?'

She tried to smile but could feel her lips quiver, so she rubbed her hand across them hoping it looked like she had an itch. 'For a time, yes. Until we decide what we're doing. I see no point in paying for a hotel in Sacramento when I could be staying in this lovely home.'

'Right, that makes sense. Well then, let's see what we can do here.'

As he moved past her his cotton sleeve brushed against her bare arm and the fresh scent of soap teased her nostrils. She'd have thought he'd smell of horses and sweat this time of day, and she was once again caught off guard.

She drew in her breath as quietly as she could, hoping her voice would remain steady. 'I think the door must be warped or something. It closes but doesn't quite catch.'

He pulled at the door and it came open easily. 'I see what you mean.'

He was standing so close it took all her self-restraint not to reach out and touch him. 'It's not safe.' Her voice sounded husky, even to her own ears.

He turned, staring into her eyes for just a moment before speaking. 'I think I can adjust it.'

He reached up, the movement sending more of his fresh scent her way. She practically held her breath as he adjusted the hinges on the back door. After a few tries the door stayed shut, even with him pulling on it.

'That's fixed for now, but if you want a deadlock installed that's best left for Denver ... or a locksmith. I'm sure I could do it, but not with just my screwdriver.'

'Thanks so much. I really appreciate you taking the time to come over. I know how busy you are. Oh, but one more thing before you go ... do you know if a lock can be put on this screen door?'

Bending over, he took a closer look at it, and then turned to her. 'Sure. The hardware store should have some handle mechanisms that'll fit this—I can fix it for you if you want.'

She let out a sigh before she could stop herself. 'Could you? Oh, look, that would be fabulous, but I hate to take any more of your time. Is it something I could do myself?' She'd seen Liam change one once—it couldn't be that hard to do if Liam had managed it.

As he looked at her, she suddenly knew what it must feel like to be a horse for sale at an auction. It made her slightly uncomfortable, but at the same time she wasn't ready to be free from his company. This whole encounter confused her on so many levels.

'You probably could, but then again it can be fiddly. I'll do it. It won't take me long.'

'Are you sure? I don't mind trying to do it myself.'

He blinked slowly, the movement being the only thing hinting he wasn't a wax creation at Madam Tussauds. She held her breath, waiting for him to seize the opportunity to flee.

'That's okay. It won't take long,' he said as he pulled out his phone and took a photo of the screen door handle. Then he shut both doors hard, and tested the door again. It stayed closed. When he faced her, his lips curled up in a slight smile. 'You want to come with me to the hardware store, or wait here?'

'I'll come, so I can pay for the lock.'

She grabbed her shoulder-bag and followed him outside to his truck.

~~*~~

Travis opened the passenger door and stood back while Alex climbed in. As he walked around to the driver's side, he cursed his stupidity. He had so much work to do before the rodeo, why had he offered to fix her door? When he got in behind the wheel he realised the scent of her perfume, which had been tantalising inside the house, was now nearly unbearable. And as he glanced sideways, seeing her tight jeans and sleeveless top, she looked irresistible.

He turned back to the road and focused on the drive. Luckily Alex remained quiet during the short trip to town.

Once in the store, he led her to the aisle with the screen doors and lifted the correct mechanism off the shelf. 'This is it.'

She smiled, looking around at all the other choices. 'That was quick. And we don't need any special tools or anything?'

'Nope, just this.'

As they made their way to the register, he noticed Alex checking out the sales table.

'I think I'll come back here later to grab some things to give the place my own personal touch,' she said, her voice sounding ridiculously excited about the store's meagre offering.

But what intrigued him was why she felt the need to give the house a personal touch if she was just staying for a few days. He let that thought stew for a bit, then back in the Rover, he decided to ask. 'Are you planning to stay long?'

'In Masons Flat?'

'Yes. I assumed you would just be here for a week or so while you work through the estate paperwork.'

She chewed the corner of her lip for a moment before she answered. 'I haven't decided. The accountant is doing some work for us on the figures and I want to give it some real thought before making any decisions.'

He'd forgotten she was meeting the accountant that morning. 'Did you remember to ask him about our offer? For the saloon?'

She hesitated before answering, perhaps weighing up her answer. 'I did. He said he knew of the offer but that my uncle didn't want to sell.'

Travis huffed out a breath. He'd expected as much. 'Then it wasn't anything to do with the accountant?'

Her eyes narrowed as she took a moment to reply. 'No, it was my uncle's decision.'

He turned, staring out the window as he started the engine. At least the accountant wasn't against it which meant there was still a chance he could buy it back. But if she was planning to sell everything, it didn't explain why she would want to personalise the house.

Unable to keep from frowning, he turned back toward her. 'So ... even if you stay for a little while, you'll have to go back to Australia at some stage, right? You wouldn't be allowed to stay indefinitely, would you?'

'Why not? I'm a dual citizen.'

An involuntary frown tightened his face. That was not what he'd expected her to say. 'I didn't know that. I assumed ... I mean, you sound Australian to me.'

'I was born in Sacramento. My mother is Australian, and my father was American. When my parents split up, Mum moved us back to Australia.'

'And your father—is he still here in California?'

'He died when I was a teenager.'

'Oh, I'm sorry—I guess I should have known that. I knew Old Man Mason had no living relations in the area.'

She looked over at him, cocking her head slowly, perhaps measuring his sympathy. 'Yes, well he died a long time ago. Then when my grandfather died, he left everything to his brother—my Uncle Steven—because my father had already passed.'

'And Old Man Mason left everything to you because he had no children.'

She shrugged. 'So it seems.'

He released the brake, and put the car in reverse, then turned to her once more. 'And you're personalising the house because you might stay a while?'

When her only reply was a smile, he drove off, completely at a loss as to whether what he'd just heard was good news or bad.

~~*~~

Alex stayed quiet on the short drive back, and when they pulled up at the house it seemed a good time to change the subject. She'd already told him far more than she should have. After all, if he was trying to buy the saloon, he might also want to buy some of the other properties. That wouldn't be such a bad thing if she decided to sell, which was still the most likely decision, so there was no point clouding any offer he might make with too much knowledge of her circumstances.

They made their way inside and back to the laundry, where Travis took off his hat and glasses. He tore open the packet with the new handle, then rolled up his sleeves and busied himself with the door.

She wished she hadn't watched him do that—rolling up his sleeves. His forearms were tanned and muscular, making her wonder what the rest of him looked like. She winced as her face grew hot with embarrassment, eternally grateful he was concentrating on removing the handle mechanism from the screen door and not paying any attention to her.

It took no time at all and, when he finished, he handed her the two keys and she tested the lock. It worked like a charm.

'I don't know how to thank you enough. Can I pay you for your time? Or will Denver send me an account?'

Travis shrugged, shaking his head. 'No, it was nothing, I wouldn't worry about it.'

'It wasn't *nothing*—I can't tell you how grateful I am to have it finished.'

She followed him as he headed back to the front door. When he reached it, he turned to her. 'I suppose I'll see you next weekend, at

Denver's party. Oh, and in case he forgot to mention it, no presents. It isn't that kind of party.'

Still feeling awkward about not paying him, she tried to be humorous. 'Are you sure? I could at least bake a cake or something?'

He looked at her blankly.

'Sorry, inside joke. I'm not my sister.'

'Sister?' he asked, quirking a brow.

'My sister's a pastry chef. Or at least she works in a bakery. Now, that girl can cook.'

'Ah, got it. No, a cake won't be necessary,' he said as he tipped his hat and headed toward the street.

She let out a long slow breath as he drove off. Then, free from the spell his proximity had cast over her, she went back inside and began to picture what this house would be like with her personal touches—ornaments, photos, her favourite vase, her books, her paintings. Yes, the place was just a house at the moment, but with her things in it, would it be a home?

Closing her eyes, she imagined how the room would look in winter, with a fire in the corner and the lights turned down low. Her fuzzy red socks rubbed up against each other as she warmed her feet in front of the fire. Another pair of socks—dark brown—rubbed up alongside hers. She let her imagination run up those legs, up past the waist and shoulders to a face topped with dark hair and even darker eyes—eyes that drew her into their depths and held her there, unable to escape.

Then she laughed at herself. This was crazy. She barely knew the man. And even if today he'd been less brooding and stern than before, chances were that he was just trying to get on her good side so she'd accept his offer for the saloon. She huffed out a breath as the realisation hit home. That had to be why he was being nice.

She grabbed her shoulder-bag from the sofa, double checked that she'd locked the back door, and then headed out to her car. She had one more stop to make before going to the grocery store to stock up.

CHAPTER 9

Travis couldn't stop thinking about Alex, replaying their conversation on the way back to his place. She'd said she might be staying a while—that she didn't actually have to leave at all if she didn't want to. She was still thinking about it, and her exact words were: *until we decide what we're doing.*

She'd mentioned a sister. That could be all it was, but a woman that alluring probably had a significant other of some sort. And the way she'd said *we* did sound like it could have been a significant other.

He banged his hand on the steering wheel. Why was he obsessing over her?

When he got home, he went inside, made a cup of coffee, and headed into his office. When he opened up his laptop it occurred to him she'd be on Facebook—wasn't everyone these days? He searched for her name but when it brought up a huge list of matches he gave up, shaking his head—this was simply too hard.

Then it occurred to him he could try a different route. He typed her name, followed by Melbourne Australia, into his search engine. There were quite a few matches, but only one seemed relevant. He opened the article from a small newspaper, dated eight years earlier, and read.

"Local tennis hopeful Alex Mason retires after injuries end her career. Australian tennis mourns the loss of a promising young player, after devastating injuries left her with poor mobility in her right arm and shoulder. Her husband, golfer Liam Bruce—"

He closed the page, his question answered. She was some sort of celebrity down there in Australia. Any wonder she had so much attitude. And she was married.

He took a sip of coffee, set it down, and sat rubbing his chin. Then again, did she sound married? She'd used "we" today, but she'd used "I" while talking about staying here and sorting through the estate. He pulled up the article again, and read further.

... Her husband, golfer Liam Bruce, is currently the golf pro at one of Melbourne's top courses.

Ms Mason has recently taken on a managerial position at a local tennis club where she will also be able to help junior players achieve their goals by running after-school and holiday coaching programs."

So, not only was she a rising tennis-star with a ruined career but she was also married to a golf professional. Country Club types. Not exactly the sort he rubbed shoulders with. Definitely explained her attitude.

Curious now that he'd opened Pandora's Box, Travis entered the words *Liam Bruce Golf Australia* into Google to see what he could find about him, but when he heard the front door open followed by his brother's whistling, he slammed the laptop shut.

~~*~~

Hilda Weston was a well-dressed and well-mannered woman in her early fifties. Alex immediately liked her.

'How do you have your coffee?' Hilda asked, a smile making her look like she could be family.

'Just black, thanks.'

Hilda directed Alex to a small sitting room, and then disappeared into the kitchen. She returned with a tray laden with fine china cups and saucers, a pot of coffee and a plate of what looked to be home-made shortbreads.

'It was kind of you to drop in to meet me. I'd have been happy to come to your place. It's not like I don't know the way.' She smiled warmly, and offered Alex a shortbread.

'I had some errands to do today and I thought it might be easier to come to you. I understand you only work part-time at the hotel?'

'Yes, just eleven to two most days—some days even less, depending on how many rooms were used.'

Alex bit into the shortbread. 'These are simply scrumptious.'

Hilda flashed a huge smile. 'I won first place at the county fair with them one year. Haven't changed the recipe one iota since.'

'You wouldn't want to.'

'I take it you'd like me to continue cleaning your uncle's home? Well, it's yours now, isn't it?'

'I'd love it ... if you have the time. I mean, it's not that I'm not capable of doing some of it, it's just that with my shoulder I find some of it beyond me.'

Hilda frowned, and tilted her head. 'You're very young to have a bad shoulder?'

'I was in a car accident—broke my shoulder and my collarbone—but life goes on, doesn't it.' She swallowed back the sorrow that always lurked within her, waiting for a chance to creep up. She rarely spoke of the accident; it was just easier that way.

'Oh, my goodness, I'm so sorry to hear that. I'll certainly continue cleaning, if that's what you want. Perhaps I'll come around one day and you can show me what you'd like me to do, and what you think you'll do yourself. Of course, for Steven, I did pretty much everything. He was getting rather frail towards the end.'

Alex liked what she heard in Hilda's voice. Hilda had clearly cared about her uncle. It was even possible that she was more to him than simply a housekeeper. Perhaps she'd been a companion of sorts? Again, she wished she'd known her uncle. Would Hilda be prepared to talk about him?

'What sort of man was he, my Uncle Steven? I've heard so little about him. My mother knew nothing about him, and my father rarely spoke of him.'

Hilda set her coffee cup down and gave Alex a weak smile. 'That's a real shame. He was truly a gentleman. Cared about people. He kept as many employed as he could at the saloon, and never worried about people getting a little bit behind with their rent in the properties he owned. I remember Sam saying something one day about how he'd have lost the hotel if anyone else owned it. Your uncle understood the ups and downs out here—the good months, and the dreadfully slow months. He helped everyone through the bad times, and didn't take advantage of them in the good times either.'

Warmth washed over Alex, hearing praise of her uncle. Both the lawyer and accountant seemed rather neutral. And the Golds hadn't had anything particularly nice to say about him either. She was glad she'd dropped in to meet Hilda today.

'Can I refill your coffee? I can make another pot.'

'That would be lovely, if it isn't too much trouble?'

As Hilda disappeared into the kitchen, the front door squeaked open and Alex turned at the sound of footsteps approaching.

~~*~~

'How'd it go over at Alex's?' Denver asked, grinning.

Travis smirked at his little brother. 'Fine,' he said, drawing out the word.

'You were there a lot longer than I'd have expected.'

Definitely fishing, but Travis wasn't going to reward him. 'Is the electrician finished already? You could have gone yourself you know.'

'He's still out there. I just came in to make a sandwich. You want one?'

'Better not. I've gotta get back out to work those two geldings. How long do you think this electrician will be?'

'Another hour or two. He's putting in several outdoor outlets, and he's talked me into putting a string of lights in all the trees; says it's the "in thing" at these outdoor parties, so I agreed to it. It's gonna look awesome—I can hardly wait.'

Travis fought the urge to roll his eyes, but couldn't keep the touch of sarcasm from his voice. 'And I can't wait for the following morning, when life can return to normal.' He lightly punched Denver in the shoulder, and then smirked again. He knew this was an important birthday, and he didn't resent his brother's enthusiasm, he just had a lot of work to do to have his young horses performing at their best for the rodeo.

'On second thought, I'll have a sandwich too, but make it snappy.'

'Yes, sir. And shall I clean your dress boots for you, too, sir?'

Denver ducked the punch, which would have been a bit harder than the earlier one, and raced into the kitchen.

Once Denver was out of the room, Travis opened up the laptop again and quickly found the page he'd been looking at. There were a number of articles where Liam Bruce's name appeared; most were results from golf matches, and a few were related to local fund-raising dinners, but there was a recent one that captured his attention.

"... Liam Bruce, the golf-pro at the prestigious McMillan Estate Country Club, is set to wed Darcy McMillan, daughter of business tycoon and estate founder, Jamie McMillan.

Mr Bruce, whose divorce from tennis player Alexandra Mason drew significant attention at the time, is the son of..."

Travis stopped reading. He couldn't care less about Liam Bruce's father—but he was intrigued to read that Liam Bruce was no longer Alex's husband.

CHAPTER 10

Alex looked up as a man who would fit in on an Italian catwalk sauntered into the room. Tall, with dark hair, he wore a five o'clock shadow that brought out the contours of his chiselled face. His deep blue eyes were piercing, and his lips looked like he had recently been engaged in a pashing session with some local hottie. His jeans, with rips in all the right places, fit him like a glove, and a pale blue shirt with the sleeves rolled up exposed tanning salon perfect skin. In fact, everything about him was perfect. And then he opened his mouth.

'Hey, Mom. I see you've got company. Does that mean your shortbreads have come out?'

He flashed Alex a smile which appeared well-practiced; even so, it made her skin tingle. She ran her hands up her bare arms as a chill made its way across her skin. This was Hilda's son?

Hilda's voice wafted from the kitchen. 'Yes, and I'll bring you a cup of coffee if you want one.'

'Yes please,' he called back.

In two strides he was in front of her, with his hand extended. She stood, and lifted her hand to shake his, but he grabbed it with both his hands and raised it to his lips for a gentle kiss.

Smooth, yes.

Over the top, completely.

Impressed? She didn't want to be, but yes, she was definitely impressed.

'I'm Harrison Weston. And you are?'

She spoke slowly—trying to sound older and wiser. Not hard, given he looked what, maybe twenty-two? 'Alex Mason.'

Somehow, he managed to stand taller as surprise washed over his face. 'As in Steven Mason's ... daughter?'

She chuckled, shaking her head slowly. 'Great-niece, actually.'

He released her hand, and bent down to grab the last shortbread off the plate. Taking a bite, he looked down at her. 'Ah, yes, that makes more sense. Welcome to Masons Flat. And do I detect an accent?'

'I was born here, well, not here, in Sacramento, but I've lived most of my life in Australia.'

'Sweet ... I'm heading down there in January. I've got a shoot coming up in Sydney.'

'Shoot? As in modelling?'

'Hmph ... thought you might have recognised me. I've been in two cable television movies, but in January I'm getting a cameo in a new Australian drama series. It's being filmed at Bondi. Suspect you've heard of Bondi?'

She laughed. 'Of course, but I haven't been there. So ... television, eh? It must be exciting.'

'Oh, it's way more than exciting—it's exhilarating. I'm hoping while I'm there I can get a gig in a movie or two. You know, start with small parts, work my way up.'

Hilda entered and placed the tray on the coffee table. She held out a cup to Harrison and handed another to Alex. Then she gave her son a mildly chastising look as she asked, 'Just passing through, or are you here for a few days?'

'I'm here for a few weeks, if that's okay with you?'

'You know you don't have to ask—your room is always ready.'

'Great, because Denver's got that big party next weekend, and the county fair the following weekend. Then I thought I'd catch up with a few friends and that before heading back down to LA. Thought I'd told you, Mom ... or did I forget?'

He bit into another of the shortbreads and then licked the crumbs off his lips with well-practiced sensuality. Alex wasn't fooled by it, but she was entertained. He was fun. He was luscious. He was ... exactly what she needed to take her mind off a certain broody man who'd been haunting her since she'd laid eyes on him.

'I take it you've only arrived in the last few days? I say that because I think I'd have heard something if you'd been here long.' He smiled—oozing charm.

'Yes, a few days ago.' She allowed an eyebrow to rise provocatively.

'Fabulous, because that means you probably won't have a date for Denver's party. Come with me. It'll be fun. I'm more than a pretty face; I can dance up a storm with the best of them.'

Alex glanced across at Hilda, who appeared to be trying to suppress a grin, but when their eyes met, Hilda's were twinkling. Why not?

'I'd love to, Harrison. Shall I pick you up? I assume you want me to be your designated driver?'

Harrison laughed. 'No, I'll drive. I don't drink—it ages the skin too quickly.'

She quirked an eyebrow at him. A man in his twenties, who didn't drink? He must be a rare find. And even rarer was the opportunity for her to let her hair down a little.

'Perfect. What time?'

'It kicks off at six, for the barbeque. How about seven? I'd die if we were the first to arrive. But that's a whole week away. We should do lunch, or dinner, before then ... get to know each other a bit, yes?'

Alex rolled her eyes. Pretentious. That's the word she'd been searching for earlier. 'Sure, just say when.'

~~*~~

Alex unpacked all her groceries, made a cup of tea and sat at the kitchen table. Then she pressed Casey's number in her FaceTime contacts. It would be Sunday mid-morning for the twins—seventeen hours later than the time in California. Talk about an awkward time difference.

'Alex! You look great—you must be getting some sun. We're so jealous.' Casey fairly squealed with delight, turning to seek confirmation from her sister.

'You do know it's been freezing here this week, don't you? I know it's only May but the weather's been shocking.' Taylor laughed.

Alex raised her cup of tea, showing off her sleeveless arm. 'Yes, well, the weather has been pretty perfect here. I've been going sleeveless and wearing sandals almost every day.'

'Rub it in, why don't you? Well, the climate obviously suits you ... or is there something more to it than that?' Casey's brow lifted as she ducked her head. 'Is there something going on we should know about? Something other than you discovering all the millions we've inherited?'

Could she still be glowing from her encounter with the charming Harrison? Surely she wasn't that gullible. She allowed herself to smile. 'It's our millions.'

'Millions?' The twins spoke in unison.

'I was just kidding,' Casey said, shaking her head.

Alex smirked. 'And I'm not.'

Taylor leaned over, hogging the screen. 'The accountant actually said that, did he?'

'Yes. It's not only the properties. Uncle Steven had bank accounts, and bonds and a stock portfolio. And now we have property, and bank accounts and bonds and a stock portfolio. It's quite astounding. I ... can barely believe it.'

Taylor stared at her, mouth wide open. 'You're having us on, aren't you?'

Alex's eyes grew wide as she shook her head slowly. 'No, I'm not. We're rich. If we don't let it go to our heads and do something stupid, money isn't going to be an issue for any of us.'

The twins looked at each other, clearly as gobsmacked as Alex had been when she'd first heard. Casey spoke this time. 'Didn't the lawyer tell you this when you saw him?'

'Probably, but not in so many words. I think I was half asleep, and the magnitude of it all sort of went over my head.'

'You can say that again. Should we come over? Do we need to sign stuff? We still trust you to do what's best for all of us, but if there's that much at stake maybe we should all be there, together?'

Alex sighed. It would be lovely for them to all be here together, but they had full lives back in Melbourne—jobs they enjoyed, partners, pets. She couldn't ask them to drop everything when there was nothing urgent needing to be done.

'Look, how about I continue on as we'd planned, and we can make some decisions over the next week or so. I'd love for you to come, but nothing has changed. I'll keep you in the loop and we can decide together what's best. There probably will be some papers we all need to sign, but not just yet. Why don't we just wait and see what needs to be done and decide then. How's that sound?'

Taylor finally shut her mouth. 'Just don't go spending it all on something stupid, will you?'

Alex struggled to wipe the grin off her face. 'Of course not. Or at least, not much. I might buy the car I'm driving. It's a red Mustang.'

'A Mustang? Wow ... now I'm really jealous.' Taylor pulled a face.

Alex raised an eyebrow. 'You didn't expect me to drive the old Buick I spotted in the garage, did you? Besides, everything is going to be a whole lot easier than we thought it would be.' She cleared her throat as she thought about how much she wished they were actually at the house, in person, and not just on the screen. Taking a deep breath, she put on a smile. 'Now, how about I take you on a tour of the house? You're going to love it.'

~~*~~

The drive to Sonora the next morning should have been pleasant; it was warm, the sun was shining, and she had the top down so the wind on her face was exhilarating. But as enjoyable as it should have been all she could think about was that something didn't seem right with the vacancies. And, given what she now knew about the ongoing resentment between the families, she had to face the fact that it was possible the vacancies could have something to do with the Golds.

When she finally pulled up at the front of Ben Thompson Realty the front door was wide open. She parked and made her way in to find just the one man sitting at the front desk.

'Hi, I've got an appointment at one-thirty with Ben. I know I'm a bit early, but is he available?'

'Ah you must be Alex? I'm Ben. I've been looking forward to meeting you in person.'

Her head tilted involuntarily—he'd said that like he knew about her more than just from her call. 'Really? Well, it's nice to meet you too.'

'Your uncle spoke of you and your sisters from time to time. He followed your career with great interest. He was quite proud of you.'

A pang of guilt washed over her. Her uncle had followed her tennis career? She'd had no idea. She'd been to California, for tournaments. She could have come to see him—if she'd known. Why had she never asked about her father's family? She should have pinned her mother down for some details. A sigh escaped before she could stop it. Ben may have noticed as he quickly changed the subject.

'And it's fine that you're early. Means I can leave a bit earlier myself. Take a seat and we'll get started.'

Alex looked around the office as she sat. It was tidy, with brochures mounted on the walls and in stacks here and there. They looked quite the real deal—as much as any estate agent office she'd ever been in. 'Are you normally open seven days a week?'

'The office is, but I'm not usually here on a Sunday. Actually, I lie. I'm often here on a Sunday, just not every Sunday.'

He flashed a wide grin, displaying perfect teeth. Other than that, there was nothing remarkable about the man who appeared to be in his thirties. He wore a gold wedding band and had a picture of his family on the corner of his desk. Seeing how young he was, she suspected he must be the son of one of Uncle Steven's friends, or perhaps even grandson.

Once they were comfortable at his desk he pulled out a file.

'They're not bad shops—decent size, good frontage. It's surprising they haven't been taken up yet. It isn't for lack of trying on our part. We've been running on-line ads for several months now. Had some in the local papers for a while too, but we stopped when we got no response from those.'

Alex frowned. 'Have many people enquired about them?'

'There've been a few. I've got notes.'

'And what stopped them? I mean, if they enquired, why didn't they go ahead?'

He grabbed a file from the corner of his desk and opened it. 'It generally comes back to money. When I mention the rent, they say they'll think about it and get back to me. Problem is no one has come back to me. And when I try to follow up with them they say they're still thinking about it.'

'Then we must be asking too much, right?'

She could see him stiffen defensively as he pulled out a large spreadsheet and placed it in front of her. 'These are the historical rentals for the town. What we're asking is in line with the rest of the town, but prospective tenants aren't prepared to pay that much given their low expectations of turnover.'

'And you don't think it might be appropriate to structure differing rent depending on the season? Like, higher in the good months, lower in the bad?'

'Are you suggesting a turn-over rental structure?'

'Well, I've never actually heard that expression, I just meant a lower rent during the times when tourism drops off.'

Ben took off his glasses and rubbed his eyes. When he put his glasses back on, he looked at her and sighed loudly. 'What you're describing sounds a bit like turnover rent, and I wouldn't recommend it as it might set a nasty precedence for the rest of the shops. Both the antiques store and the candy store are struggling—if we changed to turnover rents they might end up paying considerably less than they're paying now. You don't know how much I have to chase them for payment. Good thing the hotel is well managed—Sam doesn't seem to struggle making his payments.'

She frowned. This seemed at odds with what both Hilda and Sam had said. 'I see. And do you also manage the other vacant shops in town? There are two up near the saloon, and another couple down the street? Are you looking for tenants for those?'

'No, I've got nothing to do with them, and I'm not sure who owns them. None of them seem to be advertised anywhere.'

'That seems odd, doesn't it?'

'Not necessarily. Could be that whoever owns them is thinking of doing something different there—working through plans or whatever.'

Alex sighed, and turned to look out the window as she tried to think of ways to improve the street appeal. The front of the hotel was so lovely with the flower baskets—should she try to spruce up the front of the vacant shops somehow?

Ben cleared his throat. 'Look, your uncle gave me free rein to use my best judgement with all the shops that I manage. I hope you plan to continue the relationship.'

She thought about that for a moment, wondering if Phil Marshall might be worth speaking to. 'At this stage I have no plans on changing our relationship.' She paused, drumming her fingers on the arm of the chair as she studied him. 'What do you suggest we do to get those shops tenanted?'

He flashed a huge smile as he let out a noisy breath. 'I can run some ads in the local papers again but I think you're just throwing money away doing that—maybe just two weeks. And I'll increase the size of the online ads—that might be more effective. I expect now that we're coming into the busier time of year, there'll be more interest in them. I wouldn't stress about it if I were you. Let's give this a go for a couple of weeks.'

As he walked her out to her car, he promised he'd be in contact during the week, but as she drove off, she wasn't feeling particularly hopeful that he'd achieve anything.

On the drive back to town her mind spun as the obvious answer swirled round and round and then finally settled. The town needed a boost, for everyone's sake. People needed both a reason to come, and a reason to stay once they arrived. And a big part of that would be getting the saloon open.

But if there were some more interesting shops, that would surely help. And why couldn't she become her own tenant? That would solve at least one of the vacancies, if not both. Surely, if she could run a tennis club, she could run a small retail outlet or two, but what sort of businesses could she open?

Suddenly images of those beautiful strawberries at the market in Sacramento danced across her mind. She could open a fresh fruit and veggie shop. After all, the small grocery store in town didn't have much in the way of fresh produce on offer the day she'd been there. The town's people would flock to a fresh produce shop, wouldn't they?

Could it be that simple?

By the time she got home, she'd convinced herself opening a fruit and veggie shop was a brilliant idea. But that still left the second shop. Perhaps Casey and Taylor would have some ideas. She grabbed her iPad and checked the time in Melbourne. It was early Monday morning, so both Taylor and Casey would either be at work or getting ready for work, so she couldn't FaceTime them together, but she could send a text to both of them. Within a few minutes, she'd had replies. Two thumbs up came back regarding the fruit and veggie shop, and they both said they'd turn their minds to the other shop and get back to her.

Eager to get started, Alex went into the study and opened the cabinet with the saloon files. It was all there—the correspondence from the insurance company, the contact details for the company who'd been engaged to complete the works, and a letter her uncle had written advising he was appointing Denver Gold in his stead to be the overseer of the workmanship. She could see no reason why the works had stopped other than that they'd been made aware of his death. She'd ring them first thing in the morning to get the ball rolling again.

After setting out the papers, she went back to the kitchen, but now that she'd made up her mind about the fruit and veggie shop, she wanted to get started. And who was best to help her? Denver Gold, carpenter extraordinaire, most definitely.

She knew he was busy—he had his party coming up on top of all the things he normally did with their property—but she also knew it was in his interest as much as her own to invigorate the town. Or at least it should be.

She grabbed the car keys and within a few minutes pulled up at the front of the Gold's house.

CHAPTER 11

Travis had just put his foot into the stirrup when he spotted the red Mustang making its way up the driveway. The young gelding took a step back as he inadvertently tightened his grip on the reins. He hopped to his right, then swung up into the saddle and patted the horse's neck reassuringly before pointing him toward the car. By the time he reached the car she'd opened the driver's door.

His breath caught involuntarily when she spun around in the seat, exposing a long bare leg finished off with a skimpy sandal. The way his heart reacted to her she might as well have been wearing a negligee.

Her eyes opened wide when they made contact with his. 'Travis, hello, I was ... I mean, is Denver at home? I wanted to ask him about some work I'd like to organise.'

'Yeah, he's home, but he's out in The Beast checking the cattle at the moment. That door troubling you again? You want me to have another look at it?' He'd spoken without thinking it through, which was a big mistake.

'Oh, no, the door's fine. It's about one of my empty shops. I ... wanted to run an idea past him.'

What sort of idea could she have that needed Denver's input? And wasn't his opinion as good as Denver's anyway? His jaw tensed. Was he jealous of her attention toward his brother?

He considered dismounting, and yet standing next to her was the last thing he should do if he wanted her to go. He stayed on the horse, looking down at her without even removing his hat. Maybe she'd take the hint that he was busy.

Instead, she stepped closer, reaching up to stroke the gelding's nose. 'It's quite soft.'

'Yes.'

She reached up further and placed her hand under the gelding's mane, slowly stoking his neck. 'Wow, his coat is like satin. I've never spent much time around horses. I guess I never gave any thought to whether or not they were soft.'

A frown of disbelief momentarily tightened his brow, but why should she have spent time around horses? She lived in a big city. She played tennis. She dined at country clubs. He huffed out a breath.

The Beast's throaty diesel engine gave away Denver's impending arrival. A moment later he appeared from around the back of the barn, shut off The Beast, and walked toward them.

'Hey, Alex, here to go for a ride?' He gave her a cheeky grin as he stopped beside them.

She glanced down at her dress. 'Hardly. Actually, I've come to ask you a big favour.'

Travis sniffed out a breath at the look on Denver's face—talk about inflating a guy's ego.

'Really? Oh, that's right ... you wanted that dead-bolt done. Travis told me about it.'

When she turned and looked up at Travis, his insides roiled.

'Yes, at some stage, but that's not what I'm here about. It's ...' She seemed to lose her train of thought for a moment as Travis stared at her. He blinked and then looked across at Denver who now cracked a broad smile.

'It's ...?' Denver prompted, dragging her attention back to him.

'Oh ... I want to open a fruit and veggie shop in one of my empty properties. I know the grocery store sells produce, but I'd hardly call it an extensive array. Anyway, I wanted your advice on getting the work done to make it happen.'

Travis couldn't help but nod—it wasn't a bad idea.

Denver beamed. 'Produce ... yeah, sure, that's not hard. Some display cabinets, refrigeration, a checkout counter—all easily done.'

'Fabulous,' she said, on an exhale.

'You want me to come have a look at it, and help recommend what you'll need?'

'Could you?'

'Absolutely,' Denver said, looking at Travis with a cheeky grin.

Alex looked relieved. 'So you think it's a good idea?'

'I think it's a great idea. Old George is as lazy as a sloth; this'll make him lift his game.' Denver grinned at Alex, and then turned to Travis. 'I might drop around there sometime tomorrow morning. Would that be alright?'

Travis shrugged his shoulders, wondering why Denver was practically asking his permission.

Alex's eyes lit up. 'Perfect, thanks.' She reached into her car and pulled out her phone. 'Give me your number and I'll text you, then you'll have mine. Just let me know what time and I'll be there.'

When Denver turned, giving Travis a look so obvious he might as well have said out loud that he'd gotten the girl's number without even having to ask for it, Travis had to bite down on his lip to keep from making a smart remark.

Denver gave her his number, then continued, 'Say, we're gonna throw a couple of steaks on the barbeque shortly. Want to stay for dinner?'

Alex's eyes widened as she turned to Travis with a question on her face. 'Oh, well, I hate to intrude.'

Denver laughed. 'You're not intruding. I've invited you. How is that intruding?'

'I suppose I did turn up here right around dinner time, but it's only because I got this idea in my head and I wanted to run it past you.'

'Hey, don't apologise.' He nodded toward Travis. 'Nice to have someone to talk to besides this grumpy one for a change.'

Travis swallowed back his biting remarks—it wouldn't have been polite to let loose on his little brother in front of Alex. And it would only prove Denver right if he bit. He turned to Alex. 'Stay, by all means. I've gotta finish off with Blue here and put him out. Denver, you'll be okay to entertain our guest for forty-five minutes on your own?'

Alex ran her hands down her bare arms. 'It's likely to cool off as soon as the sun drops so I might dash home and change. And I have a bottle of wine I bought the other day which I haven't opened yet. It'll go nicely with a steak.'

Denver cocked his head. 'An Australian wine?'

'Napa Valley—is that okay?'

Denver smiled. 'Sounds good. See you shortly.'

As Travis rode back toward the arena he heard Alex say something, and then both she and Denver started to laugh. He couldn't help but wonder if they were getting a chuckle at his expense.

~~*~~

'Can I help with anything?' Alex asked as she walked behind Denver with the bottle of wine in one hand and packet of mint slices in the other.

In a moment they were standing in a large open kitchen. With its lace curtains and matching tablecloth, Alex noted the room had a surprisingly feminine feel to it for a home shared by two men. Then she remembered Denver saying it had been their parent's place—and they'd moved back when their father got sick.

'Sure, you can put the salad together while I go light the barbeque if you like. Travis is in the shower but he won't be long. Oh, and if you'll open that bottle of wine I'll grab some glasses when I come back in.'

A few minutes later they were seated out on the back deck when Travis joined them. As he stepped outside, his hair still wet from the shower, the clean scent of soap wafted toward her and a rush of excitement made her shiver.

'Need a hand with anything, Den?' Travis asked as he picked up a glass of the red and held it under his nose.

'Nope, everything's done. Give me a shout when you're ready to eat and I'll throw the steaks on.'

'I'm starving, so whenever you're ready,' Travis said, turning toward the table. He hesitated for a moment, then sat across from her and lifted his glass to his lips. When he took a sip of the wine, he looked at her over the rim of the glass.

'You've chosen well, Alex. Perfect, in fact,' he said, his lips almost curling into a smile.

She smiled as heat touched her cheeks, absurdly happy that he'd approved of her selection. She looked down at her own glass, lifted it, and took a small sip. The deep red liquid tasted of blackberries. She had chosen well.

Denver cleared his throat, then stood and headed to the barbeque. He threw the steaks on and in a moment the delicious scent of hickory and seared meat drifted toward them. Alex's stomach growled and her mouth watered in anticipation.

When she turned back toward Travis he was staring at her. She hoped he hadn't heard her stomach growl. She stared back defiantly at first, but she couldn't keep it up—his gaze was far too intense. She blinked, lifted her glass and took another sip, savouring the smooth wine as it slid down her throat and left a sweet taste in her mouth and on her lips.

She licked her lips, and bit the lower one slightly, then allowed herself to look up at Travis, embarrassed to find him watching her every move again. Again? Or still?

'Is the wine comparable to what you have down there in Australia?' Travis asked, his voice as smooth as the wine.

'It's every bit as good as any I've had at home. Mind you, I'm not much of a connoisseur. I like what I like, but I don't know much about wine.'

'Neither do I; I was just curious.'

Denver walked up and grabbed the plates off the table and set them on the side of the barbeque. Then he came back and picked up his glass. He took a drink, set it back on the table without comment, and turned to Travis.

'Do you still want me to ride out with you tomorrow while you put a few miles on that young gelding?'

Travis stared at his younger brother for a moment before speaking, and Alex wondered if there was more to the question than the obvious.

'If you wouldn't mind. It'll be good for him to go with an older, steadier horse.'

Denver took another sip of wine, set the glass down and smiled at Alex before turning back to his older brother. 'Well, I don't really mind, except I said I'd help Alex with that fit-out in the morning, and then I'm heading over to see the caterer to discuss the food and drinks for the party. So ...'

Alex looked back and forth between the brothers, sorry now that she'd asked Denver for his help. She shouldn't have bothered him with the fit-out until she'd made more enquiries about whether it was even a feasible venture. She turned to Denver. 'Look, why don't we hold off on the fit-out until after your birthday. It isn't urgent, after all.'

'No, that's cool. I don't mind having a look. I think it's a great idea, and the sooner we get started, the sooner it can open. It won't take me long to measure up and do a few sketches. Besides, I have a thought.'

Travis quirked a brow as he glared at Denver. 'Do tell.'

'How about if Alex rides out with you? She can ride Sally.' He turned to Alex, and continued, 'My mare's the gentlest horse on the property. Could even be the gentlest horse in California as far as I know. What do you think, Alex?'

She set her glass on the table and swallowed with difficulty. 'Ride out? As in, riding on a horse?'

Travis shook his head slowly. 'Denver, I don't think that's such a great idea—'

Denver shrugged as he turned back to Alex and winked. 'Sure it is. What better way to make certain you go for a quiet ride than to have a beginner with you?'

CHAPTER 12

When Alex turned up at the shop at quarter past ten, Denver was already there, one booted foot propped up against the door frame as he played with a tape measure pulling the tape out and letting it snap back in. When he spotted her, he quickly pocketed the tape measure and flashed a smile in her direction.

'Thanks again for doing this for me,' Alex said, walking up and opening the door.

'Sure thing, Alex. It'll be a fun little job.'

A musty smell greeted them as they entered the empty shop, so Alex left the door open to allow the fresh air to circulate.

Denver pulled out a sheaf of papers and a pencil, and after asking a few pertinent questions, began sketching out the location of the shelving, bins and counters. When he'd finished, he did quick measurements of the room, its windows and door.

'I'll cost out the carpentry work and get some quotes on the refrigeration units—I should have a pretty good idea of the total cost for you in a couple of days.'

'Wow, I can't believe how quickly this is all coming together. I mean, yesterday it was just a wild thought that crossed my mind, and now it's looking like it's really going to happen.'

Denver cocked his head. 'You better believe it will.'

Alex looked around the shop again. Denver's confidence was contagious. What had he called this, a fun little job? For him, yes, but to Alex it was so much more than that. It was creating something she could call her own. A slight smile touched her lips as warmth washed over her.

She turned to face Denver again as he cleared his throat to speak.

'You'll need a bookkeeper no doubt, and I've got a great contact—Cathy Brooks.'

With difficulty, Alex turned her focus back to the practical. 'Oh, good, yes I hadn't thought about that. I'll need a cash register too, I suppose. Is this Cathy a friend of yours?'

'Yeah, we went to school together. She's really good at what she does, and I'm pretty sure I've got her business card at home. I'll leave it on the kitchen table. You can grab it when you come over to ride.'

The joy she'd been feeling dissipated as his words hit home. She'd been trying to forget she'd agreed to go for a ride with Travis. Obviously, Denver hadn't.

'Are you sure this ride is a good idea? I haven't been on a horse since ... actually, I don't think I've ever been on a horse. I've ridden ponies a couple of times, but that was at school camp.'

Denver winked. 'You'll be fine. Sally is the most trustworthy horse I've ever come across. You'll have a great time. You'll see.'

~~*~~

Alex spotted Travis standing near the barn as she drove up to the house. Once again in his element, his whole body exuded quiet confidence.

When she stopped short of the barn, he directed her to where she should park. That's when she noticed the two horses tied up, both saddled, looking ready to go. The larger one was quite dark, the other a lovely reddish brown with white on its legs. She hoped she'd be riding the smaller one.

Travis was standing right there when she opened the car door. He swept his hand across in front of him. 'Your steed awaits.'

'Which one's mine?' she asked, nervously.

'That'd be Sally; on the right.'

She let out a sigh of relief as she swung her legs around and got out of the car. When he didn't move, she found herself standing far too close to him, and far too aware of his musky scent.

'Did you bring a hat with you?' he asked.

'Oh, I didn't think of that.'

'No worries, I brought one down from the house that should fit you. It was my mother's. She'd be pleased to see it being used given I'm not sure she ever wore it herself.' He reached around her and closed the door, then led her toward the horses.

He untied the horse she was to ride and rubbed the horse's forehead gently. Then he handed her the light-coloured straw hat that was resting on top of the saddle. She put it on and smiled. It was a perfect fit.

'Here, Sally really is quite gentle,' he said, encouraging her to come closer as he continued to rub Sally's forehead.

Alex swallowed hard and took a deep breath. She could do this. Wasn't it meant to be good for you to step outside your comfort zone? She reached out and placed her hand on the horse's forehead, mimicking the movements Travis had made. The horse closed her eyes and leaned into the pressure of Alex's hand. Warmth washed over her and a smile eased some of the tension in her jaw.

'See, she likes you already.' Travis must have moved closer; his warm breath touched her neck as he spoke, sending shivers down her spine.

Alex drew in a quick breath, no longer certain if it was the horse riding or Travis' company that she'd been worried about.

He chuckled softly, shaking his head. 'Come on, I'll give you a leg up.'

'No, I'm right,' she said, determined that she could do this on her own.

Travis nodded as he stepped back. 'Okay.'

Alex grabbed the side of the saddle and lifted her left leg, placing her foot into the stirrup, but as she tried to pull herself up, Sally turned her head toward her and practically rolled her eyes. She laughed nervously, and that made it even harder, so she pulled her foot out and stepped back.

Travis, to give him credit, kept a straight face. 'Here, let me show you.'

Alex moved out of the way as Travis gathered up the reins in his left hand, placed his right hand on the front of the saddle, lifted his foot into the stirrup and in one smooth motion was up in the saddle. He looked down at her, smiled, and jumped off.

'Gees, you made that look easy.'

He shrugged off the compliment. 'It is easy, when you know how.'

'I think it put me off when she gave me that look.' She took the reins in her left hand and then tried to heft herself into the saddle the way he'd done. It wasn't quite as easy as he'd made it look and part way up she had to abandon the effort.

'You nearly had it. Grab the saddle here instead.' He placed his right hand on the back of the saddle, and she wondered if she could feel his other hand on her lower back or if it was just her imagination.

She looked up into his eyes, and he just smiled. She was reading too much into this.

Clearing her mind, she put her foot back into the stirrup, and grabbed where he'd shown her. In a moment, she was up. Not nearly as gracefully as she'd have liked, but she was on Sally's back and Sally wasn't moving. A sigh of relief escaped before she could stop it.

He looked up at her, a wry smile suggesting he was holding back laughter. 'Those stirrups are a bit too long for you. Here, pull your foot out for me and I'll adjust them,' he said as he touched her lower leg, and gently moved it out of the way.

His touch sent tingles across her skin that travelled all the way up her body. Had Liam never touched her calves? They were amazingly sensitive.

'Now, put your foot back in and stand up in the stirrups. Better?'

She tilted her head questioning him. 'Better than what?'

'Yeah, it's better. Here, I'll do the other one,' he said with a laugh as he walked around to the other side.

Again, he touched her leg to get her to remove her foot from the stirrup, and again it sent shivers along the surface of her skin. This time, as he adjusted the straps his hand brushed her thigh. She drew in an involuntary gulp of air and forced herself to close her mouth.

'Try that,' he finally said, guiding her foot back into the stirrup by gripping the heel of her boot. 'And try to remember to keep your weight on the ball of your foot, and keep your heels down.'

He removed his hand and stepped back, then looked up at her, looking like he was waiting for her to acknowledge his instructions.

She swallowed and pushed an imaginary bit of hair away from her face. 'Got it.'

A moment later he was on his horse beside her. 'Ready?' he asked.

'I think so,' she replied.

'Alright then, let's go.' His horse took a few steps, and Sally fell in beside him. 'Now, when you want to stop, pull back like this. Not too hard, just a gentle pull and say whoa.'

Alex pulled back as he'd shown her, and Sally stopped instantly. Some of her tension released; at least she knew where the brakes were.

'And to ask her to turn, you do this.' He gently laid the reins against his horse's neck and immediately the horse began to turn. Then he laid them on the other side for a brief moment, and the horse turned back. 'Now, you try.'

Again, she did as he'd done, amazed at how easy this was. 'Wow, I feel like a professional now ... almost.'

A deep throaty laugh escaped him before he smacked his right hand over his mouth. 'I shouldn't laugh. We were all beginners at one time or another.'

'Yes, well, you and Denver were probably in the saddle before you could walk.'

He grinned. 'Just about.'

With each step Sally took, Alex's nerves settled further. The weather couldn't have been better, her horse was behaving beautifully, and Travis seemed to be genuinely enjoying himself. His patience in explaining things that to him were clearly second nature reminded her of the way he'd behaved when he'd fixed the screen door. It was hard to reconcile this side of him with the gruff man she'd met in the saloon the day she'd arrived in town. Had she judged him too quickly that day?

She brought her attention back to her horse as they reached the end of the driveway and Travis turned right into the main road. Sally fell in behind Travis' horse and within a few minutes, the steady clip-clopping of the horses' hooves completely transformed the last of Alex's fear to enjoyment.

Travis turned, and spoke over his shoulder. 'You doing all right back there?'

'Yeah, this is more fun than I expected. She's quite happy just following you.'

He cocked his head and gave her a smile that said, *I told you so*, without saying it. 'We'll get off this road soon and go up through Blue Gum Park—the trails are wide and clear, and it's shady.'

'Blue Gum Park? Is that the park across from my place?'

'Yep. We'll come in from the bottom and ride up through the park.'

'Riding is allowed through there?'

He cocked his head again, only this time a frown visible across his brow. 'Sure, why wouldn't it be?'

'A lot of our parks have signs saying no horses, no dogs, no motorbikes ... and the rest.'

'Horses are definitely allowed. When your uncle donated the park to the county it was on the condition that the trees could never be harvested—and the riding trails could never be closed.'

'My uncle owned the park?'

'Yes, and a great deal of other land around here. As did my family.'

She hadn't known that, but it made sense. Any wonder he'd had so much money. Once again she wished she'd known her father's side of the family better.

Travis moved his horse further to the side and slowed until Sally was up beside him. 'Your uncle used to ride a lot and made most of the trails in the park himself. He had some nice horses, but sold them all when he had the new house built.'

'I suppose he was getting too old to ride much by then. Was the house next door done at the same time?'

'Yeah, I'm pretty sure the guy who bought the land built both houses as part of the deal.'

'And is that man still living in the house?'

'No, he sold it when the house was finished. The high school principal lives there now.'

She wished she'd known who he was when she'd spoken to him about the mowing. Perhaps she would drop in on him again to ask what the kids around here did to keep busy over the summer months.

A moment later they were riding single file through the park, surrounded by eucalyptus trees. They followed what seemed to be the main trail, passing smaller ones that went off to the sides from time to time.

Travis again let Sally catch up beside him. 'How would you like to try a slow lope?'

Alex's heart skipped a beat or two as his words sunk in. Lope. That probably meant running. 'Uh ... do you think I'm ready?'

'You'll love it. Sally's like a rocking chair, and we'll just go slowly as we make our way up this gentle rise. Ready?'

'I suppose ...'

He moved his horse to the front of hers again and it started to run. He looked over his shoulder and called back to her. 'Loosen the reins a bit and give her a gentle squeeze with your legs.'

Alex squeezed her legs up against Sally's sides, hung onto the saddle and closed her eyes. There was an initial surge of power, but Sally quickly settled into a gait which didn't even bounce her out of the saddle. Either she was the best beginner in the world, or this was one incredibly smooth horse. She suspected the latter.

'That's it. You've got the hang of it.' Travis called out to her again, and then brought his horse to a stop at the top of the rise.

When she caught up to him, Alex pulled gently on the reins as they came up beside the other horse. 'I can see how people get addicted to this.'

'I told you she has a rocking chair lope. I'm glad you're enjoying it. Sally's one of the best horses we've got for beginners. She's never put a foot wrong with anyone.'

Alex leaned forward and ran her hand along Sally's now sweat-covered neck. 'And you're not going to start with me, are you Sally?'

When Travis laughed, Alex looked up and met his gaze. For the first time, she noticed the laugh lines around his eyes. They went well with the touch of grey visible in his temples, and spoke of a man who'd led a full life; a man who'd had some rough times up to now, but seemed to have come through them well enough.

And now she was genuinely glad she'd agreed to come along on this ride, and found herself hoping it wouldn't be the last invitation she'd get.

His eyes were still locked on hers when he finally spoke. 'Shall we ride on up to the top? Or do you want to head back?'

'I'm not in any rush, so it's up to you.'

He gave her a thoughtful look, perhaps weighing up the options. 'I thought you might be getting a bit sore, using different muscles. We could go back.'

'Oh, I'm pretty fit ... I run most mornings. Don't worry about me.'

When he raised an eyebrow, she regretted having said that. Was she almost goading him into taking her on a far longer ride than she was ready for?

A slow smile finally touched his lips. 'Okay then, let's keep going.'

They continued up the trail, winding back and forth, and had a couple more slow lopes along the way until they popped out of the trees onto Blue Gum Road. Travis was right; they were across the road from her place. Pride washed over her as she admired the house, still finding it hard to believe it was hers.

'We'll ride back along the road, if you don't mind. Pirate could use the exposure to cars.'

'Pirate?'

'Golden Pirate, to be exact.'

'Well then, Pirate, I guess we'll ride along the road.'

Of course, not a single car went past, but the clip-clopping of the horses' hooves did catch the attention of two young children. They asked if they could pet the horses and Travis seemed happy to oblige.

'He's so pretty,' said a young girl of about six or seven as she reached up to stroke Sally's nose while the young boy moved in front of Travis' horse.

'*She* is pretty, isn't she? Her name is Sally.' Alex corrected with a smile. 'Have you ever ridden a horse?'

'No, we don't have any horses, but we have bikes. Mom lets us ride them in the park. Is that where you were riding?'

'Yes,' Alex replied.

'Sometimes I see hoof prints on the trails, and then I pretend my bike is a horse. I've named her Princess.'

'That's a lovely name. I like the park too—tomorrow I think I'll go for a run there. It's a ripper, isn't it?'

'A ripper?'

Alex frowned, realising the little girl probably had never heard the Aussie expression. 'Oh, it's a really cool park, isn't it?'

The little girl's face brightened. 'You talk funny. Are you from Canada?'

'No, I'm from Australia. Have you heard of Australia?'

The girl tilted her head, thinking. Then she put a finger on her chin making the cutest inquisitive face. 'I don't think I have heard of Ostraya, but my cousin Laura lives in Canada and she talks funny too. They visited us last year.'

The boy pushed over to Sally, so the children swapped horses. He was either her twin or perhaps a year younger but there was no doubt they were siblings. It wasn't long before a heavily pregnant woman called out to them, and they each said a quick goodbye before dashing back to their front yard.

Alex waved to the children, swallowing back her sorrow as they departed. Then they continued along the road, this time riding side-by-side.

Travis raised an eyebrow as he turned to look at her. 'You're good with kids.'

Alex cleared her throat, regaining her composure. 'I've worked with lots of them. I used to run tennis programs after school and during school holidays.'

'Used to?'

'The club I worked for sold out to a property developer. It's a long story, but I ended up taking a more demanding job, and that was the end of my coaching. I'm hoping to start it up again soon.'

He took a long time to say anything, appearing to be considering what she'd said. 'I can see you'd be really good at it.'

'Can you?'

'What I meant was, you connect well with children, and that's half the battle.'

It wasn't a big compliment, and it wasn't based on much more than a moment's talk with a young girl, but his words warmed her heart, and made her take stock of the fact that she'd let too much time go by. Working with kids was something she loved, and she needed to get back to it. And selling all the properties would no doubt give her the money to do just that.

When a car finally came along Travis moved Pirate off the road as best he could. Sally followed and fell in behind. They rode the rest of the way back like that, single file, and when they reached the gates of Gold's Ranch, Travis hopped off and checked the letterbox. When he didn't get back on, Alex decided it might be nice to walk the rest of the way too. As she dropped to the ground she landed with a thud and a nervous laugh escaped her.

'Bit stiff?' Travis had an undisguised hint of laughter in his voice.

'Yeah, no, I'm fine.' She arched her back, and heard it crack.

And that brought a wide smile to his lips as he huffed out a breath. 'Epsom salts in the tub. Works wonders for me when I've been in the saddle too many hours.'

She kind of wished he hadn't said that because now as she looked at him it was difficult not to picture him naked, soaking in a bathtub. She quickly dropped her gaze and began walking. 'How many hours a day do you generally ride?'

'Depends on what I'm doing. I don't normally work any one horse for much more than a half hour, but some days I end up working close to a dozen, depending on what's coming up. Like the rodeo in two weeks.'

'Ah, yes, the rodeo. Will Denver ride too?'

'You bet. He and I will ride the youngsters, and when we're in a three-person team our cousin, Nick, will ride Sally.'

'Oh, so the other day when I saw you riding that horse, Sally does that too?'

'Yep, Sally can do pretty much anything you ask her to do.'

Alex reached across and stroked Sally's neck, having even more respect for her than she'd had before. 'And do you take the horses to other rodeos, or just this one?'

He flashed a slow smile. 'We go to a few each year—have to keep our name out there.'

'That must be exciting.'

He hesitated before replying, a faraway look crossing his face. 'Sometimes.'

It dawned on her he could be thinking about his wife. Denver had said she'd run off with a bull-rider. Would they be at the rodeo at Angels Camp? That would have to be awkward, travelling in the same circles. At least she hadn't seen Liam since the divorce was finalised. Perhaps Travis would bump into his ex, and her new boyfriend at the rodeo. Perhaps she should change the subject.

'And your cousin, does he have horses as well? You said he'll ride Sally?'

'He grew up next door,' he said, nodding toward a house just visible down the road. 'We all rode as kids, but now that he lives in Sacramento. He hasn't got any horses of his own, but he's happy to come out here and gives us a hand when we need him.'

'You're lucky to have him, to help out I mean.'

'Yes, he's a big help that's for sure. He'll be at Denver's birthday, then stick around for the week and work with us in the lead up to the rodeo.'

'And his family, will he bring them too?'

Travis cocked his head as another slow smile touched his eyes and lips. 'He isn't married, if that's what you're asking. His sister lives next door now—he'll stay there with her.'

'Oh, I wasn't ... I mean, I was just curious,' she said, feeling like she'd put her foot in her mouth.

He chuckled, but kept walking.

When they reached the barn, Travis took Sally's reins and led the horses over and tied them to a post, and then removed their saddles and bridles and carried the gear into the barn.

When he returned, she helped him hose off the horses, and put them into a yard with some hay.

'Now, can I get you a cool drink?' Travis rubbed his face with the back of his hand. 'I could sure use one.'

'I'd love one.'

They made their way out to the back of the house and sat at the same table where they'd eaten the night before. Travis disappeared inside, and then returned with two glasses of iced tea.

'Was there a business card in the kitchen? Denver said he'd leave one—for a bookkeeper he's recommending.'

'Yeah I did see that sitting there and wondered why. She's good.'

Alex took a long drink of the tea, watching out of the corner of her eye as he did the same. Then, what started out as a pleasant silence soon became awkward, and she pushed her seat back to stand. 'I should get going ... you probably have a lot to do for the rest of the day.'

He stood too. 'Let me grab that card for you.'

When he returned with the card, he walked her to her car. 'So, have you caught the bug?'

She turned, just as she reached the car door. 'Bug?'

'Horses. Did you enjoy the ride?'

'Oh, very much so. Thank you for taking me. They're magnificent animals, aren't they?'

He reached around her and opened the car door. 'They are indeed. Perhaps we'll do this again sometime.'

'I'd like that,' she said, supressing a sudden desire to lean forward and kiss his cheek. Then she remembered the hat. 'Oh, here, I shouldn't take this with me.' She started to remove the hat but he reached out and touched her hand.

'Hang onto it, it suits you.'

'You're sure?'

'Absolutely.'

She shrugged, getting behind the wheel. 'Thank you. It feels so comfortable I'd forgotten I had it on.'

As she drove off, she watched him in the rear-view mirror, surprised by the longing that washed over her.

CHAPTER 13

Alex kept busy the next few days with getting the saloon repairs back on track, making contact with suppliers for the fruit and veggie shop, and meeting with the local bookkeeper. She also had a meeting in Sacramento with her accountant to make sure she could access the cash to make it all happen, and by the end of the week she was confident that whether she remained in Masons Flat or not, her assets would only grow in value.

The other thing Alex did in Sacramento was shop for a new outfit for Denver's party and now, at quarter to seven on Saturday night, she checked her image in the mirror yet again while waiting for Harrison to pick her up. She loved the summer dress she'd found, with its pale blue background covered with splashes of red, white and orange flowers and emerald green leaves. She'd thanked her lucky stars when they had it in her size because it wasn't only the colours of the retro dress which suited her; its sweetheart neckline, capped sleeves, empire waist and flared skirt showed off her trim figure better than any dress she'd ever owned, while at the same time covering the scars across her collarbone and shoulder. Set off with a pair of ivory sandals with gold trim, she felt like Cinderella preparing to go to the ball.

She paced back and forth—one moment excited at the thought of seeing Harrison, and the next regretting she'd agreed to go as his date. It was thoughts of Travis, not Harrison, that had preoccupied her most of the week. The tingle she'd felt, when he'd touched her leg, his warm smile, the laugh lines around his eyes, the bits of grey in his temples, the slow easy manner he had around the horses, the strength he demonstrated as he propelled himself onto the back of his horse— all those images had been flitting across her mind, often at the most inopportune times. And in less than an hour she'd see him as she arrived at Denver's party with another man.

She checked her lipstick one last time as she heard the car pull up in the driveway, then grabbed her purse, picked up the gift she'd bought and locked the door behind her.

~~*~~

Travis watched as a young man flipped burgers and steaks on a huge barbeque, grateful Denver had decided to get the party catered so that he didn't have to stand there and cook all night. The smoke wafted up to his nostrils, the delicious scent reminding him he hadn't eaten since breakfast.

The young man turned to him. 'Hey, would you mind putting this platter over on the main table?'

He set it on a long table next to huge bowls of salads and stacks of bread rolls, then turned to face the party and began doing what he'd been doing regularly for the past half hour—scanning the crowd looking for long red hair. But instead of finding her, he spotted a group of children playing on the slide and swings, while another group paddled in the pool, under the watchful eye of a few hovering parents. For the most part, the adults mingled on the lawn area, or sat at tables set up along the edges. Everyone seemed to be having a good time, especially Denver, who was surrounded by a group of women.

When he spotted his cousins at a table on the opposite side of the lawn, he loaded a plate with a burger and a brat, topped it off with some potato salad and corn and headed across the lawn to sit with them.

And that's when a flash of long red hair caught his eye.

Nick looked up as he approached, and shifted over, but sitting where Nick indicated would've put Travis with his back to everyone. Instead, he walked around to the other side of the table across from Nick, and tapped his cousin Stacy on the shoulder to get her to move over for him. She glared at him for a second before shifting.

'Sure you've got enough to eat there, Trav?' Stacy said, nodding toward his heavily laden plate.

'I haven't eaten anything since six this morning, if you don't mind.'

'Oh, I don't mind. I'm not paying for the food. Besides, you'll need energy for all the dancing once the band gets started. Tim hates dancing so I'll be relying on you to partner me.'

Travis took a messy bite of his burger, all the while keeping an eye on Alex. She was saying hello to Denver as she handed him a present.

As she stepped back, she introduced Denver to the man next to her. She needn't have bothered; both he and Denver knew Harrison. He'd grown up in the area, and most people in town knew him. What he didn't know was why they'd arrived together. Was she his date?

Stacy said something to him, and when he didn't reply, she smacked his arm. 'Travis? How's your filly doing? The pretty one who cut her leg? Are you taking her to the rodeo next week?'

'Sorry Stacy, I was ... concentrating on my food. The filly is on the mend, but she won't be ready to be worked for a bit longer.'

'Well, if it ends up that she's too injured to be a competition horse, you could, you know, offer her to a friend ... or a relative ... as a pleasure horse. Someone who would take good care of her and only ride her lightly.' Stacy rolled her eyes and smirked.

He cocked his head. 'Yeah, that's a thought. Or I could keep her to breed from. Like you say, she's awfully pretty.'

'Well, Tammy's been pestering me about getting her a horse of her own, so if you want the filly to go to a good home, let me know.'

Nick chimed in now. 'Give it a rest, Stace. That filly's worth too much as a brood mare to become a kid's pony. I'll help you find something for Tammy if she's serious. She'll probably want a Welsh pony to start with anyway, not a valuable Quarter Horse.'

Travis gave Nick a look of gratitude, then turned to Stacy. 'I'll keep it in mind, Stace. Speaking of Tammy, where is she?'

'She's over by your horses, where else? Tim's over there with her.'

'Ah,' he said, and then, as nonchalantly as possible began to look for Alex again, but couldn't see her anywhere. He quickly scoffed down the rest of his food and then used getting a refill as an excuse to leave the table.

As he approached the spread of food, he spotted her. She and Harrison had each grabbed a burger and were standing not far from the house, talking while eating. He'd have liked to have gone over to interrupt whatever Harrison was saying that had put a smile on Alex's face, but as soon as he grabbed another burger and turned back, they'd moved away.

Movement near the dance floor caught his attention as the band members made their way to their equipment and began doing a sound test. Denver grabbed the mike and joined them.

'I want to thank all of you for coming tonight to help me celebrate this milestone birthday, but don't make the mistake of thinking me too old just because I'm thirty. I plan to dance the night away, and I want to see all of you up here at least once. Now, I'll hand over to Tommy and the Tripods to get this party started.' He let out a whoop at the end and grabbed a girl to join him on the dance floor.

The band kicked off with a loud one, and Travis stood back as couples made their way to join in. That's when he finally spotted her again. Harrison held her hand as he led her onto the dance floor, and they were both smiling.

Maybe it was a date. Whatever it was, Harrison knew how to dance and soon had Alex twirling around, her dress flowing and swishing as Harrison spun her out and back in again. They looked pretty good together, as much as he hated to admit it, making him wonder if they had been on a date prior to tonight. His jaw tightened as that thought took hold. He couldn't watch any longer.

A tap on his arm brought him back to the moment, and he turned to face Stacy with a big grin on her face. 'Come on, we're dancing.'

He allowed Stacy to drag him onto the dance floor, and they squeezed in toward the middle. There wasn't really enough room to do any fancy steps now, as the area had packed in a bit, but that was a good thing because even though he enjoyed dancing, it had always been more about connecting with a partner. Dancing with his cousin would hardly be that.

As the song finished, another started. Stacy seemed to have gained confidence, pushing back to do her spins regardless of the crowd. It was about midway through this song that Stacy backed up a bit too far, and collided with a man who lost his footing and ended up pulling his partner down with him.

Travis stepped up to find Harrison and Alex sprawled on the dance floor, laughing their heads off. He extended his hand to Alex to help her while Harrison scrambled to get up on his own.

'I am so sorry,' Stacy apologised to the pair, running her hands down the side of Alex's dress to remove a bit of dirt. 'Your dress is so beautiful; I hope I haven't spoiled it?'

Alex looked down to inspect it, but then smiled at Stacy. 'It's okay; I know it was an accident.'

When Travis suddenly realised that he hadn't yet let go of Alex's hand he did so quickly, taking one step back. He didn't drop his gaze however.

Stacy still sounded apologetic. 'And I haven't even been drinking. Best I don't get started if this is what I do when I'm sober.'

Harrison, who'd been checking out his pants, now turned to Alex. 'You're okay, I take it?'

'Yeah, of course,' Alex said, brushing his concerns aside.

'That's good, because I seem to have landed in a bit of ketchup.'

Stacy bent over to inspect the leg of Harrison's pants. 'Oh, Harrison, I'm so sorry. Let me help, you don't want that to stain.'

'No, I'd rather it didn't—these are my favourites,' Harrison said to Stacy.

'Come on, there's bound to be some soda water at the bar.' She took Harrison's hand and pulled him off toward the makeshift bar, leaving Travis standing with Alex.

When he looked down at her, she quirked an eyebrow and gave him an awkward grin.

~~*~~

Being left there on the dance floor with Travis staring at her questioningly was awkward, but she couldn't deny the tingle of anticipation that washed over her. She sighed, giving him an awkward smile.

'Shall we?' he asked, holding out his hand and flashing a smile in return.

The moment he took her hand they became a couple, swinging to the lyrics of Rockabilly Redneck as if they'd been doing it all their lives. Harrison had danced well, but it had been obvious he was more interested in showing off—stepping back and doing his own thing at every opportunity—but Travis was dancing *with* her. She couldn't wipe the smile off her face as he swung her around and pulled her in close with his strong arms. That first song was followed by a similar one, and they continued dancing, picking up the pace a bit. But when the second song ended, the band took the tempo down a notch, and as the lead singer sang out "Hey ... hey, baby ..." Alex couldn't resist swaying slowly to the song—one she hadn't heard in a long time.

They kept dancing, only this time Travis pulled her in even closer, and when her chest pressed against his it stirred feelings inside her that she hadn't dared to feel for a long time. When she again swung out wide, she had to remind herself it was just a dance, and that Travis was simply being a gentleman, dancing with the woman who'd been stranded on the dance floor because of his partner.

As the song came to an end, he cocked his head toward the bar. 'That's thirsty work. Can I get you a drink?'

When she nodded, he placed his hand ever so gently on the small of her back and guided her off the dance floor. She halfway expected to find Harrison there, perhaps still fiddling with the ketchup stain or talking to Stacy, but neither of them were anywhere to be seen.

'What can I get you?' asked a young man from behind a table that tonight made do as a bar.

Alex thought hard for a moment, finally asking, 'Have you got a light beer?'

'Absolutely. And you sir?'

Travis cocked his head. 'I'll have the same.'

The man turned and grabbed the beers, popped the tops and handed them the cans. 'Did you want a glass?'

'No, I'm right thanks,' Alex replied, nodding.

Travis smiled, and pointed toward what looked to be a small gazebo where only a few people stood. 'Do you want to catch your breath over there for a moment?'

Alex smiled and shrugged her shoulders, pleasantly surprised he wanted to talk. 'Sure.'

As they approached the gazebo Alex realised that on the other side of the small rise were a tennis court and a pool. Did all ranches have pools and tennis courts? She wouldn't have thought so, but then again, this was California.

When they stopped walking, she turned to him. 'You sure seem to know your way around a dance floor.'

Travis gave her a crooked smile. 'My ex was a big dancer, so I learned enough to get by.'

'Oh, I'd say you were doing better than just getting by. I've barely got the hang of it, but you made it easy—all I had to do was hang on.'

He smiled and took a mouthful of beer. She did the same.

'You say your ex liked to dance? And is she here tonight?' She was surprised that she'd dared to ask that, but he was the one who'd brought up his ex-wife. She glanced toward the dancers, assessing the women and trying to pick out one who might seem his type. When he didn't answer, she turned to him.

His brows came together in a deep frown for a moment. 'No, we don't really socialise these days. She ... moved to Southern California some time ago.'

'Hmm, I suppose that makes it a bit easier. Not bumping into her unexpectedly, I mean.'

He cocked his head, a smirk on his face, yet there was pain reflected in his eyes. 'Yeah, well, we didn't exactly part on good terms.'

Did he miss his wife? Was his heart still broken? Alex couldn't remember if Denver had said how long ago it happened. Could he still be in love with her?

Travis turned away and sighed, then took another long sip of beer. 'Sorry, I shouldn't be talking about her. That's ancient history.' His smile looked forced, but his words were encouraging.

She wanted to tell him about Liam, but she wasn't sure this was the right time. 'Sometimes it is best to leave the past in the past, where it belongs. Oh sorry, that came out wrong. If you want, or need, to talk about it ... that's not what I meant.'

'I know what you meant. I suppose we've all made mistakes in the past. Best to learn from them, and look to the future, right?'

There was truth in his words, but what mistake had she made with Liam? She hadn't done anything wrong. Liam was the one driving that night yet not once had she blamed him for what happened. Her mind began spinning, threatening to drag her down. No good would come from dwelling on the past.

She lifted her beer and tapped it against his. 'To the future. Yes, indeed.'

As she took a sip, she looked up at him. He was watching her, his eyes burning into her with an intensity she hadn't experienced in ages. Then he sighed, and quirked a smile. 'Hey, it's a party, and here I am making you sad. Have I dredged up old memories? If so, I apologise.'

She was considering giving him a brief explanation about Liam when Travis' phone rang. He pulled it out of his pocket and checked the screen. 'Sorry, I've gotta take this.'

He began to walk away, but not before she heard him greet the caller. 'Sweetheart, I didn't expect to hear from you tonight—where are you?'

Nausea swept over her as she realised how close she'd come to divulging far too much about herself, simply because a man was being polite to her.

CHAPTER 14

'There you are,' Harrison said as she walked toward him.

'I'm not the one who disappeared, remember?' She laughed, hoping that didn't sound possessive.

He pointed to the wet patch on his leg. 'Got it out. Stacy was right about the soda water, but then she dragged me over to where her husband and daughter were looking at a couple of horses, and I got caught up. We all went to school together, but I hadn't seen her for a few years. Lots to catch up on. I didn't mean to desert you.'

'That's okay, I was only stirring. You want to show me your moves again?'

'Do I ever, baby,' Harrison said as he flashed a cheeky grin.

It was exactly what she needed to put the exchange with Travis behind her. He grabbed her hand and led her back to the dance floor, but when they got there his dance style became even more about him. It was fun, but not the same as the dances she'd just had with Travis.

She couldn't help looking around from time to time, trying to spot Travis, and wondering about this "sweetheart" and if she was going to show up here at the party.

After three dances, she'd had enough. 'Harrison, I need another drink. You?'

'No, but you go ahead. I'll find another partner, if that's okay with you?'

'Definitely—I'll be somewhere over near the bar.' She breathed a sigh of relief as she walked away. Then she spotted Denver with a group of friends, so once she got her drink she walked over to him and he introduced her to everyone, calling her his "boss". She played along, pleased when the group started to thin out eventually leaving her and Denver on their own.

'No one special here tonight?' she asked, taking a sip of some sparkling mineral water.

'What do you mean? Everyone here is special.' His brows waggled mischievously.

'You know what I mean.' She nodded toward a group on the edge of the dance floor. The three women were giggling and looking over at him like love-struck school girls.

'Well, there is one who's a bit special, but I haven't told her yet.'

Alex wasn't quite sure what he meant by that so just pressed on. 'Those three over there look like they're dying for you to go over to them.'

He turned toward them, and then winked as he faced Alex again. 'I'm trying to spread myself around, you know. I can't go showing too much favouritism to anyone in particular tonight, now can I?'

She laughed. 'Why not? It's your birthday; you can do whatever you like.'

While Denver gulped the rest of his beer, she took a moment to scan the area but Travis was nowhere to be seen. Had the caller been his girlfriend? Had he nicked out to meet her somewhere? Surely he wouldn't leave his brother's birthday party? She clenched her jaw, berating herself—it was none of her business if he had.

Denver tossed his empty can into a barrel and turned back to face her. 'I saw you with Travis. You're a fast learner, but he's only a beginner. Wanna dance with a real partner?'

'Oh, I don't know—maybe I'll finish my drink and let you grab one of those girls over there. Don't want them to think I'm trying to hog all your attention.'

He laughed, and gave her a wink. 'Yeah, okay. Watch and learn. Come on, I'll introduce you to them. They're all good friends of mine.'

Denver led her to the group and introduced her. Then he led the prettiest of the three out onto the dance floor and stood waiting for the next song to begin. People moved out of the way, clearing space for them and when the music started everyone stayed back.

Alex watched in awe—they were spectacular. The woman's white dress flared up, revealing an underdress of black satin which twirled as she spun. Her feet moved with lightning speed as Denver spun her around and pulled her in for a dip. She jumped back up with the ease of an Olympic athlete, leaving Alex to wonder if they'd competed.

The woman next to her leaned in and whispered in her ear. 'He should've hung onto her. They were together all through high school, then he went off to college in Sacramento and she married one of his best friends. Funny, we all thought he'd marry her. Even so, they still look terrific together, don't they?'

That wasn't what she'd expected to hear. She turned to look at the woman who'd spoken, deciding perhaps she was the one. She was stunning as well, with long dark hair and almond-shaped eyes giving her an exotic appeal. Alex continued to watch her as the woman's attention went back to the dancers. Yes, she could be the one.

Alex turned back to the dance floor as Denver and the woman were doing their finale. Everyone applauded and cheered, begging them to dance another. That's when she finally spotted Travis.

He was standing next to a dark-haired woman with a young girl of about eight leaning up against her chest. The woman's hands were on the young girl's shoulders, and Travis held one of the little girl's hands. They were nearly straight across from Alex, on the edge of the dance floor, but with everyone's attention fixed on Denver she figured it was safe to stare.

So, he did have a girlfriend. And the girlfriend had a daughter. Any wonder he recognised her ability to connect with children. Maybe it was something he struggled with. Her jaws tightened as she assessed the woman. The top of the woman's head didn't even reach Travis' shoulder, and everything about her was dainty. She wore tight jeans and cowboy boots and a sparkling singlet top which showed off her perfect figure. Even from a distance Alex was pretty certain the woman was gorgeous. She was everything that Alex was not.

Anger bubbled up in her, or was it jealousy? She cursed her idiocy, knowing full well she should be grateful he was off limits. She needed to be making business decisions based on logic, and not factoring in a budding romance with someone who might yet prove to be an enemy. He'd taken her for a ride on a gentle horse, and then he'd saved her from feeling alone at a party where she knew no one. Both actions were kind, but so what? Logic told her she was being ridiculous, so why did she find it so hard to think clearly?

As the dance ended, the little girl turned and looked up at her mother asking a question. Travis leaned down and whispered something in the woman's ear. And that's as much as Alex cared to watch. She turned her back to them, speaking once again to the woman beside her.

'You said Denver let her get away, but where's her husband? Doesn't he mind her dancing with Denver?'

'No, he and Denver are still best of friends—he's not jealous. Besides, he knows that Denver knows he'd kill him if Denver tried to steal her back.' The woman was smiling as she spoke, and her voice was full of laughter, but her eyes suggested it was more than a joke. 'Ah, watch this, looks like he's going to dance with Annie now.'

Alex turned, and much to her surprise Denver was now standing with the young girl, the one who'd been with Travis. 'Annie?'

'Yes, his niece.'

'Niece?' Alex didn't even try to cover up her confusion.

'Yes, Annie is Travis' daughter. Isn't she as cute as a button?' The woman turned to face Alex, frowning. 'Sorry, I figured you'd have known that.'

With her mind racing, Alex had to quickly re-evaluate everything she'd been thinking. Travis was a father. So the woman could be his ex-wife.

Perhaps his earlier kindness did mean something. And maybe she cared more than she wanted to admit. Maybe he did too.

All this was too much to take on board right at the moment. She turned back to the dance floor and sure enough, Denver was dancing with the little girl. He'd taken his dancing down a notch so Annie could keep up, but she was amazingly good for a child. After a moment, Alex looked for Travis again, but he was nowhere to be seen so she just kept watching the dancing.

A few minutes later someone tapped her on the shoulder. She suspected Harrison had returned but, when she turned, she found herself staring straight at Travis.

'Sorry about leaving you before when Annie rang. I had to go meet her.'

She struggled to find enough breath to speak. 'That's alright. No need to apologise.'

He looked down at her, his eyes smouldering. Alex considered excusing herself, finding the intensity too much, but then he pointed toward the gazebo and nodded. 'No, I shouldn't have walked off like that. Look ... can we talk for a bit?'

Surprise brought an involuntary frown to her face. She wiped it off quickly, and then shrugged. 'Yeah, okay.'

They made their way back to where they'd stood before, positioning themselves so they could still see a bit of the dance floor.

Travis flicked his head toward the dancers. 'Denver's good with her. She's his favourite niece ... well, his only niece, but even so.'

Alex took a sip of her drink. 'She dances well. Puts me to shame.'

'She's been doing it pretty much from when she could walk. Between Denver, and her mother, she's had good teachers.'

'So I take it that was your ex? The woman I saw you standing with?'

'Yeah, that was Karen.'

Alex sighed quietly, chewing the inside of her mouth.

Travis took a deep breath, and then launched into an explanation. 'Karen was meant to bring Annie up after the rodeo—she'll be here for the summer. That's why I've been trying to get these horses ready for the rodeo. I'm hoping to sell them so I can take things a bit slower for the next couple of months. Getting the call from Annie tonight was ... unexpected.'

'I see.'

He cocked his head, continuing in a voice that had gone gruff. 'Karen's partner, Cody, got himself a job up near Seattle, so without any warning they decided to drop Annie on their way up north. Not that I'd have minded if they'd asked, but it might have been nice to get a bit of warning.'

'And is he here too?'

Travis frowned. 'Cody knew he wouldn't be welcome here—he stayed with the truck while Karen brought Annie in. They won't be staying for the party—they're heading on up to Sacramento tonight.'

Alex was beginning to get an entirely different picture of Travis. He was serious, but how much of it might be because of his responsibilities as a father, perhaps overcompensating for the marriage break-down? She took another sip of her drink, trying to think of something positive to say, when Annie raced up to them.

'Were you watching, Daddy? Did you see how good I'm getting?' Annie asked as she raced up, giggling.

Travis laughed, and as he did his whole demeanour lightened. He wore his pride like a badge of honour, his eyes sparkling when they met

Alex's. 'Annie, can I introduce you to a friend of mine? This is Alex. Alex is a tennis player, and she coaches.'

Alex sucked in a breath as her left hand automatically flew to her shoulder. She was more than a bit surprised that Travis remembered that. She swallowed, forcing a smile onto her face. 'Hello, Annie. It's nice to meet you.'

Annie turned to face Alex with wide eyes. 'You play tennis? And you're a coach?'

Alex laughed. 'Well, yes I suppose—but not necessarily a good one.'

'Can you coach me while I'm here? My friend Naomi said I'm really good for a beginner but that I need lessons. She's had lessons—lots of them.'

Alex pursed her lips as she thought. She had been meaning to get back into coaching; maybe this was a good opportunity? 'Were you on a team at school?'

Annie put her hands on her hips. 'No, not at school. Naomi has a court at her house. Mom let me go to her house after school whenever I wanted to. So can you give me lessons?'

Alex didn't want to dampen her enthusiasm. 'Sure, I'd be more than happy to coach you, Annie.'

Annie's face broke into a beaming smile. 'Thank you, thank you, thank you.' She turned to her father, rolling her eyes dramatically. Then she broke into giggles again when he reached down and tickled her under the armpit.

Warmth washed over Alex as she watched them. She didn't even try to disguise her smile when Travis caught her eye. It was a strangely beautiful moment—one she certainly hadn't expected to experience tonight.

But just then Harrison walked up, breaking the moment's spell. 'There you are—ready for another dance?' He held out a hand to her as he indicated toward the dance floor with his other hand.

She glanced at Travis, and then down at Annie, before turning back to face Harrison and holding up a finger in a *wait just a moment* gesture.

When she looked back at Annie, she was staring at her hopefully. 'Will you come tomorrow?' Annie said, her voice pleading.

'Tomorrow?' Alex looked at Travis, who simply raised his eyebrows and shrugged. She took that as approval. 'Okay, Annie, maybe some time in the afternoon?'

'Come whenever you like, I'll be waiting. Don't forget.'

Alex laughed, and then looked at Harrison, who quite obviously had no idea what they were talking about, but she doubted he cared either, especially when he nodded toward the dance floor and simply said, 'Ready?'

Annie was still frowning when Alex turned back to her. 'I won't forget. I'll let everyone have a good sleep in, so I'll come after lunch.'

Travis cleared his throat in a fatherly fashion. 'Speaking of sleeping, it's past your bedtime Annie. How about we go get you settled into your room?'

'But they haven't even sung happy birthday yet—or cut the cake. Can't I stay up longer?'

As Alex and Harrison walked off toward the dance floor, she heard Travis saying he'd get the cake organised soon. She gave one last glance over her shoulder, heat rushing to her cheeks when she realised Travis was watching her walk away.

CHAPTER 15

Alex woke early, grateful she'd mostly drunk mineral water because even though her feet were a bit sore from all the dancing, she didn't have even the slightest headache. Harrison had dropped her off just after one, and she'd fallen asleep dreaming of dancing to rockabilly music. She'd woken up fresh, ready to face playing tennis with an energetic child.

One thing weighing heavily upon her mind, however, was her interactions with Travis. She would have loved to talk to Casey and Taylor right about now and get their take on what had happened at the party, if it weren't for the blasted time difference. She'd have to wait until she returned later this afternoon to call them. Perhaps it was just as well, because seeing Travis today might be a completely different experience than the previous evening—in which case there might not be anything to discuss anyway.

After a quick breakfast she headed out to the garden. The mowing company was doing a great job, but it wasn't their responsibility to look after the garden beds. In search of some tools she made her way into the garage and took a closer look at the old Buick while she was there. It was dusty, but didn't appear damaged.

She shrugged, wondering if she should have at least taken if for a test drive before purchasing the Mustang, but then she shrugged. She loved the Mustang, and it hadn't been that expensive. Besides, it had been ages since she'd treated herself to anything even remotely indulgent.

Armed with garden gloves, pruning shears, a small spade and a fork for pulling weeds, she settled herself at the front and began to tidy up the largest of the garden beds. It was a relaxing way to spend the morning before the lesson with Annie.

~~*~~

Travis kept watching over his shoulder the whole time he worked the gelding, wondering what Annie was doing, but each time he looked she was still in the same spot, standing on the lowest rail with her arms crossed over the top rail and her chin resting on her arms. She had grown so much since Christmas. She was like a mini-adult now.

When both he and the gelding had had enough, he rode over to the fence and took off his hat to get a bit of the cool breeze.

She grinned. 'You look good when you take off your hat, Daddy. Cody doesn't—his hair sticks to his head.'

Travis tried to hide his grin—he knew exactly what Annie meant. Lots of men suffered from hat-hair. It gave him great pleasure to hear that Cody was one of them. He patted the gelding's neck and raised an eyebrow. 'Wanna cool him down for me?'

Annie's eye flew open wide. 'Can I?'

'Sure. Just walk him ... and take it easy.'

By the time Travis slid off the horse, Annie had squeezed through the fence and now stood with her back to it. She looked like a younger version of Karen, in her tight jeans and cute little cowgirl boots. He was proud to be her father, but also more than a bit frightened as he suspected she was going to be a handful as soon as she discovered boys.

Shaking off those thoughts, he went about shortening the stirrup leathers to the highest hole. She accepted his offer of a leg up, climbed on with grace, and took the reins like an expert. The horse began walking slowly, at first with Travis at his side. When she looked down at him and frowned, he moved to the fence to watch.

They looked good together, his daughter and this young gelding, and he was proud of how well she rode him. It was kind of a shame he'd be selling him. Then again, Travis knew there'd never be a shortage of horses for Annie to ride wherever Karen and Cody lived. He hoped they were taking Annie's welfare into account with this move of theirs.

He wondered if they'd given any thought to Annie when they decided to move. It was risky after all, taking Annie out of state without consulting him. He could challenge it, and he'd have a good chance at winning. But would he want full custody of Annie? Would he and Denver provide the right family balance for a young girl? Wouldn't she need her mother as she grew into a teen? He'd have to give it more thought—perhaps see how the summer went—see what Annie wanted to do.

Rubbing his chin, he once again focussed on her riding. 'Heals down, Annie.'

Annie glared at him, rolling her eyes. 'I know, Dad.'

When she dropped her heals, he grinned.

She did a few more laps of the arena, then stopped in front of him and jumped down. They walked the gelding back over to the barn and Annie hosed him down while Travis put the tack away. Then they gave him a feed and made their way to the house for some lunch.

Travis stood at the kitchen sink while Annie slowly finished her peanut butter and jelly on white bread. After she washed it down with a glass of milk he smiled. 'You best go change into shorts and your tennis shoes. Alex should be here soon.' Just saying her name made his heart start thumping. He took a deep breath, willing it to settle.

She raised an eyebrow. 'Are you going to play too?'

'Me? No way.'

'But you will watch, won't you? I've been practising—I want you to see how good I've gotten.'

He could have kissed her for giving him a valid reason to hang around for a bit while they played. 'Yeah, I'll watch.'

~~*~~

Alex had been anxious from the moment she'd gotten into her car, and now, seeing the sign reading *Welcome to Gold's Ranch*, her heart began racing even faster. She wanted to think it was excitement at having a tennis student again after such a long hiatus, but she knew it had as much to do with her student's father as with her student.

Annie raced out the front door the moment Alex pulled up, and as she opened the car door Annie grabbed her hand, giggling.

'Alex! You came. I can't wait for my lesson.'

'How nice to have such an enthusiastic student,' Alex replied, smiling.

She squeezed Annie's hand, then let go to grab her cap and water bottle off the back seat. When she turned back around Travis was standing there behind Annie. Dressed in a long-sleeved cotton shirt with the sleeves rolled up, jeans and western boots, he was clearly not joining them for tennis. A mixture of relief and disappointment settled over her.

'Hi Alex. Thanks again for doing this. You know you don't have to.'

Alex made a face and shrugged. 'You make it sound like it's an imposition. Actually Annie is doing me a favour, getting me motivated again with something I've been away from for far too long.'

Travis placed his hands on Annie shoulders, looking at Alex. 'Did you bring a racquet, or do you want to use one of ours?'

'Would you mind if I borrow one of yours? It's not something I thought to bring with me from home.'

He leaned down and spoke close to Annie's ear. 'Can you please go in and grab the racquets and balls, and meet us over at the court?'

As Annie raced back into the house Travis smiled and nodded toward the court.

Alex got out and closed the car door. 'You do know you've built me up for quite a fall if it turns out she's a better player than me.'

Travis laughed. 'She's eight. I don't think she'll be better than you.'

'I wouldn't count her out because she's young.'

'We'll see. I'm pretty sure she spends more time with the horses than with a tennis racket, but hey, I think it's great that she's got so much enthusiasm. Hopefully, if she concentrates on sports, she won't discover boys so quickly.'

They made their way around the side of the house toward the court, and Alex was surprised at how tidy everything looked. You could hardly tell there'd been a party other than by the flattened grass, the wooden dance floor, and some tables leaning up against the side of the house.

When they reached the court, Travis opened the gate and ushered her inside. While they waited for Annie to return, she could feel Travis watching her every move. Although it was unsettling, it wasn't unwelcome. But she had to break the silence.

'So ... how's Denver this morning? Has he even surfaced yet?' She gave Travis a conspiratorial wink.

'Actually, he was up early, and spent the morning cleaning up out here while I worked the horses.'

'What, no hangover?'

'Not really. I think he spent way more time dancing than drinking. He'll be tired by tonight, but he's okay.'

'And what about you?' she asked.

'I'm not much of a drinker anymore. Not since Annie was born.'

Alex blinked slowly, thinking about her father, and wishing things had gone differently for him.

They both looked up as Annie raced onto the court, the racquets tucked under one arm and a tin of balls in her hand. 'Can I serve first?'

~~*~~

Alex watched as Travis poured glasses of lemonade for the three of them. She'd enjoyed this first lesson with Annie, but had definitely taken notice when Travis disappeared from the sidelines, presumably to go back to his horses. She was glad he'd returned as they'd finished.

'Did you enjoy the lesson?' Travis asked, looking at Annie.

Annie grinned from ear to ear as she set her glass on the table. 'It was awesome, Dad. Alex is the best coach I've ever had.'

'And have you had many coaches, sweetheart?'

His sarcasm was dripping, but Alex wasn't too sure Annie would have gotten it. Until Annie grinned.

'No, just Alex. But I know she's the best coach anyway.'

Alex smiled at the compliment. 'And Annie is by far one of the quickest learners I've coached.'

'That's great to hear,' he said, pulling a chair out to sit across from Alex. Then he faced Annie. 'So, when you get rich and famous, you'll remember your Dad, won't you sweetie?' He made a sad face which only served to make Annie giggle.

'Sure I will, even if you are old and wrinkly, and in a wheelchair.'

'Hold on there, I won't be that old. And I certainly hope I'm not in a wheelchair, knock on wood.' He tapped the table, then reached over and tapped the top of Annie's head.

Annie giggled again, turning to Alex. 'When can I get another lesson? Can I have one every day for the whole summer?' She gave Alex a cheeky smile that suggested she knew it was a lot to ask for, and then smacked her hand over her mouth trying to hide it.

'Every day?' Alex pulled a face that she hoped conveyed incredulity.

Annie's eye opened wide. 'Yeah, why not?'

'Hmm, I could probably do two or three times a week ... until I work out what I'm doing.'

Annie's eyes grew wide, and Travis focussed on her as well, both clearly waiting for further explanation.

'You do know I'm from Australia, right Annie?'

'Sure, but that's okay.' Annie frowned, shaking her head.

'Well, I hope it is,' Alex said with a chuckle. 'But what I meant is just that ... I mean, I may not ... oh, I don't know what I meant. But for the time being, two or three times a week works for me.'

Annie's face beamed, but Travis stared at her with an eyebrow raised, as if waiting for even more explanation.

She seriously didn't know yet what she wanted to do. There was nothing pulling her back to Australia in any great hurry, but did she want to stay here? The house was fabulous, and she'd soon have the fruit and veggie shop to keep her busy, but that didn't mean she had to run it indefinitely. She could sell the business and the freehold, or sell the business and keep the freehold. But if she started up tennis coaching with school kids over the summer, it would tie her down for at least a couple of months. Was that what she wanted? It would mean a delay to getting anything happening in Australia, but then again, it was winter there.

Annie finished her lemonade, and then wiped the back of her hand across her mouth. She cocked her head as she appeared to remember something, and then turned to look directly at Alex. 'Will you come to the rodeo with me next weekend? Dad says he's going to be too busy to hang out with me, and wants me go with Cousin Stacy, but I don't want to hang out with them—Tammy's just a baby.'

'Annie, you can't ask that of Alex. Besides, Tammy isn't a baby. She's not that much younger than you ... what, she's maybe six or seven?'

'Dad,' she dragged the word out and rolled her eyes. 'She's six, and trust me, she's a baby. She can't even ride a horse yet—I know, because I asked her last night. I'll die if I have to hang out with her at the rodeo. Can I go with you, Alex?' She turned back to Alex, her eyes imploring.

Alex remembered what it was like when she was Annie's age, and her mother made her do things with Casey and Taylor who were two years her junior. At that age, two years was a quarter of one's life, and it seemed an insurmountable difference. 'I hadn't really thought about going, but I suppose I should. You know, I've never been to a rodeo.'

'Never?' Annie's eyes flew open wide with disbelief. 'Then you have to go. Everyone goes. Dad and Uncle Denver will be riding. And there's gonna be barrel racing and all kinds of other stuff. Mom wanted to ride, but Cody has to be at his new job so they couldn't stay.'

When Annie's eyes dropped to the table for a moment, Alex wondered if she missed her mother, but when she looked up, she had a smile back on her face. 'It'll be so much fun—and even more fun if I can hang out with you.'

Taking a deep breath, Alex grinned. 'Well then, I guess it's a date, Annie.' She looked at Travis, who shrugged apologetically. 'I couldn't think of anyone I'd rather go to my first rodeo with.'

Annie beamed. 'For all four days, right?'

Travis turned back to Annie. 'Sweetheart, I think you're pushing your luck there a bit. The frog jumping goes all four days, but you don't have to watch every one of the frogs. Let's say you just watch some of them ... maybe a few on Saturday and the finals on Sunday?'

Annie didn't answer straight away, but finally sighed. 'Okay, but we have to watch all the rodeo, right?'

Alex looked at Travis, marvelling at the look of pride on his face. Then she turned back to Annie. 'Of course, I wouldn't dream of missing any of the rodeo.' She hoped she wasn't getting in over her head with this.

'Thank you,' Annie said as she got up and ran around the table to give Alex a big hug. 'It's going to be so much fun, you'll love it. I promise.'

CHAPTER 16

Alex shifted at the kitchen table, moving her iPad out of the glare of the late afternoon sun as she chatted with her sisters using FaceTime.

'I think it's great that you're getting back into coaching, even if it turns out to be just the one girl. But I bet lots of kids will take up the offer of lessons over summer. And seriously, you'd be mad if you didn't take advantage of getting two summers this year.' Casey's face wrinkled into a half frown. 'Or are you thinking of staying even longer?'

Alex moved the screen again, fiddling with it to avoid answering her sister. Did she want to stay longer in California?

'I don't know what I'm thinking at this stage. I mean, it's really comfortable here ... and I know this is going to sound stupid, but sometimes I feel like I've come home ... like this is where I belong.'

Casey shook her head back and forth slowly. 'No, it doesn't sound stupid. You spent the first five years of your life in California, so I'm not surprised it feels like home.'

Alex sighed with relief that Casey got it, but that wasn't the only thing. 'And of course we have a huge financial interest to look after here.'

'Yes, that's true. And we're grateful you're there with your financial brain to sort through it all for us, right Taylor?' Taylor bumped her shoulder into Casey and took the centre of the screen for a moment, nodding and smiling.

Alex squinted, thinking. 'When you get right down to it, what have I got to go back to in Melbourne? A tiny little apartment, no job, not even a pet.'

'Hey, what are we, chopped liver?' Taylor said, pushing over in front of the screen again. 'You do have all your family here, you know.'

'I didn't mean it that way. I just meant ... oh, you know what I meant. You both have everything you want there in Melbourne ... I have nothing to go back to.'

The twins looked at each other and smiled. Taylor answered. 'You're right, it sounds like things are going really well for you there, but we miss you, that's all."

Alex sighed. 'You have to come over—both of you—for a visit, if nothing else. After all, we've got a beautiful house to live in.'

Casey turned to Taylor, who rolled her eyes at Alex. 'Yeah, and you've probably already claimed the best bedroom.'

Casey gave Taylor a high-five, and then turned back to the screen. 'And you say there are good looking cowboys there in Masons Flat?'

Alex grinned, remembering Denver's party and all the men she'd seen. She raised an eyebrow and pursed her lips as she pretended to give it some thought.

Casey glared at her. 'Come on, spill it. I can tell you're hiding something. What's going on over there ... what's making you think you might want to stay?'

'I suppose it's a few things.'

'Such as?' Casey quirked a brow.

'Well, for one thing, it's summer here now.'

'Uh, yeah, we established that, but that won't last. What else?'

Alex took a deep breath, trying to put her wispy thoughts into words. 'You can't imagine how good it feels, knowing I can walk down any street without fear of bumping into Liam or any of our old friends. And then there are those shops and the saloon restorations. It's all very exciting.'

'And the cowboys. You didn't answer me about the cowboys.' Casey, who had been in and out of more relationships than anyone else Alex knew, was quite possibly nearing the end of her current relationship.

Alex grinned. 'There are certainly some good looking and *single* cowboys here in Masons Flat if last night's party is anything to go by. And they've got moves on the dance-floor like you've never seen.'

The twins looked at each other, eyes wide. Casey replied. 'I do like the sound of that. Maybe a trip over isn't such a bad idea. If I put in for some time off now, I could possibly get away next month.'

'Oh, I could probably swing some time off next month, too,' Taylor chirped in, 'of course it would have to be the end of the month. We've got Summer's wedding coming up, and I'm going to be a bridesmaid, remember?'

Alex had forgotten. Summer was Frank's daughter, which would have made her their step-sister if their mother and Frank had married. Summer was a couple of years younger than Casey and Taylor, but she and Taylor had hit it off due to a shared interest in cooking. 'When, exactly, is the wedding? I should put it in my diary. I assume I'll be invited?'

'You have been invited, and Mum's already accepted for all of us. She's even bought a dress—like a proper mother-of-the-bride sort of dress,' Taylor replied.

'Wow, you're going to think I'm losing it, but seriously, I don't remember a date being finalised.'

Casey pulled a face. 'Maybe I forgot to mention it. Anyway, it's at their place, in Willows, on the fifteenth of June. They're doing up the barn so we can all get drunk and stumble back to the house if need be. Oh, and their place is huge so we're all staying there.'

'All of us? You mean, like, Mum and Frank too?'

Taylor pushed Casey over so she could answer. 'I think so. They have this huge ranch house, with like six bedrooms or something, but they've also booked all the rooms at the bed and breakfast so whoever isn't at their house will be in town. It's all sorted—so you have to come. I figured you'd be back well before then, but you'll need to book a flight soon.'

'Okay.' Alex ran a hand through her hair, and then reached up and rubbed her shoulder. She wasn't excited about another long flight, but Frank and Summer were family—she'd have to go.

Now Casey moved in front of the screen. 'You know, Alex, we haven't forgotten about the money, but we're also not counting our chickens before they're hatched. You said you were going to see the accountant. We mightn't be as rich as you think we are once the tax office gets their hands on it.'

Alex shook her head. 'The accountant says it should all be okay.'

Taylor leaned over in front of the screen again. 'Let's talk about it when you're here. We'll know a lot more by then.'

When they'd said their goodbyes, Alex curled up on the sofa to look for a Sunday evening movie, but as she sat there scrolling through what seemed like millions of channels, all she could think about was a tall cowboy and his beautiful daughter who wanted tennis lessons all summer. She hadn't looked forward to anything this much for a long time.

Had she misinterpreted Travis at first? The gruff man who had interrupted her and Denver at the saloon had, according to Denver, a chip on his shoulder when it came to women. And at the time she'd wondered if it was all women, or just her. Yet the more she got to know him the kinder he seemed. He was, perhaps, a bit on the serious side but who was she to judge him for that? She'd seen the gentle side of him when he was working his horses, and the kind side of him when he rescued her on the dance floor.

And then Annie came into the picture and everything started making more sense.

Spending time with Annie would give her the perfect opportunity to get to know the real Travis Gold on a deeper level. But was that a good thing?

~~*~~

Annie hadn't argued with him when Travis told her it was time for her to take a bath and go to bed. Between riding the horses and playing tennis she'd had a full day, and then hadn't stopped talking about the coming rodeo all through dinner.

He'd been thrilled when Alex had agreed to hang out with Annie at the rodeo, but now, alone in the living room and staring at the television screen, he wondered if it was the smart thing to do. It was a lot to ask of someone he barely knew. And wouldn't it have been better for Annie to hang out with Stacy and Tammy, her family? Then there was the risk that Annie might get too attached to Alex, spending so much time with her.

But was it really Annie he was worried about?

He couldn't deny his physical attraction to her. When they'd danced it had taken all his self-control not to wrap his arms around her, and he'd hated for each one to end. Dancing with her had been the most enjoyable thing he'd done with any woman since Karen had walked out. And later, when they were talking, there was definitely a connection. That was the first time he'd even come close to talking openly about

Karen, with anyone other than Denver. If Annie hadn't called when she did, who's to say how that conversation might have gone?

He rubbed his forehead, and then ran his hands through his hair. Alex Mason was a problem for him, but her being a Mason was only part of it. There was also the fact that she could disappear back to Australia at any time. He was a fool to even think about getting involved with her.

CHAPTER 17

When Alex drove up to the saloon the following morning, she wasn't surprised to see Denver's truck parked out the front. She walked across to the hotel, got two coffees, and then made her way over to the saloon.

Denver turned when she walked in, and rubbed his hands together. 'Hope one of those is for me?'

'You bet,' she said, handing him a cup. 'You're still happy to keep an eye on the work, right? I mean, I don't want to put you out at all.'

'Absolutely—I promised your uncle I'd see it through and I see no reason not to.' He lowered his voice. 'To be honest, these guys are pretty good at their jobs, and should be done in about three weeks.'

Alex pulled the top off the coffee and blew on it before taking a sip. 'Still—it's comforting having you look over it. So, tell me, if you owned the saloon, are there other improvements you'd do while it's closed?'

Denver beamed. 'I'm glad you asked that. I'd been planning to talk to your uncle about a few things, but never got the chance. The floor is looking pretty tired. It's got character, but even so I'd strip it back and refinish it. And some of the bar stools could use new leather on the seats so I'd be inclined to do all of them.'

'That sounds reasonable to me. I was wondering about the mirror too—there seems to be damage to one corner of the frame. Should I get someone to have a look at it?'

Denver laughed. 'No, don't touch that—it's good luck. That's a bullet hole, left over from the days when the miners drank too much and cheated at poker. You can't buy that kind of character, and you definitely don't want to repair it.'

Alex cocked her head, remembering the story of the poker game where her family had won the saloon. Could that have been the game? 'A bullet hole? Well, there you go. From a distance it looked just like it had been dropped or something. I'll have to take a closer look at it when the lights are on.'

'Should I go ahead and organise the flooring and the bar stools? I know a few people who could do the work and I think they'd get it done in the time frame you want.'

Alex nodded. 'Would you mind? I mean, I'd love to get it done, so long as their prices aren't absurd.'

'They won't be—I'll make sure of that. But to get a good job done while the saloon is shut is worth a bit extra. I'll get onto it right away and let you know.'

Alex did a quick mental calculation. Three weeks meant the saloon should be back open before she had to leave for Summer's wedding. She'd give all the old employees a call and let them know roughly when they could restart work, then she'd have to look into getting a manager organised. She'd hoped to do it herself, but that was before the girls reminded her about the wedding. She'd speak to Sam—perhaps he could help out since he had a night manager at the hotel. Or if not, maybe he'd know someone.

She took another sip of her coffee and looked at Denver over the rim of the cup.

He gave her a big grin. 'That must have been some serious thinking you were doing—I could almost hear the cogs turning in your head.'

She couldn't help but laugh. 'Ah, yes, I was thinking about how my uncle had been the manager at the saloon and how I'd either need to take on the role myself or find someone else to do it. Three weeks isn't terribly long, is it?'

'No, it's not, but I wouldn't be afraid to do it yourself. You strike me as being pretty capable.'

She tilted her head, a warm smile escaping. 'Thank you, for the vote of confidence.'

'To be honest, the employees pretty much run the place. Your uncle liked keeping active but in truth I think he was more of a figurehead than an actual worker. His assistant manager, Darleen Clarke, is about as capable as they come. And it's not like she can't call you if she needs to ask something.'

That was encouraging to hear. Everything would work out, hopefully. 'That's great to hear. Oh, and I've spoken to that bookkeeper—she sounds great. Have you gotten any closer with costing out the fit-out works?'

Denver pulled out his phone and scanned through his contacts. 'Sorry, I meant to give this guy a call about the refrigeration units. The rest will be easy after that. I'll work out the total cost after he's had a look.'

'Thanks, Denver, this is all so new to me—I don't know if I'd have had the courage to take it on without your help.'

'You don't give yourself much credit, do you? You'd have been fine, but I'm happy to give you a hand. That's what neighbours do. Now, I better make tracks. I've gotta give Sally a bit of a workout this morning, and then help Travis with a couple of the youngsters. Can't believe the rodeo has come up so quickly. Guess I had my mind focussed on my party.'

'It was a great party. I had a wonderful time.'

Denver looked at her quite seriously for a moment, giving her the feeling he was about to interrogate her, but then he seemed to change his mind. 'Glad to hear it. Oh, and I've been playing that CD you gave me for my birthday. It's great! I've never even heard of half those artists, but they're fantastic. Who'd of thought Australia had so many great country singers.'

Alex smiled, said her goodbyes, and then went in search of Sam to run her idea past him.

~~*~~

By four o'clock Alex had organised for Phil Marshall to do market appraisals of all her properties, and had spoken to the accountant who was still working through some projections for them. Both hoped to have everything complete within two weeks which would give her everything she needed to take with her so she and her sisters could make an informed decision about whether or not to sell up.

Just before five she spotted her neighbour, the high school principal, coming home. She raced out to meet him, asking about the possibility of a summer tennis program. He met the idea with enthusiasm, saying he would run it past the students and parents to see if there was any interest.

An hour later, Alex had her return ticket to Australia. It would be a quick trip, but she wanted to get back because the saloon would be open, the fruit and veggie shop would be nearly ready to open, and if the students were interested the tennis program would be about to start. And then, of course, there was Annie. Alex wouldn't say anything to Annie until right before she went, on the off chance Annie might lose interest before then in any case. It wasn't likely, but you never knew how long kids would stay interested in anything.

The following morning, Alex called Ben Thompson.

'Have you had any enquiries about those vacant shops?'

'Oh, hi Alex. Sorry, I meant to call you yesterday. The short answer is no, nothing serious. I've had a couple of calls, but they weren't prepared to pay anywhere near the rent we're asking.'

'Okay—well, you can tell the next person who rings that there is only one shop left.'

She explained her plans and when he finally replied his tone was less than enthusiastic, perhaps because he'd lost the opportunity for a commission.

'Good for you, Alex. I'll put a leased sign in the window, and perhaps with the jubilee coming up someone will make us an offer for the other shop.'

'What's happening with those other vacant shops up the other end of the street? Were you able to find out anything about them yet?'

'Not yet, but now that you remind me, I'll do a bit more investigating, see what I can come up with.'

Her voice didn't hide her disappointment. 'Oh, well, let me know what you find out.'

'I will. I'll be in touch as soon as I've got something to tell you. Enjoy the rodeo ... I assume you'll be going?'

'Yes, as a matter of fact. And you?'

'No, someone's got to man the fort, but I'm letting most of my staff have the weekend off. Enjoy it, and don't let any of this worry you. It'll all get sorted out before you know it.'

She hung up, feeling less than satisfied with his lack of results, but would put off making any decisions about him for a bit longer.

With nothing else needing to be done before Annie's lesson, she'd drive past the school to look at their tennis courts. Then she'd head over to the Gold's early, and maybe watch Travis work some of the horses for a little while. That wouldn't be such a bad way to spend a little time if Annie wasn't ready.

~~*~~

Travis was surprised when he spotted Alex leaning on the fence, watching as he finished working with the third horse for the morning. He still had one more he wanted to work this morning, and hadn't expected her until after lunch. He'd hoped to take a break, have a bite to eat, and watch their session. Now, having lost concentration on what he was doing, he rode over to the fence, took off his hat, and absentmindedly ran a hand through his damp hair.

'You're early.'

'Hey, Travis. Yeah, sorry, hope it's okay?'

'Not a problem. Annie's in the house, probably just watching television or something.'

When she didn't make a move to go, he put his hat back on and sat waiting for her to speak.

'How's the training going anyway?' She smiled, and appeared interested.

He patted the horse on the neck. 'Great. This guy's been a dream to work with. I reckon he'll sell for sure.'

'He's pretty, isn't he? I love the colour. Chestnut, right?'

'Yes, that's right.' The gelding was one of his flashier ones, with two white socks and a wide blaze. Lots of people went for these showier horses even if they didn't necessarily perform as well.

'It must be hard to see them go, after putting so much time into them, and seeing how well they come along. I'd have thought they'd become sort of like pets?'

'Sometimes, but it's the business we're in. We can't keep them all.'

She looked toward the barn, where the last horse he wanted to work was still tied up. 'If you don't mind me asking, what sort of money do they sell for?'

He cocked his head as his face tightened in a frown. Was this just general curiosity or did she want to put a figure on what he was worth? He huffed out a breath, realising she could just be interested in buying a horse for herself.

'I wouldn't let my fillies go for less than eighteen thousand. The geldings, probably around twelve to fifteen, depending on what sort of promise they're showing. They're extremely well bred, and good natured.'

'Wow, that's not bad money is it?'

'Depends on how you look at it. What's my time worth? And Denver's? And the feed we pour into them, and vet bills, when we're unlucky.'

'Oh, I hadn't thought of all that.'

'No, why would you? Unfortunately, some buyers don't either. Those prices are the young horses. If they start earning money for us, the prices go up. We sold a horse last year for forty thousand. And my stallion is worth a lot more than that.'

She blew out a weak excuse for a whistle. 'Forty thousand. Wow ... for a horse. Who'd of guessed.'

'That's nothing compared to what some of those dressage, cross-country and show jumping types pay for horses. A lot of them are well over a hundred thousand, and the rest. There's big money in horses.'

'And here I thought all the big money was in tennis.'

When she rolled her eyes he couldn't suppress a smile. She was just making conversation. Why did he have to be so suspicious all the time anyway?

Now it was his turn to ask questions. 'What about you? Did you ever think you'd make it to the top? In tennis, that is.'

She reached up and rubbed her shoulder with her left hand, then looked down at the ground almost like she was embarrassed. She'd mentioned the tennis programs, but nothing about her aspirations for her career, or the injury he'd read about on the internet.

She looked up and met his gaze, and just like they had the first time he met her, her eyes flashed like fool's gold.

When she didn't answer, he broke the silence. 'Sorry. Didn't mean to pry.'

She let out a loud sigh, and her eyes softened. 'Don't be sorry, it's okay to ask. Yes, I had big aspirations. I was good—made it into the top one hundred—but a car accident brought my career to an end. I can still play well enough to coach kids, and have a social game, but I was never going to be able to compete again.'

He knew that, but she didn't know he knew. 'Wow, I'm sorry. It must have been hard. I can't imagine what it'd be like if something happened and I couldn't ride any longer.'

'It wasn't easy, but it was years ago. You'd think I'd be able to laugh about it by now, wouldn't you?'

'Laugh? No ... I wouldn't say that.'

Annie must have seen Alex drive up, because now she was running toward them, yelling hello to Alex.

'You're early. Want some lunch?'

Alex laughed, and stepped back from the fence, readying for impact. Sure enough, Annie raced up and threw her arms around Alex, giving her an almighty hug. Alex extricated herself from Annie's grip, and laughed. 'Depends, what are you offering?'

'Well, I'm having peanut butter and jelly, but you can have sliced ham if you want. Dad usually has ham.'

Alex frowned, cocking her head almost seductively. 'What sort of jelly have you got?'

'I'm having grape, but I think we also have strawberry.'

'Hmmm ... strawberry sounds yummy.'

Annie grabbed Alex's hand and started dragging her toward the house, then looked back at him. 'You coming, Dad?'

'Not yet, sweetheart, I still have one more horse to work, but you two go ahead and have your lunch. I'll drop around to the court to watch you a bit later. Gotta make sure you aren't wasting Alex's time, you know.'

He winked, but even so Annie bit. 'I'm good, Dad, and I'll be getting better every time we play. You'll see.'

CHAPTER 18

'Can you stay for a swim?' Annie asked, with a slight whine in her voice.

Alex wasn't prepared for that question and gave a flustered reply. 'Swim? Oh, well, I haven't brought my bathers.'

Annie frowned. 'What are bathers?'

'You know, swim gear. What you wear to go for a swim in.'

Annie rolled her eyes dramatically. 'A swimsuit.'

Alex turned when Travis, who was approaching them from the courtside bench, spoke. 'That sounds like a great idea, Annie. Alex, why don't you race home and grab your suit, assuming you just meant you didn't have it with you here right now.'

She hesitated; tempted to say she didn't have one at all. 'Yes, I think I did bring something with me ... for the hotel pool.'

'Great. Race back and get it, and we'll have a swim, and afterwards I'll barbeque some steaks. That is, if you don't already have plans?'

Alex thought hard for a moment. She hadn't shaved her legs, and her bathers weren't the most flattering she'd ever owned. But more to the point, was she ready for ... this? She reached up to rub her shoulder, but caught herself, and quickly pulled her hand away. Annie and Travis were both staring at her, waiting for a reply. She hated to disappoint Annie.

'Sure, okay, that sounds fun.' She hoped they hadn't noticed how breathless her voice had sounded. 'Should I make a salad or something?'

'You don't need to bring a thing. Just yourself,' Travis said.

Twenty-five minutes later Alex was ready. She'd taken a quick shower then donned the one-piece, dark blue and not entirely ghastly bathers, covered them with an oversized tee-shirt and a pair of shorts, put her hair up in a messy bun, and thrown some clothes into a tote bag to change into afterwards. She sighed deeply as she got back into her car.

Alex spotted Annie on the front porch when she pulled up in front of the house. Before she'd even stopped, Annie raced over to the car. Annie grabbed her hand and dragged her toward the pool, telling her how much fun it was going to be because they had floating lounge chairs, but that if she didn't like those, they also had pool rings.

As they approached the pool, Alex heard splashing. She didn't see him at first, but then realised Travis was already in the pool, swimming under water. When he materialized at the shallow end of the pool, Alex did a double take. His dark hair was slicked back, and beads of water trickled down his bare chest as he stood up in the waist-high water. He was muscular—far more so than Liam—and olive-skinned. It took all her self-control to pull her eyes away from him when she heard Annie running past her.

'Dibs on the red chair,' Annie called as she reached the far side of the pool. She grabbed the chair and dove into the deep end. In no time at all she'd climbed into the chair, her hair slicked back like her father's as she lounged back, pretending to smoke an imaginary cigarette.

Alex took her time, setting her tote bag down on a deck chair, and kicking her sandals off under the chair. When she pulled her shorts off and threw them on top, a slight shiver ran down her spine. She wasn't sure if it was from the spring air or the company, but at least it was a good excuse to leave the tee-shirt on.

Committed to do this, she made her way to the pool stairs near where Travis stood. One at a time she eased down into what she discovered was only lukewarm water.

Travis watched her with a lopsided grin on his face, probably wondering why she still had her shirt on.

Once the water reached her waist, she bent her knees sliding down to where the water covered her shoulders. Then she pushed off the bottom and did a breast-stroke across the pool, keeping her head up and her hair dry.

After several laps she'd had enough and made her way back up to the deck chair where she stood ringing the water out of her tee-shirt. Within a few moments, Travis followed, and moved one of the chairs over next to hers.

'Thanks for coming today. Annie hasn't really got any friends around here. There's her cousin but Annie tends to get rather exasperated with her after a while.'

'I enjoy her company. She's a clever girl, and not a bad tennis player, I must add.'

Travis beamed with pride, then grabbed a towel and dabbed the water off his face and torso before plopping into the deck chair beside her. Once again, Alex found it hard not to stare.

'Oh, I'm a horrible host. Can I grab you something cool to drink? We've got a ton of light beer left over from the party, not to mention every sort of soft drink you could imagine.'

'I wouldn't mind a mineral water, if you've got one.'

'Pretty sure we do. Annie,' he called out to her, 'do you want a drink?'

'Orange soda, please.'

'I'll be right back.'

As he made his way back to the house, Alex watched until he disappeared out of view. When she turned back to the pool, she realised Annie was watching her watching him. She ducked her head and covered her face with her hands. In a moment, Annie was next to her, giggling.

'You like him, don't you? I can tell by the way you look at him.'

Alex couldn't prevent her eyes flying wide open at the direct question. 'Um, er ...' Gees, kids were so smart these days—she'd have been clueless at Annie's age.

'Hey, it's cool. He's my dad, and I want him to be happy. You make him happy.'

Alex swallowed hard, unsure how to respond to Annie's frank question.

'Shush, here he comes. I won't say anything, pinkie-swear,' Annie said as she held up her little finger.

Alex raised her hand and they interlocked pinkies for a few seconds. Annie immediately started to giggle again.

Travis huffed out a breath. 'What are you two conspiring about? I saw you do a pinkie-swear, Annie, and that's generally reserved for extra special secrets.'

'Never you mind, Daddy, just girl talk.' She giggled again, took the orange soda he offered, and dove back into the pool where she proceeded to climb back into the chair. She popped the top of the can and placed it in the cup-holder, then once again pretended to smoke her imaginary cigarette.

'Thank you,' Alex said as she popped the top of her can of sparkling mineral water. She tried to focus on Annie while he settled back into his deck chair, then she turned to him. 'Is her mother a smoker? I only ask because she keeps pretending like she's smoking.'

'Yes, Karen's terribly addicted. She tries not to smoke around Annie, or at least that's what she tells me, but I suspect it's easier said than done.'

'It's a horrible habit. My father was a heavy smoker ... and drinker. I'm pretty sure that's part of what drove my mother back to Australia. She didn't want her three daughters around all that.'

'You have two sisters?'

'Yes, Casey and Taylor—they're twins.'

'And are they tennis players as well?'

'No, they're more creative types. Casey's a florist, and Taylor's a baker.'

'Ah, that's right. I remember you saying something about a sister who bakes.'

Alex tilted her head, trying to recall, but it really didn't matter. 'They're two years younger than me, so I know how Annie feels about her young cousin. It gets easier, later.'

Travis smiled, and Alex realised he might have felt the same way about Denver when they were kids. Pesky younger siblings were no doubt universal.

'How often do you get to spend time with Annie?'

'Officially, I'm entitled to have her every other weekend, but I agreed Karen could take her to Southern California, and keep her for most of the year if I could have her for the summer vacation. I think I told you they pulled her out of school a little early so Cody could get to Washington for this new job of his, but I'm not sure when school will start up at their new place. Guess Karen will let me know at some stage.'

'And the holidays? Do you get to see her for Christmas, or Easter?'

'I went down there for Christmas last year and Annie and I stayed at the Disneyland Hotel for a couple of nights. We had a blast. Got to the park the moment it opened and stayed until it shut. You should have seen her eyes when they did the Electric Light Parade.'

Alex sighed. 'That's something I've never done.'

'What, the Electric Light Parade?'

'No, Disneyland, full stop. I've never been. I'd like to go one day. We have theme parks in Australia, but nothing like Disneyland.'

Travis cocked his head and a quizzical expression crossed his face. 'Seriously? Not even when you lived here as a child?'

'I was only five when we moved to Australia. And we only came back once to visit my father. He took us skiing to Tahoe but it wasn't like he was flush with money or anything.'

'Well then, you've gotta go. It's just as much fun for adults as it is for kids—maybe even more so. There's also one in Florida now, and it's even bigger, but I'd rather go back to Los Angeles. Nothing like the original as far as I'm concerned.'

'I agree. When I go, it'll be to Los Angeles.'

A deep furrow appeared between Travis' eyebrows for a moment. When he spoke, his voice had dropped an octave, and it resonated with kindness. 'Well, if you're still around at Christmas, maybe you could come with us. I promised Annie I'd take her back again this year—as much as we tried to see everything, there was a lot we missed, and she wasn't tall enough for a couple of the rides she wanted to go on. I bet she will be this year.'

Alex wasn't entirely sure she'd heard correctly. Had he invited her to go away with him and Annie? To spend time with them at Christmas? She didn't quite know how to answer. Travis started fiddling with his drink can and looked across toward Annie who was splashing about in the pool.

'Or not. How stupid of me. You have family of your own you'd want to spend time with at Christmas. Forget I mentioned it. I think I got a bit carried away, seeing as how you and Annie seem to be getting along so well. She means the world to me, and I'd do anything to make her happy.'

Shame washed over Alex as she struggled for words. 'My slow response wasn't because I didn't appreciate being included. I think I was ... it was unexpected, that's all. And it's kind of a long way off, isn't it? I mean Christmas ... I seriously don't know where I'll be or what I'll be doing ... but it was really nice of you to include me.'

Travis set his can down and turned to her with eyes that held so much intensity it took enormous effort to continue looking at him. He blinked slowly, appearing to be weighing his response.

But then Annie came over and pushed his legs out of the way so she could sit on the end of his chair. 'Did I hear you say something about Disneyland? You haven't forgotten we're going at Christmas, have you?'

A weak smile wiped the seriousness off his face as Travis leaned forward and wrapped his arms around his daughter. 'Of course I haven't. I was just telling Alex about our trip last year, and how much fun it was. Can you believe she's never been to Disneyland?'

Annie's eyes grew wide and her mouth dropped open like a fish gasping for air. 'Never? How come?'

'Hey, I live something like ten thousand kilometres away. It's not like Disneyland is a couple hour's drive down the road for me. Give me a break, eh?'

Alex reached over and rubbed the top of Annie's head, making Annie giggle. She squirmed free from her father and ran back over to dive into the pool.

'So, who's hungry? Shall I go light the barbeque?' Travis called out loud enough for Annie to hear.

'I am,' yelled Annie from the pool.

His tone was light with the change of subject to food. Had he so quickly dismissed the awkward moment they'd just had?

He stood, and for a moment before he headed over to the house his eyes followed Annie's every move. There was love in his eyes, pure, and unadulterated.

Alex bent down and fiddled with her sandals, then collected her things as she waited for Annie to join her. She could get used to this family if she let herself, but was that what she wanted? She hadn't even decided if she wanted to stay in California, and here she was entertaining the idea of spending considerable time with them.

She looked up in time to see Travis heading to the back door, still wearing nothing but his bathers, and the thought of his arms around her, like they'd been on the dance floor, sent shivers down her spine. As she turned back to Annie, Annie lifted an eyebrow and shrugged her little shoulders. Alex would definitely have to be more careful about when and how she looked at Travis in Annie's presence.

CHAPTER 19

What had he been thinking, asking if Alex wanted to go to Disneyland with them? For one thing, Christmas was his special time with Annie. And for another thing, he barely knew Alex. And for a third thing, she was a Mason and there was still the stupid feud.

He'd been trying to let go of the whole feud thing, but she wasn't helping. After all, she'd still done nothing, and said nothing, about their offer. He couldn't allow himself to lose sight of that. Not yet, anyway—not until he had the full measure of this woman's integrity. She was attractive, and there was more chemistry between them than he'd felt in a long time—he'd give her that. And Annie seemed taken with her. But that didn't mean he should drop all his defences and make a fool of himself.

After he'd showered and dressed he went around and lit the barbeque. Then he grabbed some steaks out of the fridge and pulled the husks off some corn—ready for the barbeque.

By the time he'd finished, he'd regained a bit of control. He'd been an idiot out there by the pool, and he wasn't going to let his defences down again in a hurry. Alex was good company for Annie, and her agreeing to hang out with Annie at the rodeo was more than he would ever have asked, but he had to scale things back afterwards. Lessons, yes. Barbeques and afternoons by the pool, maybe not so much.

The patter of feet told him Annie was on her way in, with Alex right behind her. She smiled as she walked past him, and disappeared into the house. Five minutes later Alex re-emerged, wearing a sweater that brought out the green in her eyes. Why on earth did she have to be so darn good looking?

'Can I help with anything?' she asked as she came up beside him.

She stopped only a matter of inches away. She smelled like something from the garden—roses perhaps. Or jasmine. Or both.

'You can make a salad if you like. Everything's in the fridge, bottom drawer.'

While she busied herself making the salad, Travis grabbed plates and silverware, and set the table out on the back deck. He took his time, fiddling with placemats, grabbing napkins, finding four matching glasses. He didn't trust himself to stand next to her again—not while she looked and smelled so good.

Annie saved the day when she appeared carrying a deck of cards and saying she wanted to show Alex some card tricks. She stood patiently while Alex finished making the salad, and then dragged her off to the dining room table, leaving Travis alone with his thoughts.

With her no longer in his proximity, Travis started to breathe easier. And then Denver walked out to join him.

'Is that Alex in there with Annie? Is she staying for dinner?'

'Yes, and yes.' His voice was cool. Normal. Back in control.

'Well, I must look and smell nasty. Better grab a shower and change into something a bit more presentable.'

Travis looked him up and down. Denver's jeans were filthy, especially on his calves where they'd rubbed up against his horse's sweaty sides. At least his shirt didn't look too bad.

He quirked a brow as he answered. 'Don't bother—it'll take too long. Just don't sit right next to Alex and she might not notice the smell.'

Denver smoothed out his shirt and tucked it into his jeans a bit better. 'Seriously? You think this is okay?'

'You've never worried about it when it's me and Annie.'

'Yeah, but Alex is a guest.'

'She's Annie's tennis coach, not your next conquest. Chill.'

Denver cocked his head, and that meant trouble. 'No, but is she yours? That's the real question here, isn't it?'

He took a deep breath, willing himself to ignore his brother's teasing. 'We're having steak and salad, and there's a loaf of garlic bread in the freezer that I can put in the oven.'

'Garlic bread? You sure you want that?' Denver grinned, lifting an eyebrow.

'Go wash your face and hands. And then make yourself useful by grabbing some cold drinks to put in the ice bucket,' Travis said.

As Denver headed toward the bathroom to wash up, Travis could hear him laughing. It was obvious maintaining control throughout dinner would be a challenge.

~~*~~

Alex covered her mouth when she started to yawn. She was having a lovely evening and was a bit cross with herself as she turned to her host to apologise. 'I'm sorry to be yawning, guess it's been a long day. It's certainly no reflection on the company, or the lovely dinner. Thank you so much for inviting me.'

'It's been our pleasure,' Travis said, setting his napkin onto his plate. 'It's good of you to give Annie some lessons. Denver and I never really took to tennis the way our mother hoped we might—we were too focused on the horses.'

'I did wonder why you have a tennis court. I mean, it seems a bit odd ... on a cattle ranch?' She looked over at Denver but it was Travis who answered.

'Our mother grew up in Santa Barbara, having both a pool and a tennis court. It was something she insisted on when they built this house. She wanted her children to have a choice of activities—not just riding horses.'

'Oh, so she didn't want her boys growing up to be cowboys, I take it?' Alex had a vague memory of a song she'd heard with those lyrics.

'That was part of it. Like most parents, she wanted the best for us. She was really disappointed when I got married before I finished my degree. Then she was even more disappointed when Karen and I started following the rodeos, and I dropped out of college altogether.'

Annie, who'd gone in to watch some television, reappeared and when Alex turned to look at her she caught the tail-end of her yawn. Annie rubbed her eyes and then flashed a big smile.

Travis reached over and pulled Annie onto his lap. 'Don't think I didn't see you yawning, Annie. It's time for you to hit the hay.'

'Aw, Dad, another half hour?'

'Say goodnight to Alex. And don't forget to brush your teeth before you climb into bed.'

Annie did as she was told and left, head down, shoulders drooping. Alex knew the feeling. It was the most enjoyable evening she'd had in quite a while. One side of her, just like Annie no doubt, wished it wouldn't end.

Alex stood. 'Let me give you a hand with the dishes.'

'Nope, that's Denver's job tonight. You're the guest. Can I get you a coffee or a cup of tea?'

'Oh, I'd love a peppermint tea, if you've got one.'

Travis went to stand, shaking his head. 'Peppermint ... I'm not too sure—'

'I'll get the drinks,' Denver said, cutting him off as he got up. 'We got a box of teas as part of a Christmas basket a couple years ago, so there could be peppermint in that. I'll have a look. Usual for you, big brother?'

Travis nodded, and then Denver disappeared inside.

And now Alex was alone with Travis.

She pushed her chair back to cross her legs, turning it slightly so she was angled toward Travis. 'I've had a really lovely day, thank you. Your family makes me feel so welcome here in California. I find myself forgetting, from time to time, that I'm ten thousand kilometres from my sisters. Thank goodness for the internet. At least I can FaceTime them at night.'

He rubbed his jaw, looking at her thoughtfully. 'Do you speak to them every day? I suppose you must miss them.'

'A bit, but I didn't speak to them every day at home, so I don't speak to them every day now. Besides, the time difference makes it tricky.'

'Have they ever been here? As in California?'

'They were born here, but they were only a bit over two when we moved to Australia.'

'And they've never been back?'

'There was the trip I mentioned ... the three of us came to see my father for Christmas. I was fourteen, they were twelve.'

He nodded slowly, thinking. 'That's right. I suppose you all have pretty established lives there in Australia.'

Alex smiled. 'Sort of. I mean, they like their jobs and—.'

'I found the tea—we did have peppermint.' Denver interrupted as he came through the screen door juggling three mugs. He set the steaming mugs on the table and plonked himself back down on the other side. 'So, Alex, I meant to mention, I spoke to that friend of mine about the flooring. He can get the work done over the next week or so without a problem—and as for the bar stools, the guy wants to come look at them tomorrow but he thinks he'll have plenty of time to do the work over the next two weeks. You'd want him to replace them with the same leather, right?'

She quirked a half smile. 'Sure, if that's what you think.'

'That's what I'd do, if it were my decision.'

As Travis watched the two of them talking a frown broke out on his forehead. He opened his mouth, to say something, but then seemed to change his mind and instead he picked up his mug of coffee and took a sip, then hung onto the mug, staring at it, rocking forward and back slowly. Alex looked over at Denver, who gave her an *I-have-no-idea* kind of look, and they both picked up their mugs and drank.

As she continued to watch Travis she couldn't help wondering if his change in demeanour was to do with them talking about the saloon. She wanted to say something, but she didn't know what. She'd sell it back to them if she was going to sell everything, but that was a decision yet to be made. She chewed her bottom lip for a moment, wondering what to say, but was saved by Annie's return.

She looked at the mugs, pouting. 'Nothing for me?'

'Hey, you should be in bed,' Travis said, scowling at her.

She pouted again, but then leaned into her father and kissed his cheek. Then she walked around the table and gave Denver a big hug, giving Alex a cheeky grin the whole time.

'I hadn't said goodnight to everyone. Good night, Alex. Thank you for the lesson. Can we do it again tomorrow?'

Alex pulled out her phone and checked her diary. 'I have a few things I need to do tomorrow, but I could come around for a quick session Thursday morning if that's okay?'

Travis took a deep breath, and Alex figured he would say no, but then he shrugged his shoulders and gave her a half smile. 'Sure. That's fine by me. I'll be busy working horses but you can see yourself in.'

Annie clapped her hands excitedly. 'Great, I'll see you Thursday morning then. What time?'

'How does nine o'clock sound?'

'Perfect. Goodnight everyone.' Annie dashed back inside, letting the screen door slam behind her.

Travis set his mug down and turned to her. 'If you're busy you don't have to do this.'

'No, it's no burden, trust me. I miss coaching. Besides, this has inspired me.'

Travis and Denver both looked at her inquisitively, but she decided not to elaborate. No point talking about the possible program until it was a certainty.

She picked up her mug of now cool tea, drank the last of it and stood up to go. 'I should go. Thank you, both, for your hospitality.'

Travis stood, too. 'I'll walk you out. Denver, you get to clean the barbeque.'

'Lucky me,' he replied with a laugh. 'Night, Alex. Guess I'll see you Thursday.'

Alex walked to her car with Travis following her. Once inside she rolled down the window before starting the car. 'Thanks again. It was a lovely meal.'

'Made lovelier by your company, I'm sure. Annie's quite taken with you, and she's over the moon with the lessons.'

'I wasn't kidding ... about it not being a burden. Spending time with Annie has made me realise just how much I miss coaching.'

Travis cocked his head, and she was tempted to explain, to mention how her whole life had gone topsy-turvy when she lost both her job and her husband on the same day. But now probably wasn't the time for that.

He took a step back and pretended to tip his hat toward her, except he wasn't wearing one. It made her smile. 'Well, for Annie's sake, I'm glad you're enjoying giving her the lessons.'

'I am. Thanks again, for dinner, and if I don't speak to you Thursday, I'll see you early Saturday morning, for the rodeo.' A rush of warmth surprised Alex—it was good to be part of this, to be helping out, even if only in a small way.

'Good night, Alex.' He stepped back and made his way up onto the porch.

As she drove off, she could still see him standing there in the pale glow of the porch light.

~~*~~

Denver grinned when Travis walked into the kitchen. 'You kiss her goodnight?'

'That's none of your business.'

'You're a fool if you didn't.'

'And why, pray tell, would you say that?'

'Seriously? Man, you two are so made for each other it isn't funny,' Denver said, shutting the lid on the barbeque.

Travis glared at him. Why on earth did he put up with his antics? He knew why—because he loved his brother, and all kidding aside, wondered if his brother saw something he'd refused to see himself.

Denver pulled a face. 'I mean it. You look good together, you're both as serious as each other, and Annie is crazy about her. But that's not the half of it. I watched you on the dance floor Saturday night. There was so much chemistry between the two of you even I could feel it.'

Travis continued glaring for a moment while he considered his words carefully. 'Look, for all we know she could be married, or in a serious relationship. She's here to assess the properties, do some improvements to maximise her values, get rid of them, and then go back to Australia.'

'How do you know that? She seems pretty relaxed and comfortable here—not at all like someone who is pining to get home to a loved one, if you ask me.'

'And did I?'

'Did you what?'

'Ask you?'

Denver smirked. 'Don't let this opportunity slip through your fingers just because of what happened with Karen. She wasn't right for you—I knew from the start. So did Mom.'

Travis clenched his jaw to keep from saying something he'd no doubt regret later. There was no reason why he should defend Karen. After all, Denver was right—his mother hadn't ever taken to her. He and his father were the only ones who got caught up in her spell. But that was ancient history now.

'And what has any of that got to do with Alex? What "opportunity" are you referring to? You do know she's a Mason, right?'

'Trav, forget the whole Mason thing. I know Dad couldn't let it go, but seriously? She's as hot for you as you are for her. I can see it plain as I can see how dirty my jeans are. And by the way, I should have changed them at least, even if I didn't take a shower.' He twisted so he could see his pant legs, scowling.

'I'm not sure what you think you see in her, but the truth is, she lives ten thousand kilometres away. She mentioned it twice today—ten thousand kilometres. Perhaps her way of reminding me how much water separates us. She's doing me a huge favour, helping out with Annie, but maybe that's her way of paying us back for the work you've been putting in at the saloon and this other shop she wants to set up.'

'Nope. She's paying me. Everything's strictly business.'

Travis rubbed the stubble on his chin. Could Denver be right? Could Denver see something he was refusing to acknowledge? But if so, why had she looked ill when he'd mentioned Disneyland? Her face wasn't that of someone who had the hots for the inviter so much as the face of someone who was horrified at the thought.

And perhaps he should be horrified too, for having made the suggestion.

CHAPTER 20

The whole drive home Alex couldn't stop wondering why Travis Gold had to be so infuriatingly nice. It simply made everything she had to do harder. It had been easier to keep things businesslike when he was grumpy and abrupt.

One side of her did like the idea of staying here, living here—coming back to her roots.

The other side of her missed her mother and sisters, and the familiarity of Melbourne, of knowing where everything was and how to get there.

But she'd have liked the decision about staying or leaving to be made with a clear mind, objectively weighing up the pros and cons. Now there was this other factor to consider—this matter of the heart, involving not only an interesting man, but one with a ready-made family she could probably slot into to as easily as sliding into an old pair of slippers.

As she pulled into the driveway and shut off the car, she cringed, recalling her reaction to his comment about her going to Disneyland with them at Christmas. The comment had caught her off guard and she'd reacted horribly. Travis would be perfectly entitled to think her a complete philistine. And yet he'd been the perfect gentleman the whole rest of the evening anyway.

She needed to talk about this. Desperately. Which meant a call to her sisters.

Once inside, she sat at her kitchen table and pulled out her phone finding a missed call and message. She played the message, listening to Harrison's voice asking her if she planned to go to the post-rodeo dance at Angels Camp, and if she'd like to go with him.

She hadn't thought about Harrison once since Saturday night. When he dropped her home he hadn't even turned off the car's engine. She'd been relieved, figuring he felt as she did, grateful not to have gone to the party alone, but under no obligation for a goodnight kiss or "night cap". So why did he want her to go to the rodeo dance? For the same reason?

Well, it was out of the question. She'd be hanging out with Annie for as long as that took, and she neither knew nor cared how long that might be.

A smiled crept onto her face, its warmth radiating through her. But was the joy she felt from the thought of spending time with Annie, or with Travis? Did it matter? Were they not a package, inseparable, a two-for-one deal? She chided herself, horrified she'd thought of them as any sort of "deal". And yet, was that wrong?

She checked the time. Casey would be at work, but if she was lucky she might catch her having a late lunch. She punched the FaceTime contact and closed her eyes.

'What's wrong?' Concern laced Casey's voice when she answered.

Alex sighed. 'Nothing. Nothing at all. I just needed to talk, and you were the first one who came to mind.'

Casey sniggered. 'Must be about a man.'

'Yep.'

Casey brought her hands up and rubbed them together with a wicked smile on her face. 'Oooooh, I can't wait to hear. Give me a minute and I'll ring you back. I've got a hospital delivery to make so I'll just finish putting the rest of the arrangements in the van and give you a call once I'm on the road.'

Alex made a cup of tea, grabbed her phone, and not long after she sat at the table Casey called back.

'So ... do tell. You've met someone? Is he one of those hunky cowboys you've mentioned?'

Alex was glad they were now on the phone, and not FaceTime—Casey wouldn't see her blush. 'Yes, and no. I mean ... oh, I don't know what I mean.'

'This must be serious. My sister, the level-headed one, is confused about a man—and she's almost tongue-tied. This is big. Taylor's gonna be sorry she missed this.'

Alex frowned. 'Stop teasing me. This is serious.'

Casey dropped the humorous tone. 'Sorry, it's just so rare to find you in this state of delirium. So ... is this the first man you've shown any interest in since Liam?'

Alex sighed, wishing now that they were actually having a coffee somewhere and that she could see Casey's facial expressions. 'Yes.'

'This is great news, isn't it?'

'I don't know. Is it?'

'Of course it is. And he must be special. What's he like?'

Alex gave Casey a full run-down starting from the day she met Travis in the saloon, through to tonight's dinner. Casey listened, saying "uh-huh" in all the right places, but for once in her life, not interrupting.

Alex sighed. 'And now I don't know what I want to do, and how I'm going to behave next time I see him.'

'Wow. Sounds to me like you're falling in love, big sister.'

Alex shook her head, hopelessly trying to shake the confusion from it. 'Yeah, but with Travis, or Annie?'

'Sounds to me like it's both of them. Is that a problem?'

'I don't know. I seriously don't know what to do.'

Casey didn't reply straight away, and when she finally did it was with all seriousness. 'I don't know why you think you have to *do* anything. Just go with it. Enjoy their company. Come home for the wedding. See if you miss them. If you do, great. If you don't, well then at least you'll know. It's not like you have to decide anything, is it? I don't get why you're so stressed about it.'

The muscles in Alex's face softened as her tension dissipated momentarily. 'But ...'

'Look, I know what you're thinking, but seriously, you need to move on—let go of the past. What happened was horrible, and completely unfair, but you can't let it define you. You're so much more than your past.'

Alex's heart swelled with gratitude. Casey was there for her. Everything would work out. 'You're right. I have to let go of it.'

'Yes. You're a wonderful catch for any man—don't let Liam make you think otherwise. Enjoy this cowboy and his gorgeous daughter, and just see how things go. She'll go back to her mother at the end of summer, and you can come home ... or you can stay ... whatever feels right.'

Alex sighed again, but this time it was with relief. Casey, as usual, was right. Alex had to learn to live again, and maybe this little town was a good place to start.

CHAPTER 21

'Weren't they great? Did you see how well Daddy rode?' Annie was glowing with pride as she jumped up off her seat when the team penning event concluded.

Travis and Denver had just finished, and although they weren't in first place their time was probably good enough to show off the potential of the young horses. Travis should be pleased with their results.

'I'm starving. Can we go get another corndog?' Annie began fidgeting, biting her lower lip.

'Another one? You've already had two.'

'My tummies rumbling, so I must be starving ... and they're so good.'

Alex sighed. 'Now? Your dad's in the next event—don't you want to stay and watch?'

'We can come right back. I think I need to find a bathroom—now.'

Alex bit her lip, doubting they'd be lucky enough to get these same seats when they returned, but the pale look on Annie's face confirmed the need to find a bathroom quickly.

They made their way past more good-looking men than Alex had ever seen in one place. Then again, maybe it was the faded jeans, rolled up shirts exposing strong arms, and cowboy hats—every one of them had a cowboy hat—which made them seem better looking than they might otherwise have been, but either way Alex was acutely aware of each one as they squeezed past.

When they found the large toilet block, Alex waited outside the entrance as Annie dashed inside. 'I'll wait right here.'

Annie hadn't been gone more than a few seconds when Alex heard her name and turned to see Harrison standing a few feet away. He came up and gave her the evil eye for a moment.

She did a mock face-palm as she remembered the message from him, and the fact that she'd never returned his call. 'Gees, I'm bad. Sorry. I meant to ring.'

'Did you? I took your non-response as a no, and now here you are?'

'Yes, sorry.'

'And you're alone?'

'No. I mean, I am for the moment, but ... no, I'm not here alone.'

Harrison grinned. 'Are you sticking around for the dance?'

She shook her head. 'I don't think so. What about you?'

'Oh, definitely. I just came early because I decided it would be good to have a look around. I'm not really into horses, or cows, but it's interesting to watch. You never know, I might need to play a cowboy at some stage, so it could be good research.'

Suddenly a loud commotion broke out and people started screaming and pushing and shoving. Alex got caught off guard with a heavy bump and started to lose her balance backwards, but Harrison grabbed her arm just in time.

'What the ...?' Harrison's face darkened with anger; or was it fear?

And then the sound of thundering hooves rose above the screams. Alex stood, paralysed with indecision. Turn right? Turn left? Stay still? But then Harrison once again grabbed her arm and pulled her back moments before a horse raced toward them, scattering people who were jumping out of its way. Harrison kept pulling her by the arm until they were well off to the side, but Alex had a clear view of the horse. It looked terrified, dripping with sweat and covered in foam. Its saddle was underneath its belly, and straps were twisted around its legs. It struggled to remain upright as it kicked out and half reared, before finally coming to a stop, shaking with either fear or exhaustion.

Finally, a cowboy walked up to the frightened animal, speaking softly and moving slowly. It seemed to recognise him, or else it was soothed by his manner. When he finally had hold of it, another man approached and within moments they'd removed the saddle and straps, and the horse seemed to breathe a sigh of relief.

The cowboy who was leading the horse turned his attention to the onlookers. 'It's okay everyone, nothing more to see here. Make way and we'll take this little filly back to her owner.'

The crowd applauded softly, and then backed away. A murmur of voices and relieved laughter broke out as the two cowboys led the horse away.

Harrison turned to Alex, rubbing her arm. 'Holy crap, that was close. Where'd that thing come from? Are you okay?'

She laughed—the same relieved laugh she'd heard from the entire crowd a moment earlier. 'Yeah, I'm fine. It must have thrown its rider.'

Harrison glared in the direction of the departing cowboys, and yelled out. 'Yeah, well, someone could have been hurt.'

The cowboy carrying the saddle turned and looked at Harrison, shaking his head. 'Not my horse, man, I'm just trying to help. It's a rodeo, dude, get over it.'

Alex smiled at Harrison, hoping to settle him down. 'Like he said, it's a rodeo. It was an accident. Things ... happen.'

Harrison seemed to regain his composure and sighed loudly. 'Yeah, sure. Took me by surprise, that's all. But you look like you could use a drink. Do you want to go get something?'

In all the chaos caused by the horse, Alex had momentarily forgotten about Annie. How much time had passed? She had to be out of the bathroom by now, but where was she?

'Annie?' Alex yelled over the murmuring crowd, calling several more times, louder each time. With no response, she turned to Harrison. 'I was with Annie, Travis' daughter. She went into the bathroom, moments before you walked up. I have to find her.'

'Hey, calm down, she'll be here somewhere. She probably saw the commotion with the horse and stayed put. Why don't you go look inside?'

Alex agreed, and raced over to the bathroom, calling Annie's name as she walked in. There was still no reply even when she called several more times.

When she came out, Harrison was still standing where she'd left him, fiddling with his mobile phone. That gave her an idea. Maybe in the confusion Annie had gone back looking for her father. She rang Travis, but the call went straight to his voicemail. She began to speak, trying to control her voice, but it was as if she'd just run a marathon—her breath catching in gasps. 'Travis? It's Alex. Is Annie with you? Please call me.'

She ended the call but continued to hold the phone in front of her face, willing it to ring. When it didn't she began looking again.

'I don't think she could have gone far,' Harrison said, half shrugging and looking like he'd rather be anywhere else.

Alex could barely speak as a wave of nausea washed over her. 'I have to find her. She's only eight. If anything happens—.'

Harrison grabbed both her upper arms and gave her a gentle shake. 'Hey, we'll find her. Don't panic. Did you have assigned seats somewhere? Would she have gone back there?'

Alex tried to remember exactly where they'd been sitting. 'She might have tried to go back. Or she might have gone to her father's horse-truck. I have to go. I have to look for her.'

Harrison released her arms, and stepped back. 'What was she wearing? I'll stay here and keep looking in this area, and you go back to where you were.'

'A red cowboy hat ... and her hair is in long braids. She had her denim jacket with her, so if she got cold she might have it on.' Alex shivered at the thought of Annie getting cold, but she refused to let her imagination go wild. She'd be found, probably with Travis. If Alex could find Travis, she'd find Annie. She looked over her shoulder toward the area where he'd parked his truck, then looked back at Harrison, swallowing back her emotions as she tried to decide where to head first.

'You go ... I'll stick around here. I'll ring you if she turns up. And same, let me know when you find her so I can stop looking.'

She tried a weak smile, nodding as she turned and raced off in the direction of the arena where they'd last been sitting.

~~*~~

Travis tied his horse to the side of the truck and pulled the saddle off. The young gelding had done well; probably well enough for him to get an offer before the end of the rodeo. Both fillies had already sold. He smiled, pleased with everyone's efforts for the day and grateful to be going home and not trying to get back here for the dance later tonight.

He pulled out a container of water and poured it over the gelding's back, then scraped the excess off and rubbed him down with an old towel. He rubbed his neck in that special spot the horse particularly liked, just below his jaw, then threw a light-weight cotton trailer sheet onto him and led him into the horse-truck to tie him in next to the two fillies that were also done for the day.

As he walked out of the truck, he spotted Alex. She was racing toward him looking distraught. His heart skipped a beat.

'Alex? What's wrong? Where's Annie?'

'She went into the large toilet block—the bathroom—and then this horse came barrelling toward us and there was so much commotion and everyone was panicking and screaming, but then she wasn't anywhere.'

Disbelief raged through him and his fists clenched involuntarily. 'Start at the beginning, I'm not following.'

'We were watching you ... and Annie said she wanted another corndog, and then she said she needed to go to the bathroom. I waited outside, but she never came out.'

'What were you saying about a horse? Was Annie injured? Could she have been kicked or trampled?'

'No, nothing like that—no one got hurt. I don't know how much time passed while they got the horse settled and took it away. I went into the bathroom, looking for her, but she wasn't there. We looked for her. And called her name. She was ... nowhere.'

Travis swallowed hard, trying to make sense of the situation. Annie was a smart girl. She wouldn't have gone off with a stranger. He looked at Alex again as her words finally sunk in. 'You said "we". Who was with you when she disappeared?'

'Harrison had come up—'

His teeth clenched at the name, then he cut her off. 'Harrison. You were talking to Harrison when you were meant to be looking after *my daughter*.'

Tears began to well in Alex's eyes as she shook her head back and forth, slowly. 'It wasn't like that. He walked up only a moment after she went into the toilets, and then the horse ... it couldn't have been more than a few minutes in total, I'm sure of it.'

His head throbbed as rage threatened to overpower logic. He looked at Alex—sobbing now—but it was disgust that rose in him, not sympathy. She'd lost his daughter. He'd trusted a Mason—the thing his father had told him to never do—and *she'd lost his daughter*. He took a deep breath. She was still his best bet to find Annie.

'Where haven't you looked yet?'

'Here. This is the last place. I went back to where we were sitting, but she wasn't there so I thought maybe she'd come looking for you.'

This ... could ... not ... be ... happening. All he could see was Annie's smiling face, giggling as he tickled her. She had to be safe. Somewhere. She had to be. 'What about your car? Could she have gone there?'

Alex's eyes lit up. 'I didn't think to check there.'

Travis looked around. There were a number of other competitors hanging around grooming their horses, and Denver and Nick would be back soon. He closed the door on the truck and turned to Alex.

'Come on; let's go check your car. She's probably standing there, waiting for you to return,' he said.

Alex took off—at a jog first, and then she sped up. Travis kept pace with her easily. When they reached her car there was no one there. They split up, both walking up and down the rows of cars, hoping Annie was simply in the wrong aisle, but Annie was nowhere to be found. When they met back at her car, Alex lost it.

Her words came out between deep sobs. 'I am so sorry. I think we need to ring the police.' Then tears welled in her eyes and, when they began to run down her cheeks, she rubbed her hand across her face smearing black makeup everywhere.

Something gave in him as he watched her. This wasn't her fault; it had simply happened.

'Yes, I think you're right—I'll ring them now.' He pulled out his phone, and that's when he remembered he'd switched it off earlier. There'd been several missed calls; Alex, a couple of numbers he didn't recognise, and his cousin, Stacy.

Hope welled in him as he pushed Stacy's number. When she answered the first words out of his mouth were, 'Have you got her there with you?'

CHAPTER 22

Alex wiped her tears away and tried to swallow but her throat seemed blocked. She bit her lip, trying to hold back the sobs that wracked her body. She'd never been terribly religious—Mum had only taken them to church a couple of times when they were young—but now she prayed. She asked that Annie be there with Stacy, safe and unharmed. She asked for forgiveness for having lost her focus for those few horrible moments. And lastly, she asked, if it was possible, for Travis to find it in his heart to forgive her.

She'd seen the disgust in his eyes. She'd heard it in his voice. Now she watched, helplessly, as he waited for Stacy to reply.

When relief washed over his face, and he looked at her and nodded, Alex looked up at the sky and said a silent thank you. Then she stepped back, leaning up against her car, taking in deep settling breaths. Tears streamed down her cheeks again, but this time, out of relief.

Travis spoke into his phone. 'I'd switched it off—I didn't want it ringing while I was competing and I'd forgotten to put it back on.'

Then he was listening, nodding, and repeating "uh huh" every now and then.

Finally, he looked Alex straight in the eye as he replied to Stacy. 'That's perfect, Stacy, you're an absolute life saver. Thanks so much. I'll see you tomorrow night sometime.'

There was a pause, and Travis continued to nod. Then, 'Yes, I'll ring as soon as I'm home. Thanks again.'

He popped his phone back in his pocket and turned to Alex, suddenly looking old and tired. 'Stacy found her; she was throwing up in the bathroom. And when Tammy saw Annie throwing up, she got sick too.'

'Oh, no, I hope it wasn't those corndogs.' Another pang of guilt stabbed at Alex. She'd wondered about letting her eat those greasy looking things—she should have said no to the second one.

He stared at her, looking almost too exhausted to reply. When he did speak his words came out slowly. 'Stacy said when they came out to look for you there were people everywhere because a horse was causing all

157

kinds of commotion, and Stacy wanted to get the girls out of there. She grabbed them and left. She'd tried to ring me but couldn't get through, and she didn't have your number. She said to apologise to you if she gave you a fright but she didn't know what else to do.'

Alex wiped her hand across her face and sniffed back her tears. It was over. But she still couldn't stop shaking. She ran her hands through her hair and tried to compose herself before answering. Finally, she spoke anyway.

'Stacy did the right thing—I don't blame her. They caught the horse relatively quickly, but it might not have been. And with both girls being sick, no, I certainly don't blame her for leaving.'

Travis cocked his head, drawing in a loud breath before replying. 'It gave us both a fright, but don't blame yourself.'

Alex swallowed hard, and then spoke in a voice she could barely hear herself. 'You did.'

He raised an eyebrow, studying her. 'Yeah, maybe I overreacted for a moment. And then when you said you were talking to Harrison ...'

'I was still watching for Annie to return. We'd only been talking a couple of minutes when that horse came running up.'

Travis sighed. 'Are you okay to drive home?'

Looking around at all the cars jammed into the parking lot, Alex wondered how long it was going to take for it to clear. The rows were close together, and there were giant SUVs on both sides of her. She'd have to wait for one of them to leave before she'd even be able to get her doors open to get into it. She took a deep breath and let it out with a noisy sigh.

'I'm not sure,' she finally replied.

'Look, why don't we leave your car here, and come back for it tomorrow? It should be fine. I suspect there'll be a number of cars left, with people staying for the dance and drinking too much. You can come back with me. I could use a hand with the horses in any case, since Denver and Nick are staying for the dance. Actually, if one of them is sober enough, they can bring your car back tonight.'

Alex swallowed hard, and then took another deep breath. 'Okay, if you don't mind? I can't seem to stop shaking.'

'You had a fright—both with nearly being knocked over by a frantic horse, then thinking you'd lost Annie. We both had a fright, in actual fact.'

His gaze was intense, but his deep brown eyes no longer held the horrible disappointment she'd seen earlier. When he reached out to her she took his hand, and they headed back to his truck.

When they got there, Denver and Nick had already loaded the last two horses and they were standing there looking around, no doubt wondering where Travis had gotten to. Travis told them what had happened, and Alex filled in a couple of blanks.

Denver seemed unfazed—like it was an everyday occurrence. Maybe it was, for him. Or maybe, she'd simply overreacted out of guilt.

'Gees, Alex, bummer of a way to end the day—but I don't mind bringing your car back. It's no drama at all. Just means neither of us can drink too much, Nick.'

'I wasn't planning to in any case, given I was already going to be driving,' said Nick, quirking a smile. 'It's you that's got to behave now, cuz.'

Travis patted Denver on the back. 'Thanks, Den. This is probably a good outcome, given we're competing again tomorrow and I don't want you having a hangover. We don't want anyone reneging on their offer to buy these youngsters because you've made the horses look bad.'

'Never gonna happen, you know that.' Denver laughed off his brother's concerns, and put his hand out to Alex. 'Keys?'

She dug in her purse and handed them to Denver. Then she remembered Harrison, and quickly sent him a text saying Annie was safe. When she looked up, they were all three staring at her.

'I had to let Harrison know we'd found her. He stayed near the toilets, in case she came back there.'

Travis raised an eyebrow, but didn't say anything.

Denver simply shoved the keys in his pocket, then reached into the passenger side of the truck and pulled out a duffle bag. 'Oh, so where's your car parked, anyway?'

Travis explained the location, and then asked if all the horses were good to go.

'Yep, all tied exactly the way you like them. See you back home later. I won't be too late ... probably by midnight.'

'Okay, Cinderella, don't go turning into a pumpkin on me.'

Denver laughed at the comment, then threw his duffle bag over his shoulder and cocked his head toward Nick. 'Let's go grab something to eat, and then get ready for the dance.'

Nick smiled at Alex as he turned to follow Denver, so she gave him a weak smile in return.

At the sound of Travis clearing his throat, she turned to find him staring at her. 'Ready? We'll get these horses home and then get you something to eat. I'm sure you'll feel better after that.'

CHAPTER 23

Travis had been right—after a bowl of leftover stew and some sourdough bread, Alex could view the day's events more objectively. Yet every time she looked across the table at Travis, she remembered the look in his eyes when she first told him Annie had gone missing. Would she ever completely regain his trust? Did she deserve to?

'Better?' he asked, his face carrying a few less of the deep crevices that had darkened it earlier.

'Much.' She sighed. 'I truly am sorry about today—I would never have forgiven myself if anything had happened to Annie. You know that, don't you?'

When his frown lines began to reappear she regretted bringing it up again, but it had to be discussed—they had to clear the air between them.

'Annie's a smart girl. I was worried, but deep down I knew she wouldn't have gone off with anyone—she wouldn't have just left you either, but when you mentioned Harrison, at first I thought she might have ... gotten a bit ... jealous.' His eyes were searching hers, looking for something she wasn't sure how to express.

'Look, Harrison had only stopped to say hello—he was about to leave, and would have, if it wasn't for the horse charging through. I doubt Annie would have even seen him.'

Travis looked down, chewing his bottom lip, the frown lines still evident. When he spoke, his voice was deeper than usual. 'You came to Denver's party with him.'

Her heart was racing, but she kept her voice even. 'Yes, I did. And he drove me home. And we said goodnight, and there was nothing to it.' She swallowed, sensing where this was heading and uncertain how much she was prepared to divulge about her feelings.

'Harrison's ... he's a bit of a player I suspect, living down there in Southern California, mixing with the movie crowd.'

'Yes, he's quite the charmer, but it was nice of him to drive so I could have a couple of drinks. He doesn't drink—did I tell you that already? Says it's bad for the skin and he's obsessed with his appearance.'

That brought a smile to Travis' lips—or perhaps it was a smirk. 'He doesn't drink? Gees, he'd be about the only one in Hollywood who doesn't. Anyway, that's enough about Harrison. Shall we call and see if Annie is still awake?'

'Great idea.' She could think of nothing better than to hear Annie's voice right now—both to know Annie was safe, and to change the direction this conversation was headed.

Travis pulled his phone from his pocket, and called Stacy. Then he put the call on speaker and set it on the table so Alex could hear too.

After the hellos, Stacy gave them an update. 'Neither of them threw up once we left the rodeo, so I'm hoping it was just something they ate, and not the flu.'

'Glad they're improving. Is Annie still awake? We'd like to say goodnight to her if she is,' Travis said, not taking his eyes off Alex the whole time.

'No, they've finally passed out ... or at least I can't hear any more giggling from in there. I'd rather let them sleep. They were both in good spirits, so whatever it was seems to be passing.'

'Okay, better not to disturb them then. And you're sure you don't mind her staying with you and Tammy tomorrow?'

'Not at all. Tammy's got a stack of DVDs they can choose from and I'll park them in front of the television.'

'Thanks again, Stacy, you really are a lifesaver. I'll give you a buzz tomorrow afternoon sometime, and let you know what time I'll get there to pick her up. I owe you big time for this.'

Stacy laughed. 'You sure do, and I think a few riding lessons may be the price. After seeing all the horses at the rodeo, Tammy's never gonna shut up about getting her a horse. Nick said he'll help, but I think you'll be a lot better at it than he would be.'

'No problem, I can do that. Well, goodnight then.' Travis switched off the phone and looked up at Alex. 'Guess I'd better run you home.'

As she put her hands on the table and stood, her stomach dropped to her feet.

'What's wrong?' he asked, still sitting. 'You look like you've seen a ghost.'

She shook her head in disbelief, and sat down again. 'I gave my keys to Denver.'

Travis shrugged. 'Yes, so he can drive your car back.'

She drew in a breath, and huffed it out. 'But it wasn't only my car keys, it was all my keys.'

'Oh? Ooooohhhhh.' Travis looked down, his brows knitted in thought.

Alex rolled her eyes, amazed at her stupidity. 'I'm so sorry. I wasn't thinking.'

Travis shrugged again and placed his hands on the table, palms down. 'Look, it's not the end of the world. Why don't you stay here? You can have Annie's room.'

'Are you sure?'

'Absolutely.' He reached across and took her right hand in his, giving it a gentle rub. His touch sent warm tendrils through her whole body. Then, painfully aware of her shoulder, she had to fight the urge to run her other hand up to her right shoulder and give it a rub.

When he spoke, it helped her to change focus. 'How about a night cap? It's been a long day, and I think I could use one.'

She gave him a slight nod, afraid to speak, knowing her voice would be breathless. The feelings he'd stirred with his touch were both wonderful and frightening.

He smiled, and then stood. 'Come have a look—we've got a number of liqueurs to choose from, some I haven't even tried. Or you can have a scotch or whatever takes your fancy.'

She followed him to the bar, and then stood looking at a huge selection of bottles.

'What takes your fancy? This liqueur is nice—I've had it a time or two,' he said, pointing to a bottle shaped like a monk.

'Okay, I'll try that one then.'

He pulled two small glasses from the cupboard, and then poured the amber liquid into each one. 'A toast,' he said, handing her a glass and then gently tapping it with his own, 'to long days and new friendships.' He smiled as he lifted his glass and took a small sip.

She closed her eyes, savouring the nutty scent as it approached her lips, and then took the smallest of sips to start. The warm sweetness tasted like liquid Heaven as she swirled it in her mouth. She took a deep settling breath, her eyes still closed. 'Hmmm, that's beautiful.'

When she opened her eyes, he'd stepped closer. 'It's not the only beautiful thing in the room,' Travis said, as he took another step forward and placed a hand on her back, pulling her in close.

When their lips met, she could still taste the liqueur in her mouth, making his kiss sweeter than any she'd ever experienced. It started off soft, and slow, and warm, but when she responded it became something more.

Travis took the glass from her hand and set it on the bar next to his own. His strong hands reached for her waist and he easily lifted her up onto the bar, bringing her face even with his. She spread her legs to allow him to lean in closer as his hands cradled her face, his thumbs caressing her cheeks, his eyes burning into her. Without even thinking, her arms encircled him, pulling him up against her chest as his lips once again took hers.

As their kisses deepened, she struggled to breathe and her body tingled with anticipation. With her eyes closed she was weightless, floating in an abyss, no longer aware of time or place or propriety or restraint. Her hands caressed his muscular back, her fingers digging into the cotton of his shirt, wishing it wasn't a barrier between them.

And then he stepped back—his jagged breath a sign that this meant as much to him as it did to her. He pulled off his shirt, and then reached out and stroked her cheeks with his thumbs as his hands gently cupped her face. She closed her eyes as he came back in for another kiss—this one deep, his tongue probing, questioning, seeking.

Now she could barely breathe, but she didn't care. She pulled him closer as she yearned for their bodies to meld. And with every beat of her pounding heart, she became more acutely aware that she wanted this man. She wanted to feel his skin on her own. She wanted to merge their bodies, to feel his strength, to be one with him.

She brought her arms back to her sides, and then squeezed her hands between them, fumbling with the buttons on her shirt until they were free. She hesitated for one moment, conscious of her scar, but past caring she pulled her shirt from the waist of her jeans.

He stepped back, and helped her remove the fabric that separated them and tossed it on the floor. He stared at her, his eyes smouldering. Then he reached up and slowly ran his fingers down the scar that marked her like a brand.

She expected him to recoil—was prepared for that response—but she wasn't prepared for him to lean forward and put his lips to the scar. His kisses began at the top of the scar, then slowly he made his way along its length, and across to the hollow of her neck, sending waves of sensation through her core. When he stopped, he leaned back and looked deeply into her eyes for a moment before pulling her close again. She was on fire now, her entire body aching with desire. When his lips met hers this time there was searing heat and desperation in their kiss.

Both panting, he leaned back, admiring her with eyes that burnt into her soul. 'Will you stay with me tonight?' His voice was ragged, deep and breathless.

She slid down from the bar, bent to retrieve their shirts from the floor, and took his outstretched hand.

CHAPTER 24

Travis woke with the first rays of the sun. Alex's soft breathing immediately triggered a memory of the night before, bringing a smile to his face.

His body responded as memories of their lovemaking played out in his mind, but he needed to focus on work—he had horses to prepare and a big day ahead of him.

He slid out of bed as quietly as possible, not touching her or disturbing the sheet. As he made his way to the shower, he remembered that Nick had stayed—she'd have to face not only Denver this morning but Nick as well.

When he returned from the shower she was sitting on the end of the bed, fully dressed, her hair pulled back away from her face in a ponytail. The only giveaway of the night's activity was the smeared makeup around her eyes, and the slight puffiness of her bruised lips. He wanted to kiss them again, but knew if he started it would be impossible to stop. He kept his distance.

'Good morning,' he said with a smile. 'What would you like for breakfast?'

'I would kill for a coffee.' She smiled back, raising her shoulders in a sweet shrug.

'I think that can be arranged. Oh, and just so you know, Nick and Denver might both be out there—Nick stayed the night.'

'Yes, I heard them come in. They walk heavily in those boots. And they were laughing.'

'I didn't hear them. Guess I'm used to Denver banging around at night. I slept like a baby.'

Her face contorted into a smirk, but he could see the smile underneath. 'I've never heard of a baby making quite that much noise.'

He chuckled, but held his tongue. 'Your coffee will be waiting for you.'

A few minutes later Alex joined him in the kitchen. Whatever she'd done in the bathroom had worked—there were now no signs of the frantic activity they'd enjoyed the night before. She sat at the table, and he set a cup of steaming coffee in front of her. 'Sugar? Cream?'

'No, just black, thanks.' She picked up the cup and blew on the top of the coffee, glancing at him from under her lashes.

'What else can I get you? Toast? Eggs? Or Annie's got all sorts of cereal in the cupboard.'

'This will do until I get home. And speaking of home, you wouldn't know where Denver would have put my keys, would you?'

He held up a finger as he ducked into the entry hall where he hoped Denver would have had the good sense to leave them on the side table. Sure enough he had. He brought them back and set them beside her.

'Perfect. Perhaps I should go, before the others get up.'

Travis shrugged. 'If you like. They may both sleep in a bit, but you never know.' He pulled eggs from the fridge and set them on the side of the stove, watching as Alex took a long sip of her coffee. 'Sure you don't want some breakfast?'

She looked off into the distance before swallowing the last of her coffee and standing. 'I'd better not. So, I guess Annie won't be in any shape to go to the rodeo or the frog jump today. Such a shame.'

Travis frowned. 'I suppose it depends on whether it's the flu, or if it was what they ate.'

Her face brightened. 'Do you think that might be all it was? Because if so, I can check with Stacy a bit later, and if Annie's up for it I can pick her up and bring her out to see the finals.'

Warmth raced through him at her words. 'Would you? She'd love to see all the finals if she's better this morning.'

'Send me Stacy's number, and when I get home I'll give her a call to see if Annie's up to it.'

He walked over and pulled her into his arms for a gentle hug. When he stepped away a slight smile teased at the corner of her mouth, and her eyes sparkled with something deeper than the passion they'd shared the night before. Whatever it was, it sent tingles through his body.

He stepped back, and cocked his head. 'Can I walk you out?'

'No, that's okay—I'll just slip out quietly. You go ahead and have your breakfast. Hopefully, I'll see you later today.'

He gave her one last quick kiss, and then watched as she headed for the door.

He couldn't afford to think about her right now—he'd save all his thinking for later, after the rodeo—but he did allow himself to acknowledge one thing. He'd never wanted to be around any woman as much as he wanted to be near Alex Mason.

~~*~~

Alex couldn't stop smiling the whole way home, blushing as she remembered everything they'd done. She'd never been with anyone other than Liam—he'd been her first boyfriend, and he'd taught her everything she knew—which, if last night was anything to go by, wasn't much.

Once home in her own kitchen, she stood with her eyes closed waiting for the electric kettle to boil, recalling the feel of Travis' hands and the taste of his kisses. He was like a drug, and she wanted more of him.

And as soon as that simile crossed her mind, her sensible and protective side kicked in.

She wasn't in a position to allow herself to become attached to Travis. She still wasn't certain she'd stay here longer than the summer. How was it fair to anyone, herself included, to become emotionally involved with him? Wouldn't it be better to view the previous night as a lapse in judgement?

She longed to speak to Casey. She would know what to do—she'd had so much more experience with love. She opened her iPad to check the time difference. It was well after midnight in Australia; far too late to ring Casey when she'd have to be up for work in just a few hours.

When the kettle clicked off she jumped, but it wasn't just the kettle that startled her—it was her own thoughts. Love. Could that be what was happening? Could she be falling in love with Travis? Or was it simply a strong physical attraction? After all, she hadn't been intimate with anyone for over a year and a half. She craved his touch, wanting to feel his hands on her body again, but was that simply lust?

Staring out the window, she watched the wind fluttering the leaves on the gum trees across the street, remembering the day they'd ridden up through the park. Even that day, when sex was the furthest thing from her mind, she'd enjoyed his company. She'd enjoyed the ride, and helping to groom the horses afterwards. And then there'd been Denver's party—where she'd savoured the sensations as he'd pulled her in close while they'd danced.

Her eyes shot open. How could she even be questioning this ... of course she was falling in love with him.

~~*~~

Travis took the last bite of his eggs as Nick stumbled into the kitchen wearing nothing but a pair of jeans and a cheeky grin. He was glad Alex had gone before his good-looking cousin appeared.

'What's for breakfast,' Nick asked as he plonked himself down across from Travis.

'Whatever you want to make. I had eggs on toast, but there's plenty of milk and cereal if you prefer. Don't expect me to make anything for you.'

'Testy this morning. Didn't have a good night?'

Travis quirked a smile, not intending to give anything away. 'Testy? No. I'm just not a short-order cook. How was the dance?'

'You should have come. There were so many single ladies looking for a good time. Denver was in high demand—but I think I might have stepped on a few ladies' toes. You'd have cleaned up, with those dark moody looks of yours. The ladies always like the brooding types.'

Travis stood and walked around behind Nick, then smacked him on the back of the head—the same way he'd been doing since they were kids.

'Ouch.' Nick pulled a face as if it had hurt, but it was all an act.

'Who's testy now?' Travis headed over to the kettle and flicked it on. 'I'll make you a cup of coffee, but that's where I draw the line.'

'Have you got many more rodeos lined up over the next few months? Will you need me to do much more riding for you?'

'Doubt it. I made a couple of sales yesterday, and there's one being looked at today. That takes my stock numbers right down. Annie's here for the summer so I'd rather stick close to home and stay away from the rodeo scene.'

'That's good. Not that I mind going, you know that. I enjoy having an excuse to get back in the saddle.'

'Yeah, I know, and I appreciate it. So, how long are you planning to stick around?'

'I'll stay again tonight, and tomorrow night too, if that's okay with you? Stacy and I have some appointments on Tuesday ... then I'll head back home afterwards. I've got to be back at work on Wednesday.'

'That's fine,' Travis said as he made Nick's cup of coffee, wondering what sort of appointments Stacy and Nick would have, together, here in Masons Flat. 'Something for your parents, is it?'

Nick frowned for a moment. Then shrugged. 'Yeah ... they're thinking of moving into a retirement community—an expensive country club sort of place. Stacy and I just want to make sure we get all our ducks in a row. Nothing major, just a bit of forward planning—make sure they don't spend all our inheritance in one go.'

'They still own the main street properties, right? And the farm? I know it's not really any of my business, I'm only curious.'

'Yeah, it's okay. Stacy and Tim love running the farm and that's fine by me, because you know I was never interested in raising cattle. It'll probably go to them in the end anyway. But yeah, we need to sort out the logistics of everything else. Like, for example, there are a couple of houses just outside of town that may need to be sold, you know, that sort of thing.'

Travis walked up and handed him the cup of coffee. 'Well, let me know if there's anything I can do to help with any of it. I've got a pretty good brain for property matters—I had to learn quick-smart when Dad got sick.'

'Thanks for that—if I get stuck, I may very well ask for help.'

Before he could say any more, Denver walked in, rubbing his eyes and yawning. 'What are you getting stuck with? I'm pretty handy at most things, so don't feel like you've gotta pester Travis.'

Travis shook his head and made his way outside to start getting the horses ready for the day.

~~*~~

'She's much better, Alex,' Stacy said when Alex rang her.

'Oh, that's brilliant. I've been worried about her all night.'

'They both slept well, and had toast with strawberry jam for breakfast. So far they seem fine. I think it might have been a mixture of the corndogs and the cotton candy, not to mention the rides. Or it could have been a twenty-four-hour thing. Either way, I think Annie's fine if you want to head up to the frog jumping finals. I know how disappointed she'll be if she doesn't get to see them. And she also really wants to watch her father ride.'

'You're a better judge than I am, so if you think she's good to go, I'll come get her in about an hour.'

When they ended the call, Alex stood staring out the window again. Perhaps Annie was the key consideration in this budding romance. She and Travis were adults, and entering into a physical relationship that might end with one or both of them getting hurt was a decision each of them had to make. Allowing Annie to get her hopes up that they were going to be a couple, well, that wasn't something Alex was keen on. She'd have to give this more thought. Much more.

But not right now.

Right now, she wanted to shower, and change into a fresh pair of jeans and a clean shirt. She would enjoy the day and let the rest take care of itself.

Today was for Annie.

And as for tomorrow, well, tomorrow could be a totally different story.

CHAPTER 25

When Alex got home from the rodeo that evening, she rang Casey. She knew Casey was probably still at work but this couldn't wait.

'I'm glad you enjoyed the rodeo, and I think it's wonderful that you've found someone you're interested in, but it's a shame he didn't ask you to stay tonight as well,' Casey said, barely concealing her excitement.

'We had a wonderful day, but Annie was exhausted by the end of it—she probably hadn't slept well last night. And ... you know ... it was awkward; with his brother and his cousin right there with us the whole time we were talking.'

'Okay, I get that it might have been awkward, but sooner or later they'll find out, won't they?'

Alex swallowed hard, trying to sound positive. 'You don't think I should, you know, back off a bit?'

'Why?' Casey's frown came across clearly in her voice.

'Well, for one thing, he has this big ranch here in *California*. And he has an eight-year-old *daughter*. So I'm sure there's no way he would ever consider moving to Australia ... which would mean if we were to get serious, I'd have to stay here. And to be honest, I'm not sure I'm prepared to commit to staying here permanently.'

'Crikey Alex, do you hear yourself? Didn't you listen to anything I said last time? You like the man. And from the sound of it, he likes you too. Go with it. See what happens. Don't stop seeing him in case you *might* not want to live in California for the rest of your life. Live a little. Enjoy each day, because you never know if it'll be your last.'

'Wow, I know you're trying to be positive, but that actually sounds rather depressing.'

Casey grunted; frustration obvious in her voice. 'You know what I mean. Don't worry about what the others might think, and don't worry about forever. Enjoy his company.'

'You don't think that's selfish?'

'Selfish? Look, you've gotta look after yourself because no one else will. But I tell you what; I'd love to meet him. I'd like to see what kind of a man has gotten you, *Ms In-control-at-all-times Mason,* so rattled. He must be something special, that's all I can say.'

Alex took a deep breath. 'I knew I could count on you for stable, well-grounded love-life advice,' she said as Casey sniggered again.

'Do you want me to pick you up at the airport when you get in?'

'Yeah, sure. I'll email my flight details.'

'Cool. Now sorry to cut you off but I've gotta go. Get your beauty sleep, and make plans to see this cowboy of yours soon. He sounds like the kind of guy who'll get taken off the market if you don't let him know you're interested.'

Alex shook her head, still not entirely confident she was making the right decision, but she told Casey what she'd want to hear. 'I'll be seeing him Tuesday—tennis lesson, with his daughter.'

'Great. Why don't you suggest cooking him dinner at the weekend? Get a sitter lined up for his daughter so it's just the two of you.'

'Hmmm, that's not such a bad idea. I've always been able to cook a pretty presentable lamb roast.'

'Now you're talking. Men like meat. Feed him, and give him a couple of glasses of red, and then let him put his feet up in front of the telly. When he starts to nod off, you invite him to stay the night.'

Alex could feel the heat rising up her cheeks, and the tingle spreading across her entire body, just thinking about what it would be like to have Travis stay the night here, in her home.

Maybe ringing Casey hadn't been such a good idea after all—or had she gotten exactly the advice she'd wanted?

~~*~~

Monday disappeared in a blur of meetings, phone calls and ploughing through her uncle's files but on Tuesday morning, Alex popped into the saloon to check on the progress of the renovations. She was pleased to see Denver there.

'Hey Alex.' He gave her a big smile as he spotted her coming in.

She looked around, noting there was a tradesman working in the kitchen, another assessing the floors, and one of the barstools had been dismantled, all of which meant progress. 'Hi Denver—it's actions stations here for sure. And everything's looking great—what do you think?'

'I think it's all on schedule to be finished by the end of next week or maybe a day or two later. Here, let me show you around.'

Denver pointed out the work that still had to be completed, and by the time they'd gone over everything Alex was confident the saloon would be open before she left for Australia.

She started to leave, but then turned back to Denver. 'Are you hanging around?'

'No, I just wanted to check in.' Denver made a move toward the door, and Alex followed him. 'It's good they were able to get the floors started so quickly. This place won't know itself when all this work is done. Have you spoken to the employees with the good news?'

They were outside now, standing at the door. 'Yes, and they're all excited—especially Darleen. I said two weeks, but I'm hesitant to throw any sort of grand opening in case we miss the date.'

'You can organise that a day or two before. Trust me; word will spread quickly once the job is nearing completion. You put a sign on the door and everyone will come.'

She sighed, relieved to hear his vote of confidence. 'I really wanted it open before I go, so this is great news.'

'Go?' His face contorted into a frown.

'Yes, I have to go to a wedding ... in Australia. Please don't say anything to anyone yet. I want things to just tick along without the added pressure of that as a deadline. I also don't want to tell Annie until right before I go. She's enjoying the lessons, and I hate to disappoint her but there isn't anything I can do about it.'

'But you are coming back, after the wedding?'

She nodded. 'Of course.'

It was his turn to sigh with relief now, and he did so with the theatrics of a stage artist. 'Had me going there for a moment.'

She flashed him a cheeky smile. 'You'd miss me if I left, I take it?'

He threw his hands up in the air, spreading his arms wide. 'We'd all miss you—you're becoming one of us, for sure.'

She smiled, soaking up the sense of belonging. 'Speaking of me going ... I need someone to keep an eye on the saloon while I'm away, I don't suppose you've got any ideas? I was planning to chat to Sam, but if you've got any better suggestions I'd love to hear them.'

He spun around, nodding toward the hotel. 'Nah, Sam's your best bet. He knows everyone here in town, and he's well liked, but to be honest, Darleen knows what she's doing so I doubt he'd have much to do anyway.'

That was a relief. She'd pop in and see Sam before heading over for Annie's lesson. She had to remind herself that everything in town had managed for a long time before she'd arrived on the scene, and would no doubt manage just fine without her. She had to step back and stop being a control freak.

~~*~~

Travis stood staring at Annie while she finished her lunch. Afterwards, they headed out to the barn to finish cleaning the rest of the tack from the weekend. It didn't need to be done that moment, but it gave him a bird's eye view to watch for Alex who was due any time now.

He'd been thinking about Alex ever since he'd finished putting away all the horses after the rodeo and had a moment to himself. He'd gone to bed wishing she was there next to him. And then he'd thought about her all the next day as well. He'd been looking forward to seeing her today, without question, and yet something was making him uneasy. Something he couldn't put a finger on.

He looked down at Annie as she rubbed some oil into a bridle, her tiny fingers reminding him just how young and fragile she really was. Perhaps he had to lower Annie's expectations with regard to Alex, and perhaps his own in the process.

Picking up his rag, he grabbed another of the bridles and as he began rubbing it, he turned to Annie. 'You know, sweetheart, Alex may not be able to give you all that many more tennis lessons.'

A slight frown appeared on her face, making her look older than her eight years. 'What do you mean? Mom said she won't come get me until August. That's two whole months away. Alex can give me lots of lessons in two months.'

He drew in a breath, contemplating the best way to approach this. 'Yes, but remember when we were talking about Disneyland?'

She dropped the rag and put her hands on her hips. 'Sure, Dad, but what's that got to do with tennis lessons? That's not until Christmas.'

'I know, but do you remember why Alex said she hadn't ever been to Disneyland?'

Annie's frown deepened, and she chewed her lower lip. She was cute all the time, but particularly when she was concentrating. Eventually, she replied. 'Because she lives kazillions of miles away?'

He smiled, pleased she remembered. 'Well, maybe not quite that far, but that's exactly right, she lives a long way away.'

Annie rolled her eyes melodramatically, shaking her head. 'But that was *before* she moved here. She isn't far now. She showed me her house on Sunday. We drove right past it.'

'Yes, she's living there for the moment, but only temporarily. Like how you're living here with me now, for the summer. You'll go to Washington, and Alex will go back to Australia.'

Annie crossed her arms and shrugged. She was the spitting image of Karen when she did that. 'Yeah, okay, but not for a while, like ... not over the summer, right?'

He set the bridle down and picked up another. 'That I can't say, sweetheart. Alex hasn't said how long she's going to stay here.'

The sound of a car coming up the drive told him Alex had arrived. He dropped the bridle and rag onto the table as Annie raced ahead. As he walked up, Alex was reaching into the back seat for her bag, exposing a bit of skin as her shirt pulled with the stretch. Seeing her bare midriff sent pulses through him and made him wish she was arriving to see him rather than for Annie's tennis lesson.

With bag in hand, Alex tempted him further as she swung her long bare legs out of the car and stood up next to Annie. He wanted to kiss her, to run his hands down her back and pull her close. He wanted to whisk her off to his bedroom and repeat all the things he'd done with her Saturday night.

He wanted to do all of that, but of course he did none of it.

'Hi, Alex. Good to see you.' He kept his voice even and his hopes in check.

She smiled, but Annie spoke so she turned toward her, away from Travis.

'Alex, I missed you yesterday.' Annie threw her arms around her, giving her father a look of defiance as she peeked at him around Alex's side. 'I think we should have lessons four times a week—while we can.'

She'd heard everything he'd said to her, but Annie didn't want it to be true. She didn't want to lose Alex and she wasn't afraid to let her know it. He raised an eyebrow as he quirked a smile toward his daughter, then closed the car door.

'Four times a week,' Alex said, laughing. 'Wow, you'll get too good for me if we play that often.'

'No, I won't. I'll never serve as good as you until I grow at least another foot taller.' Annie grabbed Alex's hand and started to drag her off to the court. 'Are you coming to watch, Daddy? You should watch me—you'll be surprised at how good I'm getting. You've got time, right?'

He swallowed, grateful for Annie's invite. 'Sure thing, sweetheart, for a few minutes anyway. And for the record, nothing you achieve will ever surprise me.'

Alex looked down at Annie, then up at him through her lashes. He wondered if she had any idea of the effect she had on him, standing there, so scantily dressed, and looking at him that way. The thought of dragging her into his bedroom once again sent pulses through his whole body while chasing away the uncertainty that had plagued him earlier. Perhaps Annie didn't need to be protected from Alex's potential departure. Perhaps it was just his own feelings he needed to worry about.

'Well come on then.' Annie, who was already holding Alex's hand, grabbed his, and pulled the two of them around the side of the house toward the court.

CHAPTER 26

Alex could have ended the rally earlier but she was enjoying the improvement in Annie's ground strokes. When a movement in Alex's peripheral vision made her turn slightly, Annie took advantage of her loss of concentration and smashed the ball beyond her reach on the backhand side.

'Great shot, Annie,' Travis called out, clapping his hands slowly.

Alex turned toward him, shaking her head but grinning even so. 'Takes every opportunity I give her, that's for sure,' she replied to him before turning to Annie. 'I think this deserves a drink break, don't you?'

'You must have read my mind,' Travis said as he approached. 'Water, iced-tea or home-made lemonade; what takes your fancy?'

'Lemonade for me,' Annie replied as she made her way to sit on the partially shaded bench. 'But put some extra sugar in mine, please,' she added with a cheeky grin.

'Iced-tea sounds good to me, thanks.' Alex replied, turning back to him.

'Coming right up,' he said, heading back toward the house.

Alex walked to the bench to join Annie just as a deep frown darkened the young girl's face.

'Dad says you might not be staying here too long. He says you might be going back to Australia.' Her voice was flat, unfitting for a girl who was winning the tennis match.

Alex drew in a deep breath and exhaled it slowly. 'Yes, well, Australia is my home. When I first arrived, I was pretty sure it was going to be for a few weeks. Now, I'm not sure.'

Annie's tone softened. 'You like it here, don't you? Does that mean you might stay?'

Alex didn't want to give Annie false hope because as much as she did like it here, she also knew that when she got back home for the wedding the distance might give her a different perspective on things. She chewed her lip, trying to be diplomatic in her response. 'It's tricky, Annie. You see, all my family is there.'

179

'Do you have a big family, like I have Mom and Cody, and Dad, and Uncle Denver, and my cousins?'

'I don't have a huge family, but everyone is in Australia.'

'And that's kazillions of miles away.'

She grinned. 'It's a long way, yes. It took me almost a full day of travelling to get here—and most of that time was on a plane.'

Annie sighed, her face puckering up into a pout. 'I wish you could live here—all the time. Daddy seems much happier when you're around.'

She didn't know how to respond to Annie, but thankfully the sound of Travis returning saved her. As she turned to face him, and caught the look in his eye, the magnitude of Annie's words sunk in. He had changed. He was a different man to the one she'd met in the saloon on her first day in Masons Flat. He'd been abrupt, if she was kind, rude if she was feeling less than kind, but since then he'd become the epitome of a gentleman.

'Here you go, ladies,' he said as he set the drinks on the end of the bench.

Annie grabbed hers and drank almost half of it in a big gulp.

Travis scowled, chastising her. 'You'll get the hiccups if you drink that too quickly."

Alex picked up her glass and scooted over, making room if Travis wanted to sit, but he remained standing, watching the pair of them.

'So, who's winning anyway?' he asked.

'Annie's winning, just. She took the first set six to four, and we're three games each in the second set.'

'Am I winning? I thought you were just being nice.'

'You're definitely winning,' Alex said, with a toss of her head. 'But I am being nice. It wouldn't be fair if I served hard now would it, given our height difference?'

Annie giggled. Then her eyes flew open. 'If I win this set, that'll be two sets to love. Then you can play Daddy, and I'll be the umpire.'

Alex laughed, but Annie seemed serious.

'I mean it, Daddy, go change your shoes. I wanna see how good you are.'

'Me? I'm hopeless, you know that.'

Annie tilted her head and pulled a face. 'You afraid to play against a girl?'

Travis laughed. 'Alex is no girl. She's a woman, and an ex-professional tennis player. You just want to see me squirm, don't you?'

Annie giggled again. 'Yes. Go change your shoes.'

Travis shook his head, but when Annie glared at him, he gave in. 'Alright, alright, I'm going.'

As he walked off, Annie turned to Alex and whispered, 'This will be good. He's hopeless.'

As it turned out, he wasn't exactly hopeless, but his serves had nothing on hers. Annie not only umpired, but also took on the role of cheerleader, switching sides from time to time as she cheered good serves and returns. With the score five games to four and Alex serving for the set, she gave her shoulder a rub and gritted her teeth; playing through the pain she served as though her life depended on it.

Ace.

Annie jumped up and raced to the net. 'And the winner is ... Alex.' She grabbed Alex by the wrist and did her best to hold up her arm, like the umpires do with exhausted boxers, only the height difference made it a bit tricky.

'I told you I was hopeless,' Travis said, bending over with his hands on his knees, pretending to struggle to catch his breath.

Annie dropped Alex's hand and turned to her father. 'You played okay, Daddy. Just not good enough. Now you see why I want to keep having lessons with her, right? She's the best.'

He straightened up. 'Well, on that note, I think another cool drink has been earned. Let's go inside, out of the sun.'

They made their way into the kitchen, and the moment Annie disappeared to the bathroom Travis stepped up beside her and put one hand on her cheek, caressing it. 'You didn't have to go easy on me, you know.'

She leaned into his hand for a moment, and then stepped back. 'Easy on you? You're joking, right? That was quite a workout.'

He ducked his head around the corner, and she assumed he was checking to see if Annie was returning.

Then he leaned forward and snuck a quick kiss before heading to the fridge to pull out the drinks. She was about to make a smart-alecky comment when Annie reappeared.

'Can we have pizza for dinner?' Annie plonked herself at the table, and put on a brilliant smile as she said, 'Uncle Denver's gone out so it's just us, and pizza's my favourite.'

'Pizza? I don't think we have any in the freezer, but since it's now your favourite, I'll make sure to buy some next time I shop.'

'No, I mean real pizza, from a pizza parlour.'

'In Masons Flat? Have you seen a pizza parlour in town that I missed?'

Annie pouted, and dropped her head down onto her folded arms.

Alex looked at Travis and shrugged her shoulders. 'Well ... I can try to make us one. That is, if you've got the right ingredients.'

Annie looked up, her eyes wide with awe. 'You can make a real pizza?'

'I can try. And you can help me, if you want.'

Travis walked over to the fridge and pulled out some fresh tomatoes, a huge block of cheddar cheese, a small packet of parmesan cheese and some sliced ham. Then, from the pantry, he grabbed two containers of flour, a bottle of dried oregano, another of basil and salt and pepper.

'Ham and cheese pizza do you, Annie?'

Her eyes said it all, but even so she answered. 'Yes, please.'

~~*~~

As Travis watched Alex and Annie, heads down, stirring the ingredients to make the dough, memories of his mother floated back. This house hadn't been the same since she'd passed on, and now here was Alex, in his mother's kitchen, teaching his daughter to cook. If felt natural, and something told him his mother would be happy to see the two of them together.

Could he imagine Alex staying? Why would she? He'd read up on Melbourne the night before—universal health care, strong gun controls, weather similar to California's, and it had been named the World's Most Liveable City several times. How could Masons Flat compete?

Yet the look on Alex's face as she helped Annie knead the dough suggested a strong connection developing between them. Was it strong enough to coax her to stay? Was he foolish to hope she might decide to make this her home?

His mind wouldn't stop spinning. What had happened to his resolve to keep his life simple? Didn't that mean working this ranch, looking after the household and their various properties in town? Didn't all that keep him busy enough between visits with Annie? He'd been satisfied with the new definition of his life, hadn't he?

Of course he had, until Alex Mason arrived on the scene.

Her arrival in town—the arrival of a Mason—had revived the feud he'd hoped was buried along with Old Man Mason, but it'd done so much more than that. It had woken up feelings he'd been happier without.

'It should taste better than it looks,' Alex said, pulling his attention back to the present. She and Annie were placing slices of ham onto the base, and smothering them with cheese. Perhaps she'd mistaken the look on his face for criticism of the pizza.

'It doesn't look bad, not bad at all—far better than anything I'd have been able to do.'

When she smiled, his heart skipped a beat.

'I'll go set the table,' he said, excusing himself so that he could clear his head. He had to keep things casual—it was best for everyone that way.

After they'd finished dinner, he'd sent Annie up to get ready for bed while he and Alex cleaned up the kitchen. When Annie returned, Travis agreed they could watch a bit of television together before she had to go to bed.

Sitting on the sofa, Annie, who'd insisted on sitting in the middle, took turns looking up at him and then at Alex. Annie said nothing, but even in silence he suspected he knew what she was thinking. When she finally began to nod off, he picked her up and carried her to her room.

When he returned, Alex was sitting on the edge of the sofa fiddling with her keys.

'Are you leaving?' he asked, not sure what he wanted her answer to be.

'I probably should get going.' She continued to play with the keys, pulling them around on the ring, looking as uncomfortable as he felt.

'You don't have to rush off just because Annie's gone to bed.' He sat beside her, and turned slightly so he could look at her.

Alex sighed as she slid back on the sofa, still looking less than relaxed. 'Okay ... yeah, sure.' She hesitated for a moment, and then started talking about Annie. 'Her tennis has really improved—I can see a lot of potential in her, especially if she continues with lessons once she goes back to school.'

He looked at her, one side of him grateful that she'd chosen a safe topic, but the other side of him already feeling the loss of what might have been. He drew a deep breath before continuing on the same line of conversation. 'Weren't you letting her win?'

'No. Well I suppose I wasn't serving it as hard as I could, but each time I challenged her, she stepped up to it. I'm not kidding about her potential, if she keeps playing.'

'I'll certainly tell Karen—maybe there'll be some sort of club or something she can join at her new school.'

When Alex turned to face him, her eyes were flashing. 'Will it mean you see less of her, with them moving up to Washington?'

He cocked his head, thinking. 'Guess that depends on their school vacations. I'll still have her here for the summer each year, until she gets bored or finds a boyfriend who's more interesting than her father.'

'Hopefully that won't be for a few years.'

When she huffed out a breath, he wondered if what he'd said had brought back memories of her own youth. He sighed. 'She's growing up so fast; it seems like yesterday that she was learning to walk. You haven't mentioned any children, so I take it you haven't left any behind when you came over here?'

As sadness washed over her face, he regretted his question. 'No, we ... my ex-husband and I ... had I mentioned I'm divorced? Anyway, we hadn't ever felt ready to start a family ... and then ... well, it's just as well, given how things turned out. But I love kids. I loved coaching, and working with Annie has been marvellous. It's brought back so many good memories.'

Warmth washed through him with the realisation that Alex was exactly the kind of woman he'd hoped Karen would have become— only she never had. Karen had never lost her need for excitement, never wanted to give up the barrel racing. Getting her to stop while she was pregnant had been hard enough, but once Annie was born, she'd gone straight back to her old life, happy to leave him at home to care for their young daughter while she traipsed off to rodeos. Somehow, he doubted Alex would have behaved that way—doubted she was quite as much of a sporting-world prima-donna as Karen had been.

Just thinking the phrase made him cringe, remembering who Alex was ... or at least who he'd thought she must have been. Had he been wrong about her?

'When you get home, will you start up coaching again?' There. He'd done it. He'd opened up the conversation about the future. It was probably more abrupt than he'd intended, but at least it was out there.

She blinked hard and cleared her throat. 'When I get home ... yes, well, it's something I need to turn my mind to, that's for sure. This inheritance came out of the blue, and I guess I still haven't gotten my head around it yet.'

A frown tightened his forehead as incredulity swept over him. 'Out of the blue?'

'My father never said anything about it, and my mother—she's hopeless when it comes to anything financial—she seemed as surprised about it as I was.'

It seemed unbelievable that she could not have known about her inheritance. But if it was true, she was even more likely to sell everything and go home. She'd have no sense of connection to the town or its history, so why would she stay? He was a fool to allow himself to imagine she might.

He coughed, then stood and cleared his throat. 'I need some water. Can I get you anything?'

She shook her head almost imperceptibly. 'No thanks.'

As soon as he was out of her view in the kitchen, he put his hands on the edge of the sink and ducked his head down, trying to clear his mind. He couldn't deny the physical attraction—his desire to take her to his room and make love to her again was strong—but he also knew there were a lot of reasons not to. Not the least of which was that he was even more certain now that she'd sell everything and leave. And she still hadn't said anything about the offer he and Denver had made for the saloon. Was she intending to use their offer as leverage to get a better offer from someone else?

He grabbed a glass and turned on the tap, letting the cold water overrun the glass and pour across his hand. Then he set the glass down, cupped his hands letting the water fill them, and then leant down and splashed it onto his face. He'd been an idiot to let his desire for Alex override his common sense. She was here to sell the property, and when that was done she'd be gone.

When he walked back into the living room she was standing again, with her phone in her hand.

She looked at him, and smiled tentatively. 'I suppose I really should get going ...'

He swallowed hard, allowing her words to reinforce the decision he'd pretty much already made, and forcing his desires back down where they belonged.

'I'll walk you to your car,' he said, moving away from her as he led the way to the front door.

~~*~~

As she walked toward the door, Alex couldn't help but wonder what had changed. Had she said something that upset Travis? Up until he left to get a glass of water, she'd been certain he was going to suggest she stay the night again. She'd wanted to stay. She'd even come prepared, with an overnight bag in the car. She knew it was terribly awkward with Annie being there—it would be embarrassing if she woke during the night and went looking for her father and found them together. But even so, he could have said he wanted her to stay but thought it might be best to leave that for another night.

She yearned for his touch as he opened the door and held it for her to pass through. And as he followed her to the car, she desperately wanted to stop, and lean back into him. She wanted to ask if he'd like her to stay—wanted to know if he shared her desires—but she just couldn't bring herself to do it.

When they reached her car she stopped just short of opening the door. He stepped past her, and opened it for her. She turned, hoping he'd kiss her goodnight, but when he made no move toward her, she climbed in, pulled the door shut and started the car. She rolled down the window and smiled up at him, waiting without speaking until he leaned over and gave her a quick kiss through the window. When he stepped back rejection tore through her like a knife.

Tears burned behind her eyes as she nodded. 'Goodnight then.'

He looked over his shoulder for a moment, but he didn't walk away. Hope sprung from deep within her—hope that he'd changed his mind.

He reached in and put his hand on her shoulder, then leant down for another kiss—a kiss that said what his words hadn't.

As he pulled back from her, he met her gaze. 'I wish things weren't so ... complicated.'

She blinked slowly, trying not to sigh. He was right. There were so many factors to take into account—it wasn't just two people connecting and wanting to spend time together. 'Me too.'

His lips were in a tight grimace as he stepped back, once again tipping the hat he wasn't wearing. She smiled, and put the car in gear, wishing she wasn't leaving but knowing she had to.

She replayed their final moments on the short drive home. He'd wanted her to stay—it was obvious from his kiss—but he was right when he used the word complicated. Annie's feelings had to be considered. Becoming romantically involved wasn't a smart move, even if her body believed otherwise.

As she pulled up at her house, she remembered there'd been a missed call from a number she didn't recognise. To take her mind off Travis, if only for a moment, she pulled her phone out and rang her voicemail.

CHAPTER 27

Alex recognised the deep voice immediately. It was the man doing the quote for the refrigeration units.

'I just wanted to let you know I did all the measurements, and I left the key back with Sam like you said. I'll send my quote over to Denver. The units I'm proposing are in stock, so there won't be any delays if you decide to go ahead with it.'

The good news was uplifting—especially given how things were left with Travis. She checked the time and decided a call to Casey might also be uplifting. Casey was usually good at taking her to a happier place.

Casey didn't even say hello, jumping right in where they'd left off. 'Have you set a date for when you're cooking dinner for your cowboy?'

Alex grimaced, but kept it from her voice. 'I already did. Tonight.'

'Really? Is he there now? If so, why are you on the phone to me?'

'No, I made a pizza at his house ... with his daughter's help.'

'I thought we agreed the plan was for you to invite him to your place?' Impatience laced Casey's voice.

'Yeah, well, the opportunity hasn't come up yet.'

'But wouldn't tonight have been the perfect opportunity to invite him for a *proper* meal at your place?'

'I suppose. I didn't think of that.'

'Let me rephrase that for you ... you chickened out.'

Alex paused before answering. Was Casey right? Was her concern for Annie just an excuse because she was afraid of getting hurt again?

'He said things are *complicated*. And he didn't ask me to stay the night.'

'Wow, you two are a match made in heaven if there ever was one—you're both really overthinking this. How can you and I even be sisters?'

Harsh, but true. Alex had always known she was the serious one, while Casey and Taylor were the carefree risk takers. Time to change the subject.

'Have you bought a new outfit for Summer's wedding?'

Casey huffed out a breath. 'Yes, but we weren't finished talking about your cowboy. What's the real reason you didn't invite him to dinner?'

She drew in a long breath and let it out slowly. 'I think it would be best if I hold off getting more involved until we make a few big decisions ... like what we're doing with the properties. And I need to think about what it would mean to live here. Masons Flat is such a small town—I'm not sure I'm cut out for it.'

'Well, come back then. Sell everything, bring back the cash, and set up your coaching business here. You've been wanting to do that for years. Now's your chance. I mean ... if you don't want to stay there in California.'

'I didn't say I don't want to ... I just said I'm not sure.'

'Exactly. So why not explore this relationship while you're making up your mind. Look, I'm not trying to talk you into staying there. You're the only one who can decide if it's what you want, but what an opportunity, especially now, when you don't even have a job to worry about coming back to. And besides, you don't have to live in Masons Flat. You can live in Sacramento, or San Francisco.'

Maybe Casey had a point. Maybe she didn't have to live in Masons Flat if she decided to stay. Still, why stay in California at all if she wasn't going to live here? Something about the upcoming wedding niggled at the edges of her memory. 'Summer's wedding is in a small town, isn't it?'

'Yeah, Willows—north of the city. Why?'

'What's it like?'

'I haven't been up there, but Taylor said it's a cute town ... quaint.'

'I wonder what Summer thinks of living in a small town.'

'She grew up in woop woop somewhere, so it probably doesn't feel small to her. But seriously, you don't have to live in Masons Flat. The question is, do you want to live in California, or do you want to come back to Melbourne?'

And that was exactly the question—one she couldn't answer yet. She liked what she'd seen of Masons Flat so far, and the people all seemed nice even though she only knew most of them casually. Well, perhaps some a bit more than casually, but did she want to stay? 'I think I need to sleep on it—weigh up the alternatives.'

'Yeah, that makes sense. Think on it. Anyway, I watered your plants the other day, and I've gone through your mail. There's nothing urgent on this end. Come home for the wedding, and see how you feel. If you decide not to go back I'm sure the accountant and lawyer would be happy to handle everything. You know Taylor and I will support whatever you decide. Sleep on it, and give me a call in a few days. In the end, you really need to do what's right for you.'

After they ended the call, Alex poured a glass of wine and curled up on the sofa to watch the last of an old movie. Could she see herself living here, doing this every night? Or did she only want to stay because she could see herself sitting on Travis' sofa, snuggled up with both him and Annie?

~~*~~

After a long run, Alex spent the morning continuing to go through her uncle's files. By two-thirty she had more numbers spinning around in her head than she'd ever dreamed she'd have to worry about.

She had a quick shower then gave Denver a call, and they made plans to meet at the vacant shop.

He pulled out the plans, and walked her through the drawings that were now complete with the refrigeration units.

'Everything looks great to me, Denver. Let's do it.'

'Great. I should be able to get all the work done while you're away, so you can open up as soon as you're back. By the way ... you didn't change your mind about telling Annie about your trip, did you?'

'No, I still want to leave it until right before I go. Why?'

'Oh, it's nothing, really ... just she and Travis both seemed a bit down this morning. I thought you must have changed your mind and told them.'

'No, not yet.'

'Must have been something else then. Or maybe it's just me finding it hard to keep a secret,' he said while giving her a crooked grin.

'I'll only be gone for two weeks. Perhaps I should go ahead and tell her.'

'No, stick to what you originally thought. If you tell her now it'll feel like you're gone twice as long.' He smacked his hand to his forehead.

'Gees, I just realised, she'll probably pester me to play tennis with her while you're away.'

Alex raised an eyebrow. 'Is that a problem? My guess would be you'd be good at any sport you turned your mind toward.'

Denver winked. 'Maybe. Anyway, I'll go ahead and order everything, and get started as soon as I can.'

She thought for a moment, wondering if she should hold off to make certain she even wanted to return after the trip, but the shop was the right answer for the town even if she didn't run it herself.

'That'd be great, thanks Denver.'

'Are you giving Annie another lesson tomorrow?'

'Yes, unless I hear otherwise.'

'Guess I'll probably see you tomorrow then.'

As she drove home, Alex couldn't help but wonder if the moodiness Denver had witnessed was her fault. Maybe Travis had wanted her to stay last night. Maybe, if she'd given him a bit of encouragement, he would have suggested it. Then again, maybe his mood had nothing to do with her.

She pulled into the driveway, got out and stood staring at the beautiful home. There were a lot of things to like about Masons Flat, but maybe it would be best for everyone if she were to wrap things up here and head back home, for good.

CHAPTER 28

When Alex gave Annie her lesson the following day, Travis was nowhere to be seen. She knew he must be around the property somewhere as Denver's truck was gone, and she knew Travis wouldn't leave Annie there on her own.

But he never surfaced.

Nor did she see him any of the other times she gave Annie lessons over the following week.

Then again, it wasn't helped by the fact that the moment she and Annie finished each lesson Alex found an excuse to dash off. Between the works going on in town, the meetings with the bookkeeper and the estate agents, and the mountain of files in her uncle's study that she still hadn't completely waded through, there was always something to attend to.

But that's all any of those things were; excuses—reasons to avoid Travis.

And on the days that she didn't see Annie, she kept busy by being a tourist. She spent a full day in San Francisco, lunching at the famous Fisherman's Wharf and taking an excursion out to Alcatraz, a full day at an outlet mall, and another full day exploring a few of the Napa Valley wineries. There was plenty to see in California that didn't involve Travis Gold.

But as busy as she kept herself, she didn't stop thinking about him. Nor did she stop wondering if he was doing the same thing—finding excuses to be busy because it was far easier to avoid her than to deal with *complications*.

~~*~~

Two days before the saloon was to re-open, Alex met with Darleen Clarke, the assistant manager. Alex liked her the moment she set eyes on her. In her mid-fifties, with auburn hair and green eyes not dissimilar to her own, Darleen commanded respect with both her height and demeanour, and Alex left their first meeting entirely comfortable that Darleen would be capable of managing the saloon in her absence.

On the night of the opening, Darleen stood beside her at the door. They greeted people as they entered, ensuring everyone got to meet the new owner, and taking the opportunity to let everyone know beer was on-the-house until eight.

A few minutes after eight, Alex had abandoned the front door, and had nearly given up hope that Travis would appear when she heard his voice. She turned, and there he was, standing at the front door beside Denver. When he caught her eye and nodded, Alex's heart thumped wildly.

Denver raised a hand and yelled out to her. 'Hey, Alex, looking good!'

She put on a smile as he approached with outstretched arms.

'Place looks terrific; and the locals don't look too upset about having their watering-hole back,' he said as he gave her a hug and then stepped back.

'Yes, I'm over the moon with the turnout, and with getting to meet so many new people. This isn't the normal sort of numbers for a weeknight, is it?' She did her best to speak normally, but it was hard with a thumping heart.

Denver scanned the room. 'You might have close to this many on a Saturday night ... maybe half on a weekday.'

Travis walked up, stopping a few feet from Alex. 'Congratulations on getting the place open in good time. Looks great—love the floors.'

'Thanks, Travis. It's all come together quite well hasn't it? Mind you, I couldn't have done it without Denver's help. Now, can I get you both a drink? My shout.'

'Sounds like a great idea—I'll go get them.' Denver patted Travis on the back before excusing himself to head to the bar.

Alex could feel the heat in her face as she stood there, staring down at Travis' boots, struggling for something to say. Finally, he broke the silence. 'So, how've you been? Busy, I take it.'

She looked up into his eyes, trying to read them. He appeared to be sincere; she'd detected no hint of sarcasm. 'Yes, well, you know ... trying to get the fruit and veggie shop organised as well as this place ... and going through all my uncle's papers. Everything seems to take longer than you think it will.'

'Yes, I know the feeling.' He looked toward the bar, and she followed his gaze to see that Denver still had his back to them, waiting to be served. They wouldn't be saved by his presence in a hurry.

'And you? You've been busy? I haven't seen you when I've been over for Annie's lessons.'

He raised an eyebrow and shrugged. To a stranger his gesture might have appeared the epitome of nonchalance, but she wasn't necessarily buying it.

'Yeah, I've been trying to bring that injured filly back into some gentle work—she's healing up quicker than we'd hoped. And you know it never ends with horses. Selling a few of the young ones at the rodeo was great, but there are a dozen more coming up to replace them, plus my stallion always needs work.'

She smiled, mostly because both his voice and his words betrayed him—he was nervous, and discovering that calmed her a bit.

'Well, at least you love what you do. Makes a difference, doesn't it? I loved working at the tennis club. I never minded the long hours and extra weekend work.'

Now he grinned and his edges softened. 'I'm lucky that way—I get tired, physically, but I always love what I'm doing, even when I'm exhausted.'

Denver came up then, with a beer in each hand. 'Sorry, Alex, didn't even think to ask if you wanted anything.'

'Oh, I'm right—I'm on my best behaviour tonight, being the new owner and everything. I'm glad you could make it, but I suppose I should get back to mingling.'

Travis nodded. 'It was good seeing you, Alex. I'm glad this is working out so well for you.'

As she walked off, Denver gave her a big cheeky smile and a wink. Travis smiled, but his was laced with something else; regret perhaps? But regret that he'd been avoiding her, or regret that it was her re-opening the saloon, and not him and Denver? She hoped it was the former, but it was impossible to say for sure.

She shook off her thoughts and made her way over to the bar while Denver and Travis headed toward the pool table.

She kept one eye on Travis for the rest of the night, but didn't speak to him again other than a mouthed goodbye from a distance when she spotted him and Denver leaving. Even so, she was glad he'd come. She was grateful she'd had the chance to speak to him casually and had survived the encounter—if only on the surface.

~~*~~

Tuesday was the final lesson with Annie before she was to leave for Melbourne, so this time Alex allowed Annie to coax her into the kitchen for a cool drink, thinking it might be easier to tell her while they were chatting at the kitchen table.

Once seated, she dove in. 'Annie, remember how we talked about my family all being in Australia?' She took a sip of the tea, giving Annie a moment to reply.

'Sure, I remember.'

'Well, one of my sister's, actually my step-sister, is getting married.'

Annie took a drink, her face suggesting she was thinking hard. 'That's nice.'

'And I've been invited to her wedding.'

Annie set her glass back down on the table and clapped her hands excitedly. 'Oh, that'll be fun. Will she wear a long dress and have lots of flowers?'

Alex whooshed out a loud breath, pleased with Annie's reaction. 'That's a good question. I assume she'll wear a long dress and carry flowers, but some weddings are very different so I can't say for sure. What I can do is take some photos to show you. Would you like that?'

'Cool.' Annie's face puckered up as she chewed her lower lip. 'Is the wedding in Australia?'

'Yes, it is.'

Now she frowned. 'Will you be gone long?'

'About two weeks? Is that long?'

Annie tilted her head, and then shrugged. 'I guess not, although I will miss my lessons. I'll just have to play with Daddy. Or maybe Uncle Denver, if I promise not to thrash him.'

When Annie giggled Alex let out a loud sigh, wishing she hadn't waited so long to tell her. Annie was taking it far better than she'd expected. She gave Annie a conspiratorial wink. 'He's that bad, is he? Should I pretend I don't know?'

'No, he's better than Daddy, I just like to tease him.' She giggled again and slapped her hand over her mouth so as not to laugh too hard.

'What are you two laughing about?'

Alex hadn't heard him approach, but Travis now stood in the open doorway smiling at his daughter. When Alex met his gaze, his eyes were dark and questioning.

'I was telling Alex that I can only talk Uncle Denver into playing tennis with me if I promise not to thrash him.'

Travis turned to Alex. 'That sounds about right.'

Alex stood, shrugged her shoulders and made a feeble excuse about having to leave to get home to water the garden.

Annie glared at her. 'You should stay and have dinner with us. You can water when you get home.' Annie stood too, then grabbed Alex's hand and tugged her out the back door, making her sit at the outdoor table. 'I'll get you some more iced-tea. Daddy's going to cook hamburgers on the barbeque tonight.'

Alex looked up toward Travis, who had followed them out. 'Only if I'm not intruding?'

Annie grinned, and Travis smiled. 'You're definitely not intruding. Hamburgers it is. Guess I better make a start.'

Travis turned and went back inside, followed by Annie. By the time Annie returned with the iced-tea Alex could hear Travis banging away in the kitchen.

Over dinner, Annie told Alex all about the filly she'd started riding— the one who'd been injured. Annie was allowed to ride her in the arena, so long as she kept her at the walk. 'I can ride her every day if you want me to, Daddy. With Alex away, I won't be able to play as much tennis after all.'

He turned and looked at her questioningly. 'You're going away?'

'Yes. My step-sister's getting married.'

He frowned, his dark eyes growing even darker. 'When are you leaving?'

'I fly out Thursday evening.'

Annie looked back and forth between them for a moment before speaking up. 'It takes a whole day to get there, Dad. It's a long flight.'

'Yes, Annie, I remember Alex saying that.' Then he turned to her, the frown still present. 'But you're coming back?'

She smiled as she gave a slight nod. 'Yes, I'm just going for two weeks. I'd forgotten about the wedding when I made the arrangements to come here or I might have waited until after.'

His frown eased a little. 'Do you need a lift to the airport? I could take you.'

His offer surprised her, but then she decided he was probably just being polite. 'Thank you, but I wouldn't want to put you out like that. I've got everything organised.'

'Are you sure?'

'Yes, but thanks for offering.'

'Okay. So ... Thursday.' He nodded, the deep furrows returning.

'I leave here on Thursday but I don't actually arrive until Saturday morning their time. It's that pesky International Date Line. Anyway, that gives me a couple of days to hang out with my sisters and catch up with some friends. And I need to do some shopping. I don't have anything suitable to wear to the wedding—and I'll need to find a gift if I don't find anything in Sacramento.' She was rambling; even she could hear the nervous twang in her voice.

She was desperate to ease her nerves, so she turned and gave Annie a silly wide-eyed look. Annie giggled and rolled her eyes. She hated that she was nervous around him. After all, he couldn't possibly care. Sure, she'd been avoiding him, but he'd made it easy by never being around. He was probably glad she was going so he didn't have to pretend to be so busy all the time.

He stood and took their plates into the kitchen. When he returned, he brought out three bowls of orange sorbet.

'Hope you like sherbet.' He set a bowl down in front of her, making eye contact as he did.

'It's my favourite,' Annie said as she dug into hers. 'If you don't like it I could always finish it for you.'

Twenty minutes later, Annie returned from having gone to brush her teeth and get ready for bed. Both Alex and Travis stood, and Annie went up first to give her father a big hug and kiss, then came over and did the same with Alex.

'Don't forget I want to see the wedding. Here's our email address ... so you can send me some photos.' She set a bit of paper on the table, covered with her childish writing. The email address was Golds Ranch.

Alex smiled. 'I won't forget. Goodnight, Annie,' she said as Annie sulked off to bed.

Now alone on the back porch, they stood facing each other. Travis looked as uncomfortable as Alex felt. Annie had been a fabulous buffer and her absence changed everything.

Travis finally spoke. 'So ... you're going home.'

'Yes, well ... for a little while.' She stopped short of saying what was in her heart—that she'd been questioning whether going back to Melbourne was actually going *home*. After all, this was where she was born. 'It'll be nice to see my family.'

'I'm sure you've missed them. And the excitement of living in a big city. Masons Flat isn't exactly a cultural mecca, now is it?'

She nodded, feeling a slight frown pull at her temples. 'No, but I'm not someone who needs to go to the opera or ballet every weekend, either. Although a real pizza from time to time is sure nice.' Her attempt at humour lightened the mood, but it was only temporary.

They were both silent after that, and Alex was about to start walking, but then he cleared his throat.

He let out a sigh, his words coated with sadness. 'Sometimes I wonder if it's all worth it—trying to keep this town alive.'

She cocked her head, unsure what had brought on his melancholy. Sure, Masons Flat couldn't be compared to San Francisco or Melbourne, but it had its own charms, even if it didn't have a pizza parlour.

'Sam assures me this is normal for this time of year. That when the school year finishes and the weather gets warmer, tourists will start coming through again. And of course with the saloon back open, things are sure to improve, right?'

'Theoretically, but the hardware store is barely in the black, and the jeweller isn't exactly being run off his feet with customers. Sam's lucky—people like to eat out so both the hotel and the steak house do okay.' He then let out a loud sigh and changed the subject. 'What time would it be there now? In Australia, I mean.'

She looked up, thinking. 'A bit past mid-day. I generally ring my sisters in the evenings—or even late at night. Any time before mid-afternoon is dicey—they do like their beauty sleep.'

'I'll keep it in mind—if I ever have to ring anyone there, that is.' When he followed up his words with a smile, she relaxed a bit.

She toyed with the idea of reaching out to him. A gentle touch of his forearm. But it would be a disaster, no matter how he reacted. If he pulled away, she'd die of embarrassment. If he didn't, she'd be even more confused than ever. 'I suppose I really should be going. I have a lot to do over the next couple of days, you know, packing and paying accounts and ... packing.'

He turned, moving his arm behind her but stopping just short of touching her. 'I'll walk you out.'

She stepped off the deck onto the grass, and they walked around the side of the house toward her car. When she stopped, she didn't need to turn to know he was right behind her—his breath teased the back of her neck. She hesitated for a moment, desperately wanting to turn around and throw her arms around him, but torn with indecision. She closed her eyes, remembering Casey's words—she was thinking too much. Always. Maybe now was a good time to stop.

When she turned, her face was only inches from his chest. She looked up at him, giving him a half-smile as she swallowed hard, forcing herself to speak. 'I've missed you these past few days. I'm ... sorry I dashed off every time I was here.'

'And I've missed you. I just ... I don't know, I guess it seemed easier to stay away from you.'

He reached out and stroked her cheek—his touch almost featherlike. And that's all it took. She sighed, and melted into him.

~~*~~

He'd never wanted any woman as much as he wanted Alex at this moment. He'd been lying to himself, telling himself he neither needed nor wanted a woman in his life—especially not a Mason woman. And he'd used every other excuse he could think of to avoid spending time around her.

But he couldn't lie to himself any longer.

He wanted her, even if it was only for the night, or the summer. Even if she was a Mason. And even if she would never sell him the saloon.

He stroked her cheek, staring into her eyes, hoping his feelings came across without the need for words. He leant down, and kissed her; gently at first, almost teasingly, hoping for a response.

Relief washed through him as his hopes were answered. Her lips met his with naked desire—her tongue teasing his mouth.

A rush of blood pulsed through his veins. He could bury his feelings no longer.

He wrapped his arms around her and lifted her off her feet, then took one step sideways and set her down on the hood of her car. His hands went to the sides of her face, her legs wrapped around him. She pulled him closer, and then her hands slid up the front of his shirt.

Every molecule inside him wanted her, and her response told him she wanted him too.

His kisses grew urgent, hard, probing. She responded, gasping for breath as her hands slipped around behind him and pulled him even closer.

He was at the point of no return.

She was encouraging him.

But he couldn't carry her inside with Annie there.

Or could he?

Annie loved Alex. Sure, she'd be hurt if everything fell in a heap—if Alex turned out to be more like Karen after all—but was fear of what might happen in the future worth foregoing the present?

He pulled back, drawing in loud breaths as he stared into her eyes. The flecks of gold flashed, and she smiled. 'Will you stay? We'll need to be quiet—because of Annie—but I want you to stay.'

On the exhale of a breath came the words he longed for. 'I'll be as quiet as a mouse.'

CHAPTER 29

Alex woke in her own bed to the sound of her phone vibrating on the bedside table. A smile turned up the corners of her mouth, and her heart thumped. It would be Travis ringing to ask why she'd snuck out during the night—or perhaps even to apologise for having fallen asleep. They hadn't really talked much, after all. They'd barely had time to draw breath, let alone form words.

Thinking about him being on the other end of the phone made her tingle from head to toe, yearning for the kisses and touches she'd enjoyed only hours earlier, wanting to hear his voice, to hear him say again that he'd miss her while she was away.

As she held the phone up close, she blew out a breath of disappointment. It wasn't Travis' name that appeared. She slid the answer button across, staring blankly at the screen.

'Alex? Good morning, it's Ben Thompson. Hope it's not too early to call?'

'Good morning, Ben. No, it's not too early. Have you got good news for me?'

'Yes, but perhaps not what you might be expecting. There's a developer who wants to have a look at a number of your properties.'

'Sorry?' She sat up now, rubbing the sleep from her eyes.

'I know, it's early and I apologise, but I did try reaching you yesterday, but you never answered. Anyway, I hope you're free this morning? He said he wants to meet us at nine fifteen ... hence my early call.'

Alex jumped up and ran a hand through her hair, not entirely certain what Ben meant. 'And he wants me to be there?'

'Yes, he specifically said he wanted to meet with the owner. Said he preferred dealing directly with owners. It's somewhat unusual, but not entirely unheard-of.'

'Well, okay then, if you think I should be there.'

'Might be worth it, if you've got the time.'

It was the last thing she wanted to do, but it could be worth hearing what the man had to say. 'Yeah, that's fine. I'll see you shortly.'

~~*~~

Alex pulled up in front of the saloon and immediately spotted Ben's car. She parked and started walking down the street toward the vacant shops, and sure enough found Ben inside with a stocky grey-haired man.

'Ah, there you are Alex, thanks for coming in.'

The grey-haired man stepped up and extended his hand. 'Paul Kelly, Ms Mason. Nice to meet you.'

She reached for his extended hand, and then instantly regretted her politeness when he grasped her hand and clasped his other hand over the top in a most patronising gesture.

She bit back a snarky remark as she wriggled free from his grasp.

'Yes, nice to meet you, I'm sure. Ben says you wanted to see me personally?'

Paul gave her a smarmy smile. 'Yes, I find it's much easier to deal directly with property owners—eliminates the chance of misunderstandings and miscommunications.'

She was surprised by the implication that Ben was inept. She glanced at Ben, but he seemed unperturbed.

'How can I help you?'

'You can do me the honour of listening to my proposal, that's what you can do. Now, Mr Thompson, would you mind terribly if I spoke to Ms Mason alone?'

She turned to face Ben in time to see him wipe a wry smile off his face. 'By all means. Alex, I'll give you a call a bit later today.'

She turned back to Paul and shrugged as mistrust bubbled up in her. 'Sure—I'm happy to listen to whatever you have to say, but I'll probably want to speak to my agent before making any final decisions.'

'Yes, yes of course you will. Now, let's walk, shall we?'

He stepped back, allowing her to walk out onto the sidewalk ahead of him. Ben followed, locking the door behind them before crossing the road and heading back to his car.

Alex fell in beside Paul, keeping a reasonable distance between them as they meandered down the street toward the saloon. Eventually Paul cleared his throat.

'I understand you're not from here ... that you live in Australia. Is that right?'

'Yes. I've only recently arrived but I'm finding it very comfortable here. I like the town.'

He turned, looking back in the direction they'd just come. 'It is a pleasant sort of town, but it's got nothing on Melbourne. You're from Melbourne, right?'

'Yes. Have you been there?'

'A few years ago—it's a lovely city.'

'It is, but Masons Flat is lovely too—it's got character.'

'Oh, I agree, I agree. Or at least, it could have ... if it weren't for having so many vacant shops. It's heading toward being a ghost town, like so many other little towns that don't have any significant industry or job opportunities.'

She squinted as protective instincts kicked in. 'Things will pick up over the summer months.'

'I understand. Was it busy here in town while the county fair was on?'

'The hotel was full. Sam did well with both lodging and meals.'

'That's good. And what about these vacant shops? Have you had any interest in yours from having the extra traffic here in town?'

'Not as such, although I'm planning to set up a business in one of them.'

He nodded, but his frown suggested something more like disbelief. 'Yes, well, as I said it's too bad there are so many vacant shops. Really does feel like the town is dying. And that's a real shame.'

Alex took a deep breath. 'Well, I have no intention of letting the town die, if that's what you're getting at. Actually, what are you getting at? What's this proposal you wanted me to listen to?'

'Look, I'll get right to the point. I have a client who also thinks the town has a nice feel to it. In fact, this client is interested in buying all your holdings here in Main Street.'

Alex's frown deepened. 'I beg your pardon?'

He smiled, seeming pleased at her surprise. 'My client has big plans for this town. He'd like to purchase all your properties.' A glint appeared in his eyes as he waited for her reaction.

Disbelief softened her voice, making it almost a whisper. 'What sort of plans?'

He took a few steps, then stopped and turned toward her. 'Tourism ... which will be good for everyone. The whole town will benefit ... you included, if you intend keeping any other properties you have in the area.'

'What do you mean by tourism?'

He huffed out a breath, and then tried to cover his impatience with a forced smile. Did he seriously think she wouldn't ask questions?

'They want to turn the town into a tourist destination, of sorts.'

'A tourist destination? Here?'

He raised his arms, swinging them to engulf the whole street. 'Yes. Have you ever been to Tombstone, Arizona? They want to do something like that ... perhaps not quite as elaborate, but along those lines.'

She shook her head in disbelief. 'I don't know Tombstone.'

'The O.K. Corral? Wyatt Earp? Doc Holliday?'

'Oh, right. But here? I mean, I don't get it?'

He dropped his head. 'There's plenty of history in these hills—even if not all of it took place right here in Masons Flat. They'll draw on history from the whole area. Re-enactments, panning for gold, that sort of thing. A bit like your Sovereign Hill, in Ballarat.'

It seemed absurd, on the one hand, and exciting on the other. She'd enjoyed going to Sovereign Hill on school trips, but something about this whole thing didn't feel right. 'And they want my hotel and saloon?'

'Yes, and the rest of the shops as well. And given you've only recently inherited the properties I thought you'd probably have little attachment to the town.'

Her forehead tightened. 'Have you spoken to the other owners in the street?'

'Oh, well, I'm not at liberty to discuss any other negotiations which may or may not be taking place, but let me just say the saloon and hotel are the linchpins in the deal. Without them, it's unlikely the project will go ahead.'

Alex swallowed hard. Did Travis and Denver know about this? Were they in favour of it?

She took a few steps back, running her hands through her still damp hair as a niggling memory finally surfaced. Was this what Travis meant when he'd said things were *complicated*? She'd assumed he was referring to Annie—but maybe it was more to do with money than people. Anger bore down on her, replacing incredulity.

His eyes narrowed. 'Look, I can see I've—'

She cut him off. 'Who else have you spoken to? Have you begun negotiations with other owners in the street or not?'

'As I said, every negotiation entered into is confidential—.'

'If you want me to listen to you then you're going to have to tell me, are you in negotiations with the Golds or not?'

A crooked smile appeared on his face, but he quickly replaced it with seriousness. 'Look, I shouldn't tell you this but yes, of course, I've been speaking to the Golds. And between you and me, they were very excited at the prospect—probably would've signed up on the spot if I'd had the contract ready at the time.'

Her jaws clenched as she used every bit of self-control not to scream. She'd been played for a fool. She'd slept with Travis—twice—thinking she meant something to him. And she'd been wracking her brain, trying to find a way forward for them. How could she have been so stupid?

It had to be Travis—Denver was far too transparent to keep something like this to himself. She looked back up the street at the saloon, and then over toward the hotel as she fought back tears of anger.

This changed everything. Phil Marshall had promised he'd have the written appraisals done by tonight. She'd read them carefully and assess whatever offer this man might make at the same time.

'Put it in writing.' She fairly spat the words, certain of only one thing; she needed time to think everything through, and she'd need all the facts in front of her to do that.

'By *it* I assume you mean you'd like a written offer?'

'Yes, of course I mean a written offer. I don't own the properties outright—I'll need to discuss this with my co-owners. As it happens I'll be seeing them in the next few days, and if you want me to take any of this seriously, I'll need an offer in writing—preferably tonight. I'm leaving first thing in the morning, so put your best offer down—and then add something to it. If it's laughable, I'll toss it in the bin.'

His smug smile made her stomach turn, and she hated the idea of doing business with him, but perhaps it would be for the best.

~~*~~

Alex sat at her uncle's mahogany desk with her head resting on her crossed arms, battling the emptiness that threatened to drain every ounce of energy from her. Travis' betrayal was as complete as Liam's had been.

How could she have been such a fool?

She'd opened her heart to Travis, allowing herself to fall in love with him. And with Annie. She'd come away from their night together convinced that they would find a way to make things work. And more the fool her, she'd been certain that his asking her to stay this time meant he felt the same way.

But that's where she'd been wrong.

He clearly didn't feel the same way. Love hadn't played a part in what they'd shared. He couldn't love her—he couldn't even care about her—or he wouldn't be doing deals behind her back.

She grabbed her phone, started to press his number, but then stopped. What would she say to him? Would she scream, and accuse him of being a traitor? And to what end? She'd only make a fool of herself, wouldn't she?

Tossing her phone down, she ran her hands through her hair and screamed at the top of her lungs, savouring the strength that came with anger. Enough with the self-pity. Okay, so she'd been a fool to think that last night meant more to him than it obviously had. He'd slept with her because there had been desire, on both their parts, in the most primal sense of the word. It had been convenient, and it had been something they'd both wanted.

Only for her, the moment had been driven by a lot more than convenience and desire—she'd allowed herself to think they were in love.

He hadn't said he loved her—he'd never even hinted at it. She'd allowed herself to believe he loved her because she wanted it to be true, and because, as she'd finally come to admit, she was falling in love with him. But wanting something to be true doesn't make it so. Was any of this his fault? Had he broken some sort of promise? Had he lied by even suggesting he loved her?

No.

She gritted her teeth. Who was she really mad at? Him, for taking what she'd given him, freely? Or at herself, for projecting her feelings onto his actions?

Logic required she not be mad at him.

Self-preservation insisted she not play the victim card.

Resolve brought her around. She was a grown woman, who accepted responsibility for her actions. And that included having sex with a man who clearly wasn't in love with her.

She could accept that. She could deal with it and move on. She definitely could. But there was still this niggling little issue—one that she couldn't live with so easily.

He'd been making deals behind her back.

Her jaws tightened as her fists clenched and unclenched over and over. Any wonder he'd been avoiding her the past week. He'd claimed he was busy. Now she knew what he was so busy doing.

But then, as she allowed her anger to blossom into full-blown hatred, his voice popped into her head. Words carried on a weary sigh. Words whispered as they'd stood alone on his back porch; telling her he'd wondered if it was worth the effort, trying to keep the town alive. Had he been trying to hint at what he was doing? Had he been trying to tell her that he'd already given up on the town? To warn her of the changes afoot without breaking any confidentiality clause he might have signed?

She shook her head as she cursed herself.

No.

Stop. Making. Excuses. For. Him.

She could let him off the hook for not being in love with her because she'd projected her feelings onto his actions when it came to them having sex, but she couldn't make excuses for his behaviour in business. He shouldn't have signed anything without talking to her first. He should have had respect for the history between their families if nothing else. He should have trusted her.

She slammed her hand on the top of the desk. 'Argh!!!!'

Nausea washed over her as her blood drained from her face. Maybe they were all in on it; Travis, Phil Marshall, and this Paul Kelly. Maybe Paul Kelly coming forward the day after she'd told Travis she was going was no coincidence. Then again, Phil Marshall knew too.

She didn't know who she could trust anymore. Maybe she could trust no-one in the town. Maybe that's why her uncle had used lawyers, accountants, and estate agents from other towns.

She picked up the phone and rang her accountant, Gary Matthews.

'Gary, I met with a developer this morning, and it looks like he'll be making an offer for my properties in town.'

'A developer? Really? And he wants to buy the Masons Flat properties?'

'That's what he said. I won't be sure until I've received the offer.'

'Why? What does a developer want with Masons Flat? Did he say?'

'He said his client wants to turn it into a tourist attraction—he mentioned Tombstone, Arizona. Anyway, the reason for the call, when I get the offer, if I'm even remotely inclined to accept it, would you be able to cast your eye over it to make sure it seems reasonable?'

'Certainly, Alex. That's not a problem at all—just email it.'

'Thank you. Actually, I might get Damien West to glance at it too.'

'Not a bad idea—it's always a good idea to get a lawyer's perspective. But as for any offer being reasonable, I've commission a firm to do sworn valuations but they won't be ready for another month at least.'

'Funnily enough, I'd already asked Phil Marshall to do market appraisals of all our holdings here in town. I wanted them so I could discuss our options with my sisters. I'll shoot you a copy of his report as well. Speaking of Phil, I remember you saying you've known him a long time, and until this morning I had full faith in his abilities, partly due to your relationship with him, but am I being naïve to assume he's trustworthy? Do you think this developer could be paying him to produce lowball values?'

Gary let out a soft whistle. 'Trustworthy.' When he sighed, Alex's stomach dropped. 'Look, he's as trustworthy as any real estate agent I've ever dealt with, but the sort of property appraisals he'll be doing tend to be rather subjective, especially if they haven't got recent sales to compare to. He'll probably provide a range of values, and sure, if it was in his interest to keep your expectations low, I'd say he'd do that. I'd say most real estate agents will read a situation and do what's best for them if at all possible.'

'I figured you'd say something like that, but I had to ask.'

'Look, your uncle loved Masons Flat, as did your grandfather, although probably not quite as much. The history of your family is not only in the bricks and mortar; it's in the soil, and the trees and the winds that blow on a cold winter's day. I know that's not the answer you'd expect from an accountant, but it's true. That history is something only you can put a dollar figure on. If you don't feel it, and you want out, getting a reasonable offer from one party makes that process a whole lot easier. But, if you do feel it, no offer, no matter how generous, will be enough.'

She swallowed down her emotions—emotions that caught her off guard. Of course he was right. The original Thomas Mason would no doubt roll over in his grave at the thought of a property developer getting his hands on the town. Or would he? Mightn't he be just as likely to laugh at how much the town had grown in value and be pleased for his descendants? She was now more confused than ever.

'Thanks, Gary. You've given me a lot to think about.'

He laughed. 'By the tone of your voice I'm not certain you really want to be thanking me, but it's better that you take all this into account up front rather than think about it after you've signed on the dotted line.'

'True.' She sighed, exhaustion threatening to take hold.

'By the way, Alex, I don't suppose you ever stumbled upon those old valuations I mentioned?'

She sat up, frowning. 'Old valuations?'

'Yes, that day you came in to see me I said I thought your uncle had some done a few years back. If you had those it would give you a good basis for comparison to what Phil Marshall comes up with, but if you haven't come across them, maybe I'm wrong and he never had them done.'

'No, I haven't come across them, but to be honest I'd forgotten you'd said that, so I haven't been specifically looking for them. Do you remember when that was?'

'Sorry, no, I don't recall when—a couple of years ago, maybe longer. And he never said why he wanted them.'

Maybe it didn't matter. Maybe none of it mattered. Maybe she just had to take Phil's appraisals at face value, and compare them to the offer she'd get from Paul Kelly, and be done with it. She could simply go back to Melbourne, start up a private coaching business there, and forget there ever was a town called Masons Flat, or a man named Travis Gold.

'Well, I'll see what I think of the offer and if I need you to look at it I'll email it across. I'm taking everything with me to sit down with my sisters, and I appreciate the work you've done so far. Talk soon.'

Setting her phone down, she decided to make herself a cup of coffee. She hadn't slept much, and after everything this morning she simply wanted to curl up and never make another decision for the rest of her life. But of course she couldn't do that. She needed to find the old valuations, if they existed, to use as comparisons to Phil Marshall's figures. And she hadn't even begun to pack yet.

Armed with coffee she returned to have another look through her uncle's files.

She looked at the tall filing cabinet where he'd kept all the rental statements and accounts, and shook her head. She'd only just finished going through all those files and hadn't spotted anything looking like property valuations. Even though it seemed the logical place for them, maybe he'd put them somewhere else.

She turned her attention back to the desk. It had three pull-out drawers on the right, a thin drawer under the writing surface, and a cupboard door that opened on the left. She already knew the cupboard had a single shelf and held several bottles of whisky and some crystal glasses on the shelf.

She pulled open the top of the three right-hand drawers. This held a folder containing all the correspondence to do with the fire at the saloon: the insurance company correspondence, a copy of the police report, a copy of the letter he'd sent to all the employees explaining the situation and assuring them he would continue to pay them while the works were being done. She'd been through all that carefully—there were no valuations hiding there.

Then she pulled out the middle drawer. It held a musty old dictionary, a selection of rulers—which must have been something her uncle collected as she'd never seen so many in one place before—scissors, a calculator and a letter opener. Shutting it, she pulled out the bottom drawer. This one held hanging files, mostly to do with the house. At the front were the most recent accounts, both those to be paid and those having recently been paid. Behind that, copies of the house insurance policy and the rates. Behind that, other miscellaneous expenses to do with the house, and behind that, a copy of the building contract and sale of the land next door.

She drank the last of her coffee, and then pulled out the thin drawer in the middle of the desk—the one under the writing surface. Surprisingly shallow, it simply held a collection of pens and pencils from various companies and hotels, a small metal box of paperclips, another full of rubber bands, and a stapler and staple-remover.

Frustration would cripple her if she let it. She gave herself a mental slap on the face. The valuations, if they were done, would be several years old in any case, and mightn't be relevant even if she did find them. She had to stop looking and get on with her packing.

She carried her empty cup back into the kitchen, and as she stood running hot water into the cup, the reality of her dilemma became obvious. Even if she'd found the valuations, it wouldn't have cured her frustration, for one simple reason. Her frustration had nothing to do with valuations.

Her frustration came from the fact that she'd allowed herself to fall in love with someone who'd chosen to betray her without a second thought.

CHAPTER 30

'So, no tennis lesson today?' Denver asked on Thursday evening as they sat having dinner out on the back porch.

Travis recognised that smile. Denver knew the answer before he'd asked. He waited, curious how Annie would answer him.

'Alex has gone to Australia. She'll be gone for two weeks so you and Daddy will have to play with me until she gets back.'

Now Denver turned to his older brother, and winked. 'Oh that's right; she's gone to a wedding I believe. I knew she was going, I just didn't know when. Think you'll survive two weeks without her and having to play tennis with Annie?'

Travis stared at him in disbelief—his brother didn't have a subtle bone in his body. His comment didn't even deserve a response.

Annie giggled. 'Don't be silly. I won't be as hard on him as I will be on you. You haven't seen me play for a while—Alex has been helping me to serve better, and now you're really going to be in trouble. And when she gets back we're gonna start working on my backhand.'

Annie giggled again, and asked if she could be excused. Her favourite show was coming on shortly and she didn't want to miss any of it.

When the door had closed behind her, Denver raised an eyebrow. 'You two getting serious, or what?'

Travis let out a long slow breath. He might as well tell him. 'I think it's the "or what" to be honest.'

'Why's that? I know you've slept with her. Her car was parked out front when I came in the other night.'

Travis huffed out a breath. 'Gees, a guy can't get any privacy around here, that's for sure.'

'I take it you two didn't click in bed then?' Denver cocked his head, waiting for Travis to contradict him. Travis knew the tone.

'That, little brother, is none of your business.'

Denver smirked. 'You know, she told me she was going to this wedding a couple of weeks ago. Swore me to secrecy as she didn't want Annie to know until right before she went.'

Travis glared at him. He knew Denver got along well with everyone, and that Alex was no exception, but he hadn't thought his own brother would keep something that important from him. He shook his head, trying to convince himself it was no big deal.

They both continued eating—Travis grateful for the silence.

'What makes you say it's the "or what"?' Denver wasn't dropping it.

Travis looked up, at first toying with the idea of not answering. 'I tried to ring her today, to say goodbye, but she never picked up. I even left a message—a couple of them actually—asking her to call me back before she got on the plane, but she never did.'

Denver reached into his pocket and pulled out his phone. 'Here, ring from mine. See if she answers.'

'She'd be in the air by now—her flight was leaving around five.'

Denver shrugged. 'Too bad. Yeah, well, she was probably just busy, you know? Might have even had her phone switched off.'

'Maybe.' Travis had thought of that as well, but intuition told him there was more to it.

'You didn't have an argument or anything, did you? You can be pretty scary when you're angry about something.'

'No, nothing. She snuck out sometime during the night. Didn't leave a note or anything.'

'And you didn't ring her yesterday to find out why? Gees, bro, she's probably pissed off that you never rang her yesterday.'

Travis clenched his fists, mad at himself, knowing his brother could be right. 'I thought about it, but at first I didn't want to come across overly anxious, then I got busy with the horses, and you know how that goes. Anyway, in the end I decided to leave it until today. And then she wouldn't answer.'

Denver shrugged. 'Don't look so worried about it. You were probably snoring. The poor thing probably couldn't sleep.'

Travis knew there was more to it than that. 'If that's all it was, why wouldn't she have answered her phone?'

'Who knows—she's a woman, it's hard to say. You look like you could use a night out. I'm meeting a couple of friends at the saloon tomorrow night. We'll have a few drinks, play some pool. Come with me—it'll be good for you.'

It was tempting. Travis could use a night out, but he had Annie to think of. 'I can't exactly bring Annie with me to the saloon, now can I?'

'Ring Stacy. Maybe Annie can spend the night over there with Tammy.'

He didn't like imposing on Stacy, but maybe a night out would help take his mind off Alex. Or better yet, he could call her from the saloon—she'd be home by then, wouldn't she? He could give her an update on it. Could be a good excuse for calling.

'Yeah, alright then—sounds like a good idea.'

~~*~~

Exhaustion weighed heavily upon Alex's shoulders as she stood at the baggage carousel. She wanted nothing more than to grab her belongings and go home, but after watching the same bags going around probably a dozen times, her heart sank. She was about to go over to lodge a claim when the conveyor cranked up again and she spotted her bag bouncing down the belt with a few other stragglers. She had to fight back tears of relief. Or were her tears for something else?

She tugged her bag off the carousel, pulled it over toward the exit, and then grabbed her phone. She didn't want or need to be picked up, but both Casey and Taylor had insisted she ring them when she got in. It took a moment for the network to connect, and then she saw the little red light indicating she had voicemail. She pressed the button which showed she had four missed calls, all from the same number; Travis.

She'd seen his first call come through but had chosen not to answer it. After that, she'd put her phone on silent before later switching it off.

What was the point of speaking to him? It was blatantly obvious what they'd shared meant something entirely different to him than it did to her. Her passion had been coupled with love, and hope, and possibility. His had clearly only been about the sex. He wouldn't have been doing deals behind her back if she meant something to him. And a call to him might just give him the opportunity to try to justify his unjustifiable actions.

Once again, she chose to ignore the voicemails and rang Casey instead.

'I'm here.'

'Great! How was the flight?'

'Long. I think I'll just take a taxi home—I won't be good company in any case. Can the three of us have an early dinner tonight?'

'If you're sure—I don't mind coming to get you.'

'No, it's not worth it. But thanks. See you tonight?'

'We'll pick you up—see you at six.'

As she headed outside to the taxi stand, the freezing wind that hit her face was an acute reminder that she'd left California's summer to arrive home in the dead of winter. She'd only been away for a few weeks, but it felt longer. And that's when it hit her, while standing there waiting for a taxi; she didn't feel like she was home at all.

~~*~~

Travis stood at the bar drinking a beer, trying to convince himself he was having a good time. Denver was around the corner playing pool and every now and then Travis could hear Denver above the din, praising a good shot, or laughing at a bad one.

He was happy there at the bar, alone with his thoughts. He kept waiting for the cool amber fluid to take the edge off his voice so he could ring Alex and not sound like a stalker. It hadn't started working yet, but there was plenty of time. She mightn't even be home yet although he was fairly certain her plane would have landed by now.

Closing his eyes, he remembered exactly how she'd looked the other night. Passion had made the gold flecks in her eyes dance mischievously, and the drops of perspiration on her body had glistened in the light of the bedside lamp.

He opened his eyes, took another sip of beer, then glanced around, surprised at how completely he'd been lost in his thoughts. He'd almost forgotten where he was. Then he pulled out his phone and checked the time. She definitely would have landed by now, but it was possible she hadn't turned her phone on yet. What would she think when she played all the messages he'd left, asking her to call him? If only she'd answered his first call—he could have told her how much he would miss her while she was away.

He laughed at himself. He'd definitely sound like a stalker if he rang her and said that now. He'd already left several messages—he couldn't ring her again, could he?

He wanted her to know how much better his life was with her in it. Both his and Annie's, actually.

She was so good with Annie—but she was so much more than a role model for Annie. She'd made him feel alive again. She'd given him something to look forward to. She'd given him love.

Was that the word he was searching for? Did he love her? Was he falling in love with her?

He drained the last of his beer and ordered another, then turned to look around the room. That's when he noticed a stranger, sitting a bit further along the bar, with a phone pressed to his ear. He wasn't sure why he'd suddenly noticed him, until he overheard a bit of the man's conversation.

The voice seemed familiar—had he spoken to the man about buying some stock? He looked like he could have something to do with cattle— perhaps a buying agent—but the man's next words made him think again.

'Yeah, she's got the contract. Expect we'll hear from her in a few days after she's had time to review everything. There's just one more—.'

'Here you go,' said the bartender, sliding the beer up in front of Travis, his voice completely drowning out the rest of the stranger's telephone conversation.

Travis paid for his drink, and then swiftly brought his attention back to the stranger. Only the man had finished the call and was reaching into his back pocket as he ordered a drink. When the man leant forward, Travis spotted who was sitting on the other side of the stranger. Harrison Weston.

As Travis stared at him, Harrison turned and caught his eye.

'Hey,' he called out, spinning around on his bar stool. He stood, came over and put his hand out for a shake.

'Hey yourself, Harrison. You're still in town.' He took Harrison's extended hand for a brief shake, and then grabbed his beer.

'A couple more days—then I'll head back down south.'

'Never did hear what brought you back here. Business, was it?'

Harrison laughed. 'Visiting my Mom and catching up with friends since I had a few weeks between gigs. And I couldn't miss Denver's thirtieth, could I?'

'That was weeks ago.'

'Yes, and then the county fair. But enough about me, how are you doing? I barely spoke to you at Denver's party but I saw you guys riding at the rodeo. How'd you finish up?'

'Pretty good. Sold all my young horses, which was the goal.'

'The business is going well then I take it? Horses and cattle both, isn't it?'

'Yes. Everything's going well. Lots of work, but it keeps us out of trouble. Speaking of trouble, I heard you played some sort of bad guy in a movie recently.'

Harrison's eyes lit up at the opportunity to talk about himself. 'Yes, it was great fun. Not a lot of money in it yet, but I'm hoping to get something bigger lined up when I'm down in Australia early next year.'

Travis blinked back his surprise, still wondering if he should be jealous of Harrison. Was he going to Australia because of Alex? Only one way to find out. 'Is that right? This a business trip, or pleasure?'

'Business; my agent landed me a small part in an Australian drama series, but I've got my eyes on a much bigger prize, if I can swing it.'

Travis cocked his head. Did the prize he referred to have something to do with Alex? But no sooner had the thought sunk in, Harrison dispelled it.

'I've got a meeting lined up with an Australian agent while I'm there. They're making a lot more movies down there these days. It'll be interesting to see what kind of work they can line up for me.'

Travis' interest waned as Harrison continued to talk about his career, allowing Travis to turn his attention back to the stranger. He watched as the man paid for his drink and took a sip. The man didn't seem to be taking any notice of him or Harrison.

When he'd had as much of Harrison's self-promotion as he could take, Travis set his empty glass on the bar. 'Well, it was good seeing you. Best head over to the pool table or I'll never get a game, eh?'

Harrison looked at his watch, one of those fancy ones which seemed to be all the rage these days, and tapped its screen. When he looked up, he made a face. 'Sorry, I'm running late or I'd stay and see if I could get a game with you. Another time?'

'Sure thing,' he said as Harrison headed toward the door, 'Another time.' Then, before he could decide whether to stay at the bar or not, Denver called out to him.

'Travis, you're up next—get over here.'

Travis made his way over to the pool table, positioning himself so he could still keep an eye on the stranger, watching him as he finished his drink. Maybe he was making something of nothing. Maybe what he thought he'd heard was nothing more than business talk. He'd given a contract to a woman to peruse, and it could be any woman. But if there was nothing more to it, what had grabbed his attention?

CHAPTER 31

After warming up with a hot shower, Alex gazed out her bedroom window, taking in the dull winter sky. The grey did nothing to lift her mood which right now felt as if she'd left her joy in California.

She turned, inspecting her bedroom with a critical eye. The small room had barely enough room for her bed, a bedside table on one side and a free-standing mirror on the other. She'd known when she bought the apartment that it was a poor substitute for the large family home she'd shared with Liam, but it was all she could afford at the time. It had been one in a series of compromises she'd made after the divorce.

Now, all she could see in her mind's eye was the spacious master bedroom she'd left behind in Masons Flat. She wouldn't have thought it possible, but she missed that house. The small personal touches she'd made had turned it into her home and it was a place where she enjoyed pottering in the garden, or hanging out watching television, or even cooking in the lovely kitchen.

The image of Annie covered in flour as they'd made pizza enveloped her mind, bringing a hint of joy. Then the image panned backwards. It wasn't her kitchen she missed. That event hadn't been in her kitchen.

It was Annie she missed.

And Travis.

She missed handyman Travis, who'd fixed her door when it wouldn't lock. She missed knight-in-shining-armour Travis, who'd come to her rescue when she'd been stranded on the dance floor. She missed passionate Travis, who'd made her feel like a woman again. She even missed serious Travis, whose concern for his daughter rose above all else.

But she didn't miss the Travis who'd gone behind her back, making deals to sell out the town.

How could he have betrayed her trust like that, putting business above all else?

She dried her hair, went out to the kitchen, and spread the documents out on the table. She blinked a few times, wishing she didn't have to do this—wishing she'd never met Paul Kelly.

She picked up Phil Marshall's report and compared its figures to the offer from Paul Kelly's client. Assuming Phil Marshall's values were realistic, and that's all she could assume at the moment, then the offer was fair. Even more so, when she took into account how easy it would be. One transaction would see her and her sisters almost clear of Masons Flat. There would still be the house to deal with, but the lovely home would no doubt be easy to sell.

She, Casey and Taylor could sign the contract and be done with it. With that money, together with the funds from the rest of the estate, they could live quite comfortably without the hassle of being landlords. They wouldn't have to manage the saloon, or try to start new businesses in those vacant shops, or try to reinvigorate the town.

But that's the thing. She didn't see any of those things as a hassle.

They were challenges, for sure, but ones she'd begun to embrace. Ones she'd enjoyed turning her mind to. Okay, perhaps she'd been a bit tentative at first, but she had come to look forward to managing the saloon and running the fruit and veggie shop. And if no-one expressed interest in the other vacant shop she would think of something for that one too.

She slammed her palm on the table. She shouldn't have attempted this yet—not when she was tired, and not when she was still so angry at Travis.

Taking a deep breath, she tried to think clearly. She could have her dream. Right here, in Melbourne. She could open up a coaching school, and might not even need a part-time job. That's what she'd been aiming for all along, wasn't it? To get back into coaching children. Maybe she'd even strike it lucky and get one who was talented enough to go the full distance.

As she imagined herself coaching, it was images of Annie that filled her mind.

And then memories of the game she'd played with Travis, as Annie played cheerleader on the sidelines.

Maybe Travis wanted out so he would have more money to provide for Annie. Maybe the horse and cattle businesses weren't as lucrative as she'd thought. Maybe he saw this offer as an opportunity too good to knock back.

And there were the other owners in the street. She hadn't met any of the others yet, so she had no idea what might motivate them to sell. And no idea whether, if she held out and the whole deal collapsed, they would resent her for ruining what they might see as a once in a lifetime opportunity.

Once again, frustration overwhelmed her and her jaws clenched so tight her face hurt. Travis had gone behind her back, but worse than that, he'd shown her a life she might have had, and then snatched it away with the stroke of a pen.

Things would never be the same.

If she signed, there would be nothing to go back to.

If she didn't sign, the whole town, including Travis, would probably hate her.

She picked up her phone and looked at the missed calls. Wouldn't it be best to ring him and have it out with him? Wouldn't that be better than carrying all this anger around? A good fight, even if only over the phone, might release her tension. Or it might rile her up even more.

She rang her voicemail and listened to the first message. It was a simple hello, asking her to call him before she left. His voice gave away nothing. She moved on to the next message. The same, basically, with a query as to whether she'd received the first message. The third message was a little longer, and there was an underlying urgency in his tone.

"Alex? Hopefully the reason you're not picking up is because you're driving and can't answer ... look, I'd really like to speak to you before you go ... can you please return my call?"

Curiosity twisted in her gut as her finger hovered over the end button. Didn't he deserve an opportunity to explain his actions, a chance to tell her how much this deal meant to him and all the other owners, and how beneficial it could be to the surrounding community?

As she pressed end and hung up, clarity struck with the force of a fist. Could it be that she was the bad guy in this? After all, who was she to come onto the scene at the last minute and ruin it for all of them?

Swallowing back her disappointment, she finally saw things as they truly were. She'd thought all this time that it was coaching that would make her life full again. And that was part of it, but there was so much more that she hadn't even allowed herself to dream about. And for a moment she'd thought she'd found it in Masons Flat. The town had everything: a beautiful home; ready-made job opportunities with both the saloon and the shops; and the opportunity to coach the local children. But more than that, there was Travis and his beautiful daughter. They'd been a bonus—something she'd never dreamt of finding.

And now, because Masons Flat obviously wasn't going to provide the happily-ever-after ending she thought it might, she was blaming Travis. Blaming him for her disappointment, when he'd never promised her anything, and for all she knew he could simply be chasing his own dreams.

Fighting back tears of frustration, she took a deep breath and dialled into her voicemail again, then held her breath as she listened to the final message.

"Alex? It's me again. I was really hoping to speak to you before you go ... maybe your phone is switched off? Look, when you get this, please ring me. Don't worry about the time difference. I'll talk to you soon."

She swallowed back the emotions his voice triggered, but there was no point reading too much into it. She had to stop thinking about him— had to accept that he was, and always would be, thousands of miles away. Thinking about him wouldn't solve anything. The only thing that could be solved right now was her exhaustion.

She went back to her bedroom, set her alarm to wake her at five, and stretched out on the bed. And the moment her head hit the pillow she began to drift off.

~~*~~

Travis had nearly convinced himself he was jumping at shadows when the man at the bar stared straight at him, then stood and approached with an outstretched hand.

'Travis Gold? I'm Paul Kelly.'

Travis swapped his pool cue to his left hand and shook Paul's hand, then stepped back a foot, frowning. 'Paul Kelly? Should I know you?'

Paul laughed. 'Not yet, but I know who you are ... by name, anyway. You were next on my list to contact, so I was glad to hear that man call out to you. Have you got a minute?'

Travis frowned. 'Depends. What for?'

'I have a business proposition for you, Mr Gold. One I'm certain you'll want to hear about. Shall we go outside where it's a bit quieter?'

Travis handed the cue to Denver. 'Fill in for me for a couple of minutes? I won't be long.'

Denver shrugged as he took the cue, and Travis followed Paul Kelly outside.

Paul explained that he represented a party who was interested in acquiring a significant holding there in Masons Flat.

Travis nodded for a moment, and then his nod turned to a shake. 'Sorry to disappoint you but our ranch isn't for sale. Doesn't matter what price you offer.'

Paul chuckled. 'We're not after your ranch, Mr Gold. It's the Main Street properties we're after.'

Travis' brow tightened with surprise. 'Main Street?'

'Yes. My client wishes to acquire your properties, as well as several others in the street. If successful, I assure you, the development will be advantageous to the whole area. This town will spring back to life and the whole community will be the beneficiary.'

Intuition sent shivers down his spine. Something about this man was less than forthright. 'I take it you've already spoken to the other owners in the street?'

'Yes, you're the last. And let me say this, everyone seems quite excited about the idea.'

'Is that right?' Travis felt an eyebrow lift involuntarily.

'Absolutely. Mind you, I'm not at liberty to discuss details of any of the negotiations. There's a confidentiality clause in the contract, you see.'

'A confidentiality clause? Why, so we can't discuss it amongst ourselves?'

Paul's response came quickly, sounding well-rehearsed. 'Yes, well, I didn't have any say in that aspect of the negotiations. If it was up to me, I'd have preferred to get everyone in a room together, do a presentation of the project and get you all as excited about it as I am. But that's not what my client wanted.'

Travis cocked his head. 'And you've already spoken to all the other owners?'

'Yes.'

Could this explain why Alex had avoided him? And why she hadn't returned his calls? Had this Paul Kelly character gotten to her and made her an offer she couldn't refuse? And why would she refuse it? If she had any inclination to sell everything this would be an easy way—one buyer, one contract. And if she took it, there would be no reason for her to stay in California. And no reason for her to return his calls.

He glared at Paul Kelly and lowered his voice. 'Even Alex?'

'Alex?' Paul played dumb, but Travis didn't fall for it.

'Yes, Alex. You know ... the owner of this saloon, and a lot of the other properties. I take it you've met with her too? What did she have to say about it?'

Paul shrugged. 'Like I said, I can't disclose any details of the negotiations with the other parties, but I'd have told her what I'm telling you—that this is a wonderful opportunity which will provide benefits to everyone in the town, not just the main street owners. That, and the fact that there is no guarantee anything will go ahead unless everyone signs.'

Anger bubbled up in him. This whole thing felt wrong. If the man was being this secretive, who knew what he might have said to Alex. Had he told her that he and Denver had signed? He frowned, and his voice dropped an octave. 'What else did you tell her?'

Paul drew in a breath, and explained the concept of turning Masons Flat into a tourist destination, finishing up by saying he'd give Travis a few days to think about it. When Travis just stared at him blankly, he shifted his weight as if he were about to leave.

Travis scowled, his voice coming out in a low growl. 'That's all well and good, but that's not what I asked. What else did you tell Alex? Did you tell her we'd already signed?'

'No, of course not,' Paul said, taking a step back and wringing his hands. 'I don't stoop to telling lies. I don't need to. This is a good deal—for everyone. Like I said, I'd have preferred to have some artist impressions done and hold a Town Hall meeting and tell you all at the same time, but even so, the deal is a good one, for everyone.'

Travis hated when people talked in circles. 'And that's all you told her?'

Paul looked over his shoulder, then sighed and looked Travis in the eye. 'Look, I told her exactly what I told you. That all the negotiations were subject to confidentiality. But she, not unlike what you're doing right now, got a bit fired up. She insisted on knowing if I'd spoken to the Golds.'

Travis drew in a long breath. 'And?'

'I told her the truth.'

When Travis next spoke his voice was ice cold. 'Which was?'

'That I'd spoken to the Gold family.'

'Then you did lie to her.'

Paul stood taller, becoming defensive. 'No, I didn't. I had spoken to the Golds. Just not you.'

'Don't move.' Travis stomped back inside and straight to the pool table. 'Denver. Outside. Now.'

'What the ...?' Denver looked at Travis, then put down his cue and followed him out.

Facing Paul Kelly again, Travis growled. 'And is this the Gold you spoke to?'

Denver had a blank look on his face. 'What's going on? What's all this about?'

Paul took a step toward Denver. 'No. I don't believe we've met. Paul Kelly's my name.' He put his hand out to Denver, but Travis shoved in between them.

Travis spoke through clenched teeth. 'Look, I've had enough of your games. Who've you spoken to?'

Paul rolled his eyes, and then shrugged. 'I've spoken to Mark Gold. Mark, and his wife, Linda. Lovely couple. They were very excited about the possibilities. If I'd had the contract ready, I believe they'd have signed up on the spot.'

Denver, still looking confused, turned to Travis. 'Uncle Mark and Aunt Linda? What's all this about?'

Travis cocked his head towards Paul. 'This man is trying to buy up Main Street. He's been sneaking around talking to everyone independently. We were next.'

Denver frowned. 'Trying to buy up Main Street? What, as in all our shops and the saloon and everything?'

Travis nodded, and Paul shrunk further back. 'It's a great opportunity. They want to turn the street into a movie set in the first instance, then, after the filming is finished, turn the whole street into a tourist attraction—panning for gold, a haunted hotel, re-enactments of gunfights in the saloon, that sort of thing.'

Denver was smiling, but Travis wasn't buying it. 'What sort of idiot would come up with an idea like that?' As soon as the words left his mouth, he knew. Harrison. His sitting there hadn't been a coincidence. 'Well, you can tell your *client* that this Gold family isn't interested, so I guess that means the whole deal is off the table, yes?'

Paul's face darkened. 'Not necessarily—we have some flexibility with leaving a few of the existing shops. Your jewellery shop, for instance, isn't necessarily critical. Please, let me buy you both lunch tomorrow and we can talk about it after you've had a chance to let it soak in. It really is a fantastic opportunity. You have to think of the others as much as yourself. The town's been dying a slow death. This could bring it new life, and everyone in the surrounding area will benefit from that.'

Travis shook his head. So, he'd used guilt with everyone—hard to do if they were all in the room together. He patted Denver on the shoulder. 'Go back in and finish the game, I'll be back in a minute.'

'Okay,' Denver said after a slight pause, then left to let Travis to deal with Paul.

'There's no need to take me to lunch, because the answer is no. My family has a long history with this town, and even if my uncle has lost interest in it, I haven't. We aren't interested in selling, and you can take that back to your client.'

Travis turned on his heel and went back into the saloon, not even looking over his shoulder to see if Paul was still standing there.

Once inside, he pulled out his phone and pressed his uncle's number.

~~*~~

Travis had stayed at the saloon until well after midnight, with the volume on his phone turned all the way up so he'd hear if his phone rang. It never did.

Sitting on the edge of his bed now, he kept going over the conversation he'd had with his uncle—about how opportunities like this don't come knocking twice. His aunt and uncle wanted to live the good life for their twilight years and the money they'd get from selling their Main Street properties would enable them to go on the cruises they'd been coveting ever since Mark retired. They didn't share Travis' sense of connection to the town. They were ready to sign, and Mark had urged Travis to do the same.

His uncle's words tugged at his heart. If Mark didn't share Travis' connection to the town, then surely, Alex and her sisters wouldn't either. Was he being selfish by not wanting to sell?

He glanced at his phone, willing it to ring. There was no longer any doubt that she'd be home—probably unpacked, showered and rested even. She just didn't want to speak to him. But he needed to hear it from her mouth—that of course she'd be selling—that she'd be a fool not to, and that she was no fool—but he couldn't bring himself to call her again.

He stripped off his clothes and crawled into bed, missing her even more. He closed his eyes, remembering what it had been like, having her next to him, savouring her scent, and the soft touch of her skin. He clutched the pillow she'd used. Was the scent of her perfume still on it, or was it simply his imagination?

His uncle's words, about how opportunities like this don't come knocking twice, played on his mind again. His uncle was right. They didn't. Only his uncle didn't have the subject of the *opportunity* right. It wasn't the opportunity to sell that wouldn't come again. It was a woman like Alex.

And that's the moment he knew what he had to do.

If the mountain will not come to Muhammad, then Muhammad must go to the mountain.

CHAPTER 32

Alex and Casey sat at a small table outside one of Melbourne's laneway cafés finishing their lunch. They'd spent the last two hours shopping, and Alex had found not only a complete outfit for the wedding, but also the most adorable stuffed koala for Annie. The morning's success had gone part way to lifting her spirits, but even so a shadow hung over her that she struggled to shake.

Casey set her coffee cup on the table and stared at Alex. 'You've been awfully quiet the past couple of days. Is there something else you want to talk about, besides the decisions we need to make about the properties?'

Alex gazed down the busy lane. There were people everywhere; an eclectic mixture of tourists, business people, couriers, students and shoppers making their way along the bluestone lane, some eyeing them enviously for having scored an outside table on this cool but dry day. On practically any other day, Alex would be completely engrossed in conversation with her sister. Or, if she was here on her own, she'd be analysing the passing parade of people, listening to snippets of their conversation, wondering about their lives.

But today she found it hard to do either.

She looked at Casey and sighed. One side of her wanted to tell Casey everything, but she didn't want her problems to influence the decision the three of them still needed to make. She'd told the twins all they needed to know about Travis Gold over dinner the night she'd arrived; that they'd had a couple of dates; that they'd gotten along well enough; but that it had been nothing more than a bit of fun. And she'd told them about the offer, and that it seemed reasonable. They'd agreed to think on it, and not do anything until after they got back from the wedding.

She almost felt like she was lying to them by leaving out so much, but the reasons for her reluctance to discuss Travis that night still held. And they were the same reasons she'd decided not to return his calls. Business was business. After all, that's how Travis was treating it.

Casey looked at her with wide eyes. 'Um, Earth to Alex? Did you hear me ask if there's anything else you want to talk about?'

'Sorry, yeah, no, everything's good. I'm waking up awfully early, but I'll try to stay up a bit later tonight, and hopefully I'll sleep through the night.'

Casey narrowed her eyes, tilting her head in thought. Alex wondered if she'd seen through her feeble excuse, but Casey didn't press her for more information. Not at the moment, anyway.

Alex turned as a woman, whose American accent triggered a pang of nostalgia, began coaxing her husband to stop at a small jewellery store across from them. The man caught Alex's eye, made a face as he shook his head, and then rolled his eyes. 'She's already bought three gold necklaces on this vacation—she must think I'm made of money, right?'

Alex smiled in response, and then the man turned and grabbed his wife's hand, pulling her away from the shop window. The woman laughed when he threw his arm around her shoulders and they made their way down the laneway.

Something about the exchange got through to Alex. Just as the woman had brushed off her husband's refusal to look at any more jewellery, Alex had to brush off her own disappointment in men. She was home and spending time with her family. And they were all going to a wedding. When they got home from the wedding, they'd discuss everything, and most likely sign the contracts.

She drew in a long breath, held it, and let it out slowly. She was, yet again, thinking too much. She set her cup on the table with determination and turned back to Casey. 'I'm sorry I've been so quiet. I'm just a bit tired. Shall we make a move for home?'

'Okay.' Casey stood, and pushed in her chair, then did a beeline to look at the jewellery the woman had been admiring.

Forty-five minutes later Casey pulled up in front of Alex's place, leaving the motor running. Alex jumped out and went to the back of the car to retrieve the shopping, then stood next to the driver's door as Casey lowered the window. 'Not coming up?'

'No, I better not. I told Maree I'd come in for a couple of hours this afternoon. She's under the pump at the moment since one of the casuals just quit.'

Alex smiled, nodding. 'You're good to her. But then again, she's always been good to you, too. So ... what time do you want to leave tomorrow?'

'Not sure. Taylor's baking all the nibbles for the cocktail party tonight but might need to do a bit more in the morning, so they probably won't be ready to leave until sometime after lunch.'

Alex sighed, still struggling to get enthusiastic about all the wedding rigmarole. 'I can't believe they need a rehearsal for a wedding that's being held at their own home.'

'I don't think they *need* one, so much as *want* one. I think it's more about country hospitality.'

Country hospitality—the words had a nice ring to them; a bit like her at the saloon shouting drinks for the first couple of hours when they re-opened. Another pang of nostalgia threatened to overcome her, but she brushed it aside. 'Right then ... you'll let me know what time you want me at your place?'

'I'll give you a call in the morning. Kiss, kiss,' Casey said, tilting her cheek toward Alex.

Alex leaned through the open window, kissed her sister, and stepped back to watch as the car sped off. Then, loaded down with her purchases, Alex made her way to the building entrance. That's when she heard her named called, followed by a car door slamming.

She turned, trying to work out where the voice had come from. When she spotted him, she could hardly believe her eyes. 'Travis? What are you doing here?'

'I thought that would be obvious,' he said, walking up and relieving her of her shopping bags.

Her heart started racing, and her voice came out breathless. 'Yes, well, I suppose you're here to see me, but *why* are you here? I mean, why are you in Australia?'

He smiled, and leaned forward, kissing her cheek. 'You just said why. To see you.'

She frowned at his avoidance of the question, then fumbled in her purse for her keys and opened the lobby door. 'Okay, well, you'd best come in then.'

By the time she'd led the way up the single flight of stairs and to her door, she was completely out of breath. But it wasn't from the stairs. The suspense was killing her. Travis was here. In Australia. In her apartment. Why?

She grimaced as she opened the door, seeing the mess of papers spread all over the kitchen table, but there was no point trying to hide them. He'd know what they were—he'd already signed similar ones himself. 'Please excuse the mess ... I wasn't expecting company.'

'It's fine. Where do you want these?' He lifted the bags, looking at her with a raised eyebrow.

'On my bed, thanks.' At least she'd made her bed this morning. There was that.

As he walked away, she called out to him. 'Can I make you a tea? Or a coffee.'

'Either—I could do with some caffeine.'

She cleared a space at the table, then went around the island bench and switched on the kettle. When he returned she said, 'Take a seat. When did you get in?'

'This morning,' he answered as he sat at the table.

She grabbed two cups and put teabags in them. 'Oh, so you've only just arrived?' She hated that her voice still sounded so breathless, but seriously, why was he here?

'Yes, I hadn't thought to book a rental car so I was lucky I got one, and that it had a navigator. I'm not sure I'd have worked out how to get here otherwise. Melbourne's a much bigger place than I expected.'

She shrugged, thinking he wouldn't have been the first to make that mistake. She tried to make small talk, since he wasn't giving much away. 'And so ... is this the first time you've driven on the left?'

'No, I drove when I was in London, but that was a few years ago so this was still a bit of a challenge.'

She poured the boiled water over the teabags, and brought the cups to the table, and then stood across from him. 'And so ... you got here.'

'Yes, I got here, and I've been sitting out there trying to stay awake, hoping you'd come home soon. I tried ringing the bell, but you obviously weren't here. I was hoping you hadn't gone off somewhere exotic for this wedding.'

'Yes, well, a day later and you'd have been waiting a long time. We're heading up to the wedding tomorrow.' She fiddled with her tea bag, waiting for him to explain why he'd come. When he didn't speak, she continued. 'You haven't actually answered my question ... what, exactly, are you doing here?'

He stood slowly and stretched out his back—then, not taking his eyes off hers, he came over and stopped right in front of her. 'You wouldn't return my calls.'

As her face grew hot, she cursed her fair complexion under her breath. 'Oh, yeah, I ... uh ... kept meaning to.'

'Sure. For almost a week now you've been meaning to. Yes, well I suppose you have been busy shopping.'

She sighed, resignation washing over her. 'Travis ... look, I wanted to calm down before I rang you. I needed to think things through. And I've done that now. Actually, I've given it a lot of thought, and I've come to understand how it makes sense for everyone. I'm not mad anymore."

A frown contorted his face. 'Makes sense for everyone? You're not mad anymore? What do you mean?'

She drew in a deep breath, trying hard to work out how best to express her conflicted thoughts. 'At first, I was furious that you'd gone behind my back to sell up—I think that's what hurt the most—you not even telling me, not discussing it.'

He raised his hands, frowning as he shook his head back and forth. 'Alex, that's not—'

'Let me finish. I've had time to think about it, and to see it from the other side. Just because I was passionate about building the town back up doesn't mean others are. And it occurred to me that not everyone may have the financial capacity to ride out the slow times like my sisters and I do.'

He took a step back as even deeper furrows creased his forehead. 'Wait ... you mean you don't want to sell?'

The tone in his voice caught her off guard. 'No, of course not. I was just getting comfortable there—with the saloon, and the new shop— and I'd been discussing tennis coaching with the high school principal, and, you know ... other things.' She felt heat rising up to her cheeks again.

His frown eased slightly. 'And you feel connected enough to the town to want to stay, and help me bring it back to life?'

Now it was her turn to frown. 'Help you? But you've already signed. Paul Kelly told me you practically signed up on the spot, and that was a week ago.'

Travis' face darkened. 'That lying son-of-a ... he told you I'd signed?'

She cocked her head, looking across to the window. What, exactly, had he said? 'Well, I'm pretty sure he told me the Gold's had signed ... or were about to. Yes, I'm sure that's what he said.'

'He was talking about my Uncle Mark—Nick and Stacy's dad—he's retired and saw this as a great way to get the cash out of the place so he and my aunt could live luxuriously in their *twilight years.*'

'Oh ...' she could barely get the word out, 'I thought ... I mean ... I was so certain it was you.'

A smile crept onto his face as he quirked an eyebrow. 'And that's no doubt exactly what Paul wanted you to think—that *all* the Golds had signed. But you have to realise I wouldn't have done anything like that without talking to you first. We're the descendants of the founding fathers, after all.'

Confusion swept over her, making it hard to find her voice at first, but after a moment she continued. 'You wouldn't have signed without speaking to me? But ... I thought ... I mean your family and mine were sort of ... at odds with each other?'

He let out a loud sigh, shaking his head slowly. 'My father was desperate to get the saloon back, so yes, he wasn't enamoured with the Mason family. But once he passed, I tried to let it go. I definitely wanted your uncle to accept our offer, but it was mostly for Dad's sake—to honour his wishes. But regardless of that, the Masons and the Golds have always done what's right for the town. I made my feelings on that matter quite clear when I found out my uncle had been doing deals without telling me.'

Her knees went weak, and she reached out to the chair for support. Travis stepped forward, putting his hands on her waist to pull her toward him, and then wrapped his arms around her, holding her close. His breath was warm on her neck just before he placed a gentle kiss on the top of her head.

She reached up, her arms almost with a mind of their own, pulling him closer. 'Oh, Travis, I'm so sorry. I should have trusted you.'

He pushed her back gently, staring down into her eyes. 'What you should have done was return my calls.'

Again, heat rose in her cheeks. She'd been such a fool. All the turmoil these past few days could have been avoided if she hadn't been so quick to trust the word of a stranger and believe Travis would betray her. She'd completely mucked things up and she had no one to blame but herself.

She swallowed hard before answering him. 'Can you forgive me?'

He reached out, stroking some loose hairs back from her face. 'I can forgive you, if you can forgive me.'

'Forgive you, for what?'

'I was afraid you wouldn't feel any connection to the town—after all, you'd only just arrived. And that jerk, Kelly, made it sound like you were on board with the whole thing. And as much as I hated the idea of you selling out, it made sense. A good offer from him would save you the trouble of trying to sell the properties individually. I was so sure he was telling me the truth I came over here to try to talk you out of it.'

She shook her head. 'This is surreal, you realise that?'

'Look, I knew your properties were the critical ones, and that even if I wouldn't sign, Kelly might press on with the development if he got the saloon and hotel. I came with the hope you hadn't signed the contracts yet—or at least hadn't returned them to him. And on the plane, on the way over, I'd even convinced myself I could probably match any offer he'd made and buy your properties myself if you were determined to sell.'

Her heart ached with regret. 'We've both been fooled by that horrible man, haven't we?'

'And for that I'm really sorry,' he said, stroking her cheeks with his thumbs as he searched her eyes. Then he bent toward her and kissed her. When he pulled back and their eyes met, her breath caught.

His voice sounded deeper than she'd ever heard it—full of emotion. 'We should have trusted each other—we should have talked rather than each assuming the worst—but at least some good has come from all this. It took the thought of losing you to make me realise just what I'd found in you.'

How on earth could her heart speed up further? It was already racing uncontrollably. 'Found in me?'

A tentative smile broke out on his face. 'I didn't think I'd ever want a woman in my life again—not after the mess with Karen. Annie was enough—I was happy just to be her father. Until I met you. Oh, I used the feud as an excuse at first, convincing myself it was important. But it wasn't. I've enjoyed every minute we've spent together. And you being so good with Annie ... that was a bonus.'

She swallowed back her emotions. 'Yes, Annie's wonderful.'

He rubbed her back, sending tingles down her spine. 'She cares a great deal about you. But as much as she cares about you, it's nothing compared to how I feel about you. The thought of losing you—forever—thinking you might sell everything and not even have a reason to come back to Masons Flat. I had to see you, had to find out if there was any chance you might ... that we might ...'

He looked deep into her eyes, as if searching for the rest of the sentence. She licked her lips, and tried to swallow as her heart raced even faster. Then he kissed her.

Closing her eyes, she allowed herself to savour the moment. The room disappeared and the only thing that mattered was that she was in his arms. And then he lifted her, and carried her into her bedroom, setting her down on the edge of the bed. Her heart nearly stopped when he knelt down on the floor in front of her.

'Come back to Masons Flat with me? We'll tell this Kelly fellow to shove his contracts. We can rebuild the town, together.'

This had to be a dream. She blinked slowly, but when she opened her eyes he was still there, kneeling in front of her, gazing at her with love in his eyes.

She reached out and touched his cheek. How could she ever have thought he'd betrayed her? He'd come half-way around the world determined to find her—to save his town, and to try to bring her home. He hadn't betrayed her at all.

Her decision was an obvious one. Masons Flat was her home now. And she wanted Travis in her life even if the details of their relationship might be ... complicated. They could sort it out.

She smiled back at him, took a deep breath and leaned forward to kiss him as she threw her arms around his neck. When she finally pulled back, her voice came out in a hoarse whisper—one laced with longing.

'Of course I'm going back to Masons Flat. It's my home now, and I can't imagine not being there, not being with you and Annie.'

Passion darkened his eyes. He stood, unbuttoned his shirt and tossed it over the mirror. Then he reached out and took her hands, pulling her to her feet and into his arms.

CHAPTER 33

Alex woke to the sound of Travis breathing softly beside her. She blinked a few times, making sure he was really there, then watched as his bare chest slowly rose and fell. Indecision crippled her, toggling between her desire to touch him and his need for a bit more sleep.

She tingled as she recalled their love making the day before, and how it had felt to snuggle up to him all night—in her bed—in her home.

Her sensible side won out; she knew he needed to sleep, so she rose, wrapped herself in her bathrobe and tiptoed out of the room, pulling the door closed as softly as possible behind her.

In the kitchen, she made a cup of coffee and caught up on the news on her iPad.

Casey rang just after nine-thirty, but Alex didn't mention Travis—she simply said she'd decided to make her own way up since she didn't really need to be there for the rehearsal. She promised to be there in time for the cocktail party, and yes, she had the address as she'd found the invitation in her stack of mail. Casey sounded suspicious, but eventually let it go.

The first indication that Travis had gotten up was when she heard the water running. A few moments later he appeared, dressed in the same clothes he'd arrived in. His dark hair was slicked back with water, his face ruddy from the hot shower. She wanted to stand up and run to him. Instead, she took a sip of her coffee.

He cleared his throat. 'Forgot my suitcase is still in the car. I'll go grab it and then change and have a shave.'

'How about some breakfast first? We're in no rush.'

Over a leisurely breakfast they agreed he would come to the wedding in Willows with her. Then, since they didn't need to leave for several hours, they made love again which meant Travis needed another shower.

~~*~~

Allowing Alex to drive was a smart move. He'd made it to her place in one piece the day before, but he'd had pure adrenaline pumping through his veins. Today he was quite happy to be a passenger as she navigated them onto the freeway, through a tunnel, and then manoeuvred through a convoluted series of exits and overpasses. They crossed a bridge heading northwest, then went past housing estates, industrial areas, and eventually farm-land as they left the city further and further behind.

It hadn't been much more than an hour before they pulled into the town of Willows. Alex drove slowly down the main street, past buildings made primarily of stone and brick. And even though it was a cold day, there was a buzz of activity with kids hanging out in front of both a small grocery store, and a shop with a sign reading fish and chips.

As they left the town behind, the roads grew narrower until eventually they turned off onto a dirt road. When they finally pulled up at a large ranch-style home there were already twenty or more cars parked at the front. They were greeted by a woman who had to be one of Alex's sisters, and within moments he'd been introduced to the whole family.

Several hours later, with the cocktail party waning, he was standing alone outside on the porch, marvelling at how easily he'd fit into Alex's family. It was as if he'd known all of them for years. He hadn't been outside long when he heard the screen door squeak and footsteps coming up behind him. He turned as Alex stopped beside him, handing him a glass of sparkling wine.

'Cheers.' She smiled, and the gold flecks in her eyes shimmered, catching the rays from fairy-lights along the roof over the porch.

'Cheers,' he replied, touching his glass to hers before taking a sip.

They both turned and gazed into the darkness. It was cold tonight, and there must have been a million stars visible in the clear sky. Soft music and muffled voices drifted out through the open door behind them, but ahead of them it was still and quiet. He pulled her close, leaving his arm resting across her shoulders.

Alex sighed. 'It's lovely here, isn't it?'

'Gorgeous.' It reminded him of home, the cold air fresh and clean—not at all like what he'd experienced at Alex's apartment.

Alex took a sip of wine as she turned to him. 'It's funny; I used to wonder how Summer could live somewhere like this ... in such a small town, practically in the middle of nowhere.'

'I didn't think Willows felt small as we drove through.' He waited for her to reply, holding his breath.

She shrugged. 'I said I *used to* ... I *used* to think it was too small for me. But neither Willows nor Masons Flat feel too small any longer. Neither one is far from a city where you can get anything you need. In fact, the way I see it, both give you the best of both worlds—country living, but within a few hours' drive of what most agree are a couple of the world's best cities; Melbourne and San Francisco.'

He sighed; grateful she got it. Then he turned to face her. 'You know, Alex, when I got down on my knees in your bedroom yesterday ...'

Silence weighed heavily between them for a moment as he tried to find the right words.

'Yes?' Her voice sounded tentative.

'There was something else I wanted to ask you ... more than just about going back to Masons Flat.'

Her eyes sparkled, and though he suspected it was still just the reflection of the fairy-lights around them it was all the encouragement he needed.

'Marry me? Make me the happiest man on the planet.'

His heart pounded, awaiting her answer—hoping for the best, fearing the worst. When she was slow to respond, he reached out and touched her cheek. 'Don't say no. Say you'll give it some thought. If you want, we can just see how things go. I shouldn't be putting this kind of pressure on you. We haven't known each other long ... it's just I know we're right for each other. I've never been more certain of anything.'

When she turned and looked into the distance, he couldn't breathe. She was going to say no. He shouldn't have asked her—not here, not today. When she finally faced him, there were tears in her eyes. He swallowed hard, bracing for rejection.

'I'm not going to say yes, or no—not yet anyway,' she whispered. 'There's something I need to tell you—and it might make you change your mind.'

He sighed with relief. 'Alex, nothing you tell me could make me change my mind.'

She turned to look into the distance again and then took several deep, ragged breaths.

Putting his arm around her shoulders again, he pulled her close. 'What is it Alex? If it's about the saloon, forget it. I have. That was my father's issue, not mine. Okay?'

She pulled away from him, and now there were definitely tears in her eyes. 'It's not that. It's ...' She let out a loud breath, then spoke in a whisper. 'I can't have children. Because of the accident. I didn't only injure my shoulder. My pelvis was fractured, and ... I had internal injuries as a result. The long and short of it is ... I will never have children.'

He stared at her, disappointment draining his energy, pain constricting his chest. He drew in a deep breath, searching for the right words as her face crumbled before him.

'Oh, Alex, I'm so sorry. That's so unfair. Life is so unfair.' He swallowed hard, not knowing what more he could say.

Her head shook back and forth as she sniffed back tears. 'I should have told you sooner.'

'No, don't say that. It doesn't matter. It doesn't change anything. I never expected to be a father again. Heck, I never expected to be a husband again.'

She blinked several times, then wiped at her eyes. 'Are you ... sure?'

'I've never been surer of anything.'

'And ... you still want me, even though I ... even though it means you won't have any more children?'

He leaned forward and placed his hands on her shoulders while he stared into her eyes. 'Alex, you're all I want. You and Annie. I'm just sorry you won't get to experience the joy I felt when she was born, when I held her for the first time. It's unfair to you, not to me.'

Her eyes glistened. 'Really?'

Once again, he pulled her close, speaking into her hair. 'I want you in my life, Alex. Not being able to have children doesn't change how I feel about you. How could you even think it would matter?'

She shivered in his arms, and he held her closer. When she finally spoke, he could barely hear her words. 'Because that was what Liam said to me. He said it like it excused his behaviour—his cheating—like he couldn't be expected to stay with a woman who couldn't give him a family.'

He shook his head. 'Your ex-husband sounds like a complete fool. But I'm glad, because if he hadn't been, I might never have met you.'

When he released her slightly so he could see her face, it had softened. He swallowed hard, knowing she was in pain, but also seeing it lessen before his eyes. 'Let's get married tomorrow. Let's make tomorrow's wedding a double header.'

Her eyes grew brighter—the gold flecks sparkling now. 'We can't. In fact, would you mind if we keep it to ourselves for a while? Can we ... not rush things?'

He touched her cheek, the tips of his fingers barely making contact and yet it was enough to send pulses of electricity through his whole body.

'We can take all the time you want, just so long as we're together.'

EPILOGUE

Three Weeks Later

Movement caught Alex's eye as she and Travis finished lunch in the dining room at Masons Hotel. Hilda Weston was approaching their table.

'Welcome back, Alex, Travis.'

They'd been back from Australia for almost two weeks, but it was the first time she'd seen Hilda.

'Thanks, Hilda. Have you got time to join us for a coffee?' She smiled, indicating the empty chair.

Hilda took a moment to sit, fiddling with her purse before eventually meeting Alex's gaze. 'Sam mentioned you've decided to stay on here. It's absolutely wonderful for our community.'

Warmth raced through her at the kind words. 'Aw, thanks.'

Hilda smiled, but after a moment her smile faded and she shifted her gaze down at the table. When she spoke, her voice was soft and low. 'I'm sorry it's taken me so long to catch up with you. I ... wasn't sure what to say. I still find it nearly impossible to believe my own son could do such a thing. I raised him to be truthful, not to sneak around trying to cheat people.' Hilda started ringing her hands as her eyes darted back and forth between Alex and Travis.

Alex reached across and placed her hand on Hilda's forearm. 'Don't blame yourself. In fact, don't blame Harrison, either. He simply had stars in his eyes. Literally.'

Hilda stared at Alex's hand for a moment. When she looked up, the tension in her face had softened.

Alex continued. 'Look, no real harm's been done. If anything, I'm grateful to him. This whole experience is what helped me make up my mind about staying here. It showed me just how much this town means

249

to me.' She turned to Travis and when he smiled warmth washed over her. She looked back to Hilda, hoping her face didn't give away their secret.

'That's very generous of you, but I'm not sure I'll forgive him so quickly. His father, God rest his soul, would be appalled.'

Travis turned to Hilda. 'Alex is right. If none of this had happened who knows whether she'd have decided to stay on. Harrison did us all a favour, by accident, but even so the town will forever be in his debt.'

'You're both so sweet. And I suppose everything has turned out okay, hasn't it? But still ... him traipsing around with that *man*.'

Alex laughed. 'You're obviously referring to Kevin?'

Hilda sniffed out a breath, frowning. 'Yes.'

'He's actually quite nice. A bit flamboyant perhaps, but I suspect most movie directors are like that—artistic and driven. I liked him from the moment I met him.'

'You've met him?'

'Yes. He and Harrison came to see me a few days after I got back—to apologise for the way things turned out. They'd trusted Ben Thompson, and that's where they went wrong. Ben was behind everything. He'd brought in Paul Kelly, and called all the shots ... instructing Paul to lie to everyone. Paul made it sound like Kevin, *his client*, was calling the shots, but that wasn't the case.'

'And you're sure neither of you blame them, Kevin and Harrison?'

'Of course not. They had a dream—and counted on Ben, the so-called expert, to make it happen. It's Ben Thompson who I'll struggle to forgive. Ben lied to my face, and my uncle's as well.'

'It wasn't their fault,' Travis said. 'They thought they were using professionals.'

Hilda shook her head looking unconvinced. 'I think it's wonderful you're so forgiving, but I'm not sure I would be, if I were in your shoes.'

Alex smiled warmly, trying to let Hilda know there were no hard feelings. 'Look, the movie was a great idea. If Harrison and Kevin had come to me directly, I'd have been happy for them to use the hotel and saloon for filming. And for all I know, that might still happen. It was taking things to the next level and trying to buy up all the buildings in such a dishonest fashion that made everything come unstuck.'

Hilda's face lit up. 'You think the movie might still be on the cards? That would make Harrison so happy.'

Alex turned to Travis, and lifted an eyebrow. When he smiled, Alex looked at Hilda again. 'You never know. We'll let the dust settle for a while, and then I'll give Harrison a call.'

Hilda beamed. 'That would be wonderful. Thank you so much for not blaming him.' Then her smile faded, and she sighed heavily. 'But then, there's the other thing.'

Alex glanced at Travis, whose head was shaking almost imperceptibly, and then she turned back to Hilda. 'The other thing?'

Hilda began ringing her hands in her lap as she spoke in a whisper. 'I'll never have grandchildren. I'd always hoped Harrison would find a nice girl—someone like you, Alex. When he took you to Denver's party, I'd hoped it was the start of something.'

Alex stifled a laugh. 'Me and Harrison? Oh, Hilda, I can't believe you couldn't see it. I mean, it took me a little while to be certain, but he's clearly not interested in women. Please don't be hard on him. He seems happy, and that's all that's important.'

'You really think so?'

Once again, she turned to flash a quick smile toward Travis before answering. 'Yes, I do. Besides, even if he'd fallen in love with a girl like me, instead of Kevin, that wouldn't have guaranteed you grandchildren.' As she finished speaking, Travis grabbed her hand under the table and gave it an encouraging rub.

Hilda shrugged. 'I suppose you're right. No doubt I'll forgive him in time. He is my only child after all. And as you say, he wasn't the real villain in all this, was he? But I still don't understand how he and Kevin got mixed up with this Ben Thompson in the first place.'

'Harrison told me that he and Kevin spoke to Ben about one of my uncle's vacant shops when they first came up with the idea for the movie. They thought they might have been able to get the film project up using just a few of the shops.'

Hilda's eyes opened wider as understanding dawned. 'So this has been bubbling away for some time, has it?'

Travis cleared his throat before answering her. 'Yes, and it seems it was Ben's idea to turn the town into a tourist destination. He convinced them they needed to buy all the properties in Main Street to make it happen, but really that was just so he could get commissions on all the sales. That's why he wanted to keep the shops vacant—to make the whole thing easier to pull off.'

'I did wonder why so many shops were vacant for so long.'

'Yes, that was all Ben's doing,' Alex said.

'He's hurt everyone with his deceit, hasn't he?'

Alex shook her head. 'Yes, and all for his own personal gain. Fancy him having Paul use the notion that the project was good for everyone as a bargaining chip, when he'd been actively hurting everyone for months. With all the deceit, Ben might even lose his licence.'

Hilda's brow creased. 'But where were they going to get the money to do all this? Harrison barely has two nickels to rub together.'

'Kevin's from a wealthy family—didn't they tell you? That's how he got into directing films in the first place. I didn't get all the names, but it seems his father and grandfather both made lots of money in Hollywood.'

'And this Ben Thompson fellow, he knew this ... that Kevin was wealthy?'

'Absolutely. That's why Ben came up with the idea of making the town into a tourist destination. He was set to make huge commissions on all the sales. And that's why he brought Paul Kelly on board—so he could claim to not be involved, and to ensure Kevin didn't do any deals directly. Kevin and Harrison were pretty naïve, but that's the worst they can be blamed for as far as I'm concerned.'

Hilda shook her head. 'I never would have thought Harrison capable of behaving like that.'

'Ben's a smooth talker,' Alex said, looking at Travis. 'And so was Paul Kelly.'

Travis nodded agreement. 'It didn't smell right from the moment I met Paul Kelly, but I couldn't put my finger on it.'

Alex ducked her head momentarily before continuing. 'The secrecy should have triggered suspicion in me as well, but I let my emotions get in the way.'

'I got caught out, too,' Travis said, giving her hand a squeeze.

Alex's heart warmed. 'Now that it's over I can see why they didn't want all of us together in one room. They almost got away with it, but never would have if we'd all been in the same room together.'

Travis looked at Alex, and then at Hilda. 'Yeah, lying to each of us about the others already signing was a bit too clever.'

Hilda drew in her breath. 'Is that what they were doing? Trying to make you all doubt each other?'

Alex nodded, and then turned to look at Travis. 'It seems that way. But your uncle Mark did sign, right?'

Travis shook his head. 'It turns out he never did. His lawyer wasn't happy with the contract being subject to development approval for such a long period. They could have been locked in for a long time without any certainty the sale would go ahead.'

Silence settled over them for a moment before Hilda let out a loud sigh. 'I really appreciate how well you've both taken all this, and that you aren't holding it against Harrison.'

'Please, don't let it trouble you any further,' Alex said, giving her a warm smile.

'Look, I've taken up enough of your time. I won't stay to have coffee; I think I'll pop over to that fresh produce shop. It looks quite nice, doesn't it?' Hilda said as she stood to go, then winked at Alex, and flashed a relieved smile.

'It is nice, even if I do say so myself. Don't forget to grab some of those strawberries before they're all gone.' Alex stood, and walked around to Hilda to give her a big hug. 'Thank you, for welcoming me the way you have.'

When Alex released her, Hilda stepped back. 'We're lucky to have you, Alex. And you're a lucky man, Travis Gold. You'll be sure to take good care of her, now won't you?'

Alex's eyes flew open. Did Hilda read something between the lines? They hadn't told anyone of their engagement.

Travis came over and threw his arm around Alex's shoulders. 'You don't have to tell me twice.' He kissed Alex's cheek before moving over to give Hilda a quick hug.

As she watched the two embrace, a shiver ran down Alex's spine and she got the sense that there was someone behind her. She turned, but the rest of the room was empty.

Or at least it seemed to be.

But then a vision of a distinguished man came to mind—a man not dissimilar to her father, but taller and more rugged looking. Another chill ran down her spine as it dawned on her that some things can never be explained. That no-one would ever be able to say with one hundred per cent certainty that her ancestor and the town's founder, Thomas Mason, wasn't in the room with them.

She looked back over at Travis, cherishing the depth of her love for him, and smiled.

And it occurred to her that if Thomas Mason was with them, watching over them, right now, perhaps he would be pleased to find her discovering gold, right here in his town, almost as he'd done himself so many years ago.

THANK YOU

Thank you for taking the time to read this first book in the Romancing the California Cowboys series. If you've enjoyed this book, please consider leaving a review on Amazon or Goodreads as this helps other readers to find the book.

I'm working on the next in the series, which is Casey's story, but in the mean time you may also like to look at my other series, the Copperhead Creek Australian Romance series, which is set in the sleepy rural town of Willows, Australia, where Alex went for her step-sister's wedding!

The fictitious town of Willows is located in Victoria's Golden Triangle, the home of Australia's 1850s Gold Rush, and is inspired by small towns scattered throughout Victoria and South Australia. Each book can be read as a stand-alone featuring a new couple who find their own happy ending, but if you read the books in order you'll find characters from earlier books making reappearances as the lives of the small town residents overlap and tangle.

The books in the series are:

Taking a Chance (a FREE series prequel)
A Chance to Come True
A Chance to Get it Right
A Chance to Let Go
A Chance to Belong
A Chance for Snow
Murder at the Creek – A Copperhead Creek Mystery

ABOUT THE AUTHOR

S M Spencer grew up in the San Francisco Bay Area where she rode horses along the beaches and across the tops of the rolling coastal hills of California. In the 1980s she was offered a job in Australia, which was the beginning of an adventure of which she has never tired. Still living in Australia, she writes from the semi-rural home she shares with her husband, horses, cats and dogs, as well as the kangaroos that pass through the paddocks from time to time.

You can find all of S M Spencer's books by visiting S M Spencer's Author Page at Amazon:
https://www.amazon.com/S-M-Spencer/e/B00PGE0G9U/

And never miss a new book, or a promotion, by following S M Spencer's blog: http://smspencer.online/blog/

CPSIA information can be obtained
at www.ICGtesting.com
Printed in the USA
BVHW081227061221
623331BV00006B/137